THE MOON

HAS NO LIGHT

BY

MARIAN P. MERRITT

The Moon Has No Light

© 2017 Marian P. Merritt

For more information about Marian P. Merritt, please connect through her author's website at the following address: www.marianmerritt.com.

Cover Art by Wicked Smart Designs

ASK Publishers

Published in the United States of America

DEDICATION

For Scott, your encouragement and support mean the world to me.

With a grateful heart, I thank my Lord and Savior for all I am and all I have.

`Sola fide`

ACKNOWLEDGMENTS

No written work is the sole endeavor of one person. I'm grateful to many for helping me bring this story to life. For their keen eyes and insightful suggestions, I thank the following: my editor, Nadine Brandes, my critique partner, Sharon Srock, and my wonderful beta readers, Debbie Jamieson, Linda Rainey, Lois Roberts, Mary Gasiewski, Robin Bunting, Robin E. Mason, Sandy Adams, Sherri Overton, Susan Johnson, and Vivian Helton. The story has been enriched because of your input. Thank you.

CHAPTER 1

*D*r. Margaret Langston compared the age-progressed photo with the original one of her son. She released the paper clip binding them to the faded newspaper article. With a reverent touch, she slid her finger along the defined jaw of the square face. The dimple in his chin. So much like his father's. The eyes. Those amazing green eyes . . .

Her clinic nurse, Tara, poked her head around the doorframe. In a softened tone, she said, "Dr. Langston, Elizabeth's here with Gracie, they're in the Cinderella room."

"I'll be right there."

Empathy flowed through Tara's smile. "She's your last patient. We didn't schedule any appointments for the afternoon. We thought you might..." Her blue eyes dripped with compassion. "...might want the time alone."

Maggie swallowed the fist of emotion filling her throat. "Thanks, Tara."

Once Tara left, Maggie took a deep breath and released it. A baby needed her. A sweet special baby. Right here. Right now. After closing the folder on the photos and the stack of papers she'd collected through her twenty-year search, she stood and moved toward her patient's room to do the thing she did best—pretend.

Pretend she didn't hurt while she helped children feel better. Other mothers' children. She lifted the chart from the holder next to the door and glanced through it.

Fever, pulling on ears, crying. As she read the list of complaints, she speculated on a diagnosis for the eight-month-old then entered the exam room.

"Good morning, Elizabeth. I see little Gracie isn't feeling well." Maggie cupped her hands under the infant's arms and lifted her from her mother's lap, then sat next to her on the examination table.

Gracie scrunched her little face and let out a scream. She extended her arms toward her mother. "Oh, baby. It's okay." Maggie cuddled the baby in her arms while inhaling the delicious baby scent. "It's okay, sweetness. We're going to make it all better."

She reviewed the symptoms with the young mother while examining the child. A peek in the struggling baby's ears confirmed her suspicions—bulging tympanic membrane, red angry tissue. Yep, Acute Otitis Media.

She kissed the top of Gracie's head before giving her back to her mother. "Both ears are infected." Maggie scribbled in her chart. "I'll call in a prescription for an antibiotic. If she's not feeling better in a week, let me know."

"Thanks, Dr. Maggie. I'm ready for her to feel better. It breaks my heart when she's sick." She wrapped her arms around Gracie.

Maggie smiled. "You're a mother. It's how mothers are." She intimately knew the pain of a mom's broken heart.

Elizabeth strapped Gracie in her travel seat. After she gathered her belongings, she turned to Maggie. "You know, just yesterday, Mom was asking about you. She'd loved to see you on her next visit. She also wanted me to thank you for taking care of her granddaughter."

Maggie thought of her colleague and friend, Grace, an

attorney who had foregone practicing to be a stay-at-home mom. She'd grown up in Louisiana along the river road and lived in an awesome old plantation just outside of Pecan Pointe. They'd met at LSU and became fast friends. "Tell her I would love that. I've missed her."

Elizabeth lifted Gracie's seat and headed for the door. "I'll tell her. I keep trying to get her to leave Mississippi and move back to Pecan Pointe. She could come to the Bible study I attend at Rosie's. Maybe you could come?"

Maggie grinned. Yeah, she couldn't imagine attending a Bible study. Her faith needed more than an hour a week with other women studying useless ideals. "Is your Dad still thinking of running for office?"

"Of course, you know Dad. That's why I think it's hopeless they'll ever move back. He has too many connections in Biloxi."

Maggie hugged Elizabeth at the door. "I do know your dad, but you never know, he could run for office here. Mayor Donaldson hinted of retiring next year. I also know your Mom, she's a pretty determined lady. And, I know they are both proud of you." She ran her index finger along the baby's nose. "And this little one. Please tell her to call my cell when she's coming to town."

Maggie scribbled her number on a small sticky note, stuck it to the side of Elizabeth's purse, and held the door opened for her.

"Thanks, Dr. Maggie. She'll be excited to catch up."

"Me, too."

Maggie returned to her office, dictated her note, and rested her head on her desk.

Babies exhausted her. Zapped the last traces of energy she had.

Yet. She couldn't stop seeing them. Their scent, smiles, and pure innocence came close to filling the hollowness in her heart—a pit so deep and wide and long she feared it would never be complete again.

#

The Friday afternoon bustle filled the bar and spilled into the hotel lobby. Maggie glanced toward the clock near the registration desk. Good. I'm early. Why had she agreed to conduct an interview at a bar?

The hostess, wearing a pasted-on smile approached Maggie. "Something to drink?"

"Scotch and water." The words tumbled out. She didn't drink, hadn't touched the stuff since she'd married Craig. And heaven knew there were many opportunities in the last two decades. But today was different, it had been twenty years and there'd been no news.

Nothing.

She caught a glimpse of the television hanging from the ceiling in the corner. Images of last night's broadcast filled the screen. Two yellow, slicker suit-wearing police emerged from the trees near the lake carrying a box. Remains, the reporter said.

No, she couldn't—wouldn't—believe they carried her son.

Somewhere he still lived. Somehow he had survived. She knew it the way only a mother could.

She tried to forget. For the sake of her marriage, she tried to let it go. But she couldn't.

Now the latest news story revived the beast within. The one that tortured and gripped. The one that prodded her to remember that fateful day. The one that wouldn't let her believe Paul was gone.

She glanced at her watch, 3:00 p.m.

Surely, if the remains found near the lake last night were her son's, she'd have heard something by now. But then again, maybe it would take days to analyze the bones. Days of pure torture.

Her cell phone rested on the table. Should she? She reached for it, then paused. Was it too soon?

She grabbed the phone. Her fingers flew over the numbers as she dialed the police. "Captain Jordan, please. This is Dr. Maggie Langston."

"Hold please."

"Maggie, hello. I know why you're calling." His deep, raspy voice brought back a rush of emotion.

"Tom, is it…is it my…?" She held her breath and closed her eyes. Did she really want to know?

"We're running the forensics." His voiced softened. "We should know something soon. I'll call you as soon as I hear."

She exhaled. "Thanks, Tom."

"Sure, Maggie." His voice caught on the words.

Could the question burning for almost half her life be answered within the next twenty-four hours? What if the truth stole the last glimmer of hope? One she'd held on to like a drowning woman clutching a life ring?

Tom's voice had changed since the first time she'd met him. They'd both changed. He'd been a detective back then. And she…well, she'd aged more than she should have in the past twenty years. More gray in her brown hair, more wrinkles around her eyes, and a little paunchier around her waist. While her life had continued, with a distant husband and no children, she'd grieved for more. She'd lessened the pain with sick children who needed her, but belonged to someone else.

Heart wrenching memories took her to the park—the overturned toy truck in the sand, her husband's incredulous look when he'd arrived, search parties, the police questions—all flashes of the past tormenting today. She would never give up trying to find Paul. Or believing he still lived.

Unless Captain Jordan called with the wrong answer.

No, she wouldn't go there. Her son was out there somewhere. Her steadfast belief had plowed a gulch through her marriage—a vast gorge neither she nor Craig had the energy to cross.

The hostess returned and placed a glass on the table. "Your drink, ma'am."

With a shaking hand, Maggie pulled a ten-dollar bill

from her wallet. "Keep the change." She attempted a smile, but couldn't get past the quiver of her lips.

The young woman thanked her then moved on to the next table with the same pasted-on smile.

Maggie stared at the condensation forming along the perimeter where the liquid reached the top. She'd already proven she wasn't a good mother. She fingered the empty spot on her left ring finger. Was she about to prove she was a lousy wife too?

"Maggie, hi. I hope you haven't been waiting long." Eric, tall and lanky, slid into the chair across from her. His radiant smile and sparkling blue eyes pierced through her. His gaze locked onto hers and held.

"No. Just got here." Warning bells bellowed. She shifted in her seat and moved her hands from the table into her lap trying to escape the tightening of her stomach.

Meeting here was a mistake. Why hadn't she picked the meeting place? Had she agreed thinking that spending time with the blond-haired, confident, and energetic doctor would take away her loneliness? A pang of guilt pricked. When they'd met last year in Kansas City, she hadn't corrected his assumption she was single.

Her heart pounded with a force so strong it captured her breath. She could leave before she crossed a line she might forever regret. Her career, her marriage—what little remained—were all she had left. Was it worth taking the chance of losing both?

"Is everything okay? You look...distracted." His sympathetic gaze elevated her pulse even higher. His words floated to her as though she were underwater—drowning in her poor choices.

She bounced out of the chair and onto her feet. The purse on her lap flew to the tiled floor. Lipstick, brush, pens, wallet, all scattered with a resounding splat. Her prized possession—Paul's picture—settled near Eric's feet.

"I-I'm s-s-sorry. This is not a good day to meet." She bent to her knees and corralled the runaway contents. Her son's smiling face brought a rush of tears. No. She would not cry. She summoned every drop of willpower she possessed.

Eric scooped her hairbrush and lipstick, and then reached for the photo. She snatched it before he could retrieve it, and took the items he offered. Maggie shoved everything back into her purse and stood. When she met his gaze, the confusion there besieged her. For a moment, she wavered on a beam of indecision. His furrowed brow and inquisitive look tightened the vice squeezing her chest.

"Maggie?"

"I can't. I'm sorry. Call my nurse to reschedule at my office." She slung the purse onto her shoulder. "I have to go." Before Eric could say another word, she rushed toward the door. His upturned hands and shaking head burned an image she would not soon forget.

With each pounding step on the pavement to her car, her regret magnified. Had she actually thought for a moment of having an affair? How could she? His attention since the medical conference last year made her feel special. Needed. Wanted. It was a feeling she'd long abandoned. Yes, her patients needed her, but this was different. His attentiveness had sparked a dying ember of emotion in her. Given her a moment of realism the past twenty years had stolen. If only it had come from her husband.

CHAPTER 2

*O*nce Maggie found her car, she fumbled with the fob, slipped into the driver's seat, and then rested her head onto the steering wheel. After rehashing the scene and thinking of all the ways she could have handled things differently, she relented and started her car. She shook her head as though the action could eliminate the haunting thoughts and turned her focus to the busy road.

She steered her Lexus past rows of spindly pine trees along the path she'd driven a year ago. And the year before. Each May for the past twenty. While the day changed, that long ago Mother's Day date stayed with her.

Her palms moistened as she neared her destination.

Sunset Park—the place of stolen dreams. The place where her faith had withered to nothing more than cynical skepticism, endless void, and the last place she remembered smiling with her heart.

Her heels sank into the soft ground as she approached the empty swings. She glanced quickly at the spot. A jungle gym had long ago replaced the sandbox. Today she yearned more than ever to remember, to smell, to feel the things robbed from her so many years ago. The warmth of the black rubber seat of the swing seeped through her slacks. She kicked off her shoes and let herself drift back to that awful day. While today's park was empty, children had filled every swing that day. Several had played in the sandbox and around the tiny fort. The memories so vivid— she pressed her hand to her aching chest.

Today. This anniversary date. The only time she allowed herself to fully immerse in the memories. Each year they provided the same bittersweet emotions—pain as insufferable as being sliced with a dull, rusty knife, but yet as sweet as the first bite of a ripe summer strawberry.

She allowed the memories to sweep her under. To take her back. She desperately sought to hear the one voice disturbing her dreams.

But other greedy voices from the past dominated. Craig's: *How could you?* Her mother's: *Wait 'till you have kids. We'll see what kind of mother you'll be.* Voices she'd become proficient at ignoring, except today.

She pushed from the sand and let the motion swing her. Backward, forward, and then back again. She let her foot drag with each pass. Sometimes deepening the previous line in the dirt—sometimes wiping it away. She thought by now her parched soul had poured out all it had.

The giggles of happy children filtered through the air. When had they arrived? Had she been so lost in her misery that she hadn't even noticed? Their presence slapped as cruel irony, she wanted to be here to remember, to reclaim the event. Yet, she wanted to sink back into the darkness of her scheduled life and never feel again.

A little boy, about five, approached her. He cocked his head to one side and stared. His questioning gaze prompted her to scan the area. Children now filled every swing.

"Would you like to swing?" she asked.

He nodded. His chipmunk cheeks puffed when he grinned.

She couldn't help but smile as she stood and held the chains while he slipped onto the seat. She inhaled and drifted off into the elusive world of crayons and glue.

"Where's your mommy?" she asked.

He pointed toward a young woman feeding an infant at a nearby picnic table her focus on the baby. Maggie's smile faded.

"My name's Tommy."

"I'm Maggie."

"Would you push me? Please." He wrinkled his nose the way Paul had when he was curious.

Her heart twisted. This child was so trusting. So innocent. She walked behind him then closed her eyes. How many times had a scene similar to this one played through her head?

Hundreds? Or perhaps thousands?

She lifted the swing and released letting him fly through the humid air.

"Weeee! Higher."

One more push and guilt stabbed. She circled around the swing and faced him, nearly tripping over the edge where the grass met the worn-away dirt. Once he stopped and let his tiny shoes drag in the dirt, he searched her face. "Please keep pushing."

"I'm sorry, I don't think it's a good idea. I'm a stranger."

His eyebrows drew closer together, making him appear older than his four or five years. "My mom says, 'don't talk to strangers.'" He pointed his stubby index finger as he said the words.

"That's right, you shouldn't."

He cocked his head sideways then smiled. "But you are a nice stranger. I like you."

A smile spread her lips while her heart squeezed in her chest. "I like you, too, but I'm still a stranger and you should always listen to your mom. Okay?"

His bottom lip protruded when he nodded. "Ooookaaay."

The sadness in his eyes and the hurtful tone in his voice sliced through her. More children had entered the park. The buzz of their laughter drifted throughout the playground.

Their squeals of delight morphed into spears of pure torture and Tommy's trust of a total stranger—agonizing. I can't do this.

"Are you leaving?" Tommy asked as she turned to walk away.

She turned back. "Yes." She gulped. "Remember, always listen to your mom."

"Yes, ma'am."

A last glance revealed his white-knuckled grip on the chains and a broad, toothy grin. The urge to march up to his mother and chastise the woman for ignoring such a wonderful kid swept over her. Forceful words perched on the tip of her tongue. Be a good mother. Play with him. Love him. He may not be here tomorrow.

As she approached the woman, the sound of humming floated above the laughter of the children. When his mother smiled and waved at him, Maggie paused. Who was she to tell this woman how to raise her child? She followed the young woman's adoring gaze to Tommy.

If only she had looked up more often that fateful day.

CHAPTER 3

*T*he two-story façade of a dark, empty house greeted Maggie. Her dream house. Their dream house. At least it had been when they'd had it built. When the future in Pecan Pointe held promise. When life was black or white and not the encompassing gray of today.

She entered her tailored world of silk drapes, plush carpeting, and designer paint. Tonight, silence screamed through the empty rooms. Its intensity pierced her ears. And her heart.

This was her house. Only a house. One without warmth. Without children. And tonight without a husband.

A soft glow illuminated the marble entryway as she plopped her purse on the granite of the small table. She trudged over the polished Travertine tiles as though walking through sand and headed toward the comfort of her shower.

The stream of water blasted her skin. The overflow vibrated off the sides in an accusing chant.

Cheater, cheater, cheater.

She slid down the wall and plopped into the corner, allowing the spray to pelt her while the water carried away the last vestiges of her carefully applied makeup.

The faint image of her son flashed before her. Not as clear an image as she craved. She strained to remember all the intricate details of his precious little face.

After her shower, she wrapped herself in the thick terrycloth robe Craig had given her for her last birthday and walked to the kitchen. In the living room, shadows from the faint light of the entryway danced among the leather couch and wingback chairs like demons ready to pounce and devour.

Irony swept in and clutched with sharp talons. Tonight she wanted desperately to remember her sweet boy, yet with remembrance came the crippling pain she'd tried so desperately to avoid.

She curled into a fetal position on the couch. The coldness of the leather seeped through her damp hair, while she allowed the darkness to envelop.

The incessant ringing of the phone was soon followed by the voice of her husband leaving a message.

"Maggie, I've been trying to get in touch with you all day." Concern edged his rushed words. She wanted to read something else into his tone.

Agitation.

Annoyance.

Something she could use to justify her actions today. To say, *see, he's not a good person so it's okay*.

But reality held. "Maggie, I'm so sorry I couldn't be there with you today."

Her chest tightened. He remembered.

A part of her longed to talk to him, but she knew their conversation would hover on the shallow surface. They never risked going anywhere deep or personal for fear they'd go where neither was sure they could keep the pretense of successful, happy people.

Her life revolved around diagnosis and documentation. His, around new buildings and out-of-town meetings. She had thrown herself into work from the beginning. So had

Craig.

Work was where they'd turned when they'd needed to cope with their inconsolable grief. A place where the softness of a newborn's skin could be next to hers, where the wobbly walk of a toddler could fill the void even if just for a second, and where the hug from tiny arms had the power to sear her skin with its warmth.

He continued, "Something has come up with the contract. The builders won't approve the design until I make a few changes. So it looks like I'm stuck in Phoenix for a couple more days."

Once, long ago, her heart would have grieved this news. Tonight, nothing.

"I should be home day after tomorrow, but I'll be late. Don't wait up."

She lifted the receiver and pressed it to her ear. Should she? With her finger poised over the button to open the connection, she paused.

"If you're there, pick up."

She didn't move.

He waited.

"Call me when you get this message. G'night." The buzz of the dial tone echoed through the room.

She replaced the phone on the table in the exact position it sat before, careful not to disturb the thin layer of dust covering the area around the base of the lamp. Comfort came from things staying the same. Remaining constant. Perhaps that was why she and Craig were still married.

CHAPTER 4

*L*aney Ellerby scanned the scuffed walls of the vacant den in her Mobile, Alabama house. A new chapter in her life dawned. Empty, the house seemed larger. What had been her family's home for twenty-five years now seemed nothing more than a house.

Tears threatened to erupt as she ran her hand along the doorframe between the den and kitchen. Small pencil marks designating her son's growth spurts graced the wood. She knew she should have wiped them away, but she couldn't bring herself to do it. It would be like wiping her precious memories away.

One gap especially drew her attention, the summer of Evan's thirteenth year. A full four inches. A slow smile spread her lips. She slid down the wall to the floor and let her mind enjoy the luscious memories.

Bryan carrying her over the threshold. His sweet words engraved on her heart. *It's the beginning of our life in our new home.* Evan holding her hand tightly as she guided him through the door.

Each recollection made the day more bittersweet.

"Hello?" Emma's voice echoed through the empty

house.

"In here."

Emma, wearing her green scrubs with her wild curls corralled into a ponytail, entered the den carrying a small package wrapped with red sparkling paper. "Well, look at you, my friend. You look a little tired." She slid down the wall and sat next to Laney.

Laney smiled and wrapped flyaway hair strands behind her ears. "Just a little."

"And a little sad too?" Emma laid her head on Laney's shoulder.

"Yeah, a little…" Laney rested her head against Emma's. "…well, a lot. I will miss you so much."

Emma patted Laney's cheek. "Me too, girlie. I'll miss you."

"Remember when we moved here. I was such a mousy recluse." Laney slid her hand into Emma's.

Emma's deep-throated laughter bounced off the walls. "Remember? Oh gosh, how could I forget. It took months to get you to come over for coffee then another four months for you to join our Bible study."

Laney lowered her head. "Yeah, but you never gave up on me. For that, I'm so grateful. You've been a good friend. What will I do without you?"

Emma straightened and turned toward Laney, her dark eyes blazing. "You know wonderful things wait for you in Louisiana, right? Evan getting accepted to LSU, and Bryan's promotion there the same week you're offered this job are not coincidences. They're God-incidences." Emma squeezed Laney's hand and sat back against the wall.

"Funny how when I accepted both the youth leader job and the teacher's position at the high school, I knew with certainty I could handle it, now I'm having second thoughts. Stupid doubts."

"Are you kidding? Girl, they're lucky to have you." Emma's hand waved through the air. "Don't let those needless doubts stir up the wrong thoughts in your head.

You'll be great. Just because you've been an elementary teacher all these years doesn't mean you won't be an awesome high school teacher."

While part of her grieved losing the world she'd known for twenty-five years, another part tingled with excitement to experience what God had in store.

"What if...?" The remaining words were consumed by the emotions she struggled to contain. She met Emma's gaze. "What if...you know. What if my past gets in the way. I still haven't told Bryan."

"Honey, it's your past. It's what makes you more than qualified to work with teenagers. Sometimes God uses the broken places in us to help others. As far as Bryan, he loves you, girl. I think he would accept you no matter what."

Laney nodded. "Yeah, you know he thinks I'm the perfect wife and mother. What if he knew? What if it changes the way he feels about me?"

Emma shook her head. "Ain't gonna happen." She turned so her gaze met Laney's. "But honey, telling Bryan is something you have to decide to do. I'm still praying about that for you. When the time is right, God will prod your heart to share."

Laney sighed. She knew Emma was right. They'd both been praying that for a long time. But God had not chosen to answer yet. Only two, well, three knew her secret—Emma, her Aunt Elaine and God.

The familiar grip of condemnation wrapped around her heart and squeezed. She was neither a perfect wife nor a perfect mother.

Emma picked up the package she laid on the floor. "Here's a little something for you."

Laney found a comforting home in Emma's warm gaze. She reached for the box. "You didn't have to buy me anything."

"I know." Emma's grin teased.

Laney slid her fingernail under the tape holding the shimmering paper together. Nestled inside lay a glass paperweight with a red cross suspended inside. "Oh." She lifted the precious gift. "For my collection, thank you."

"You're welcome, sweet friend. I hope you think of me when you look at it."

Laney hugged Emma. "Are you kidding? This one already has a special place in my heart. I owe you so much." How could she ever thank Emma for introducing her to Christ?

"You don't owe me a thing. Your friendship is priceless." Emma squeezed Laney a little tighter.

"I'll miss you," Laney said.

"I'll miss you more. Besides I'm coming to visit in a couple of weeks. Finally get to taste some authentic Cajun food." A familiar smile wrapped around her friend's words.

"Laney, honey, where are you?" Her husband's voice boomed from the kitchen.

Emma slid from Laney's arms and patted her knee. "Stay put. I'll send Bryan in." Emma rose and blew a kiss.

Laney blew a return kiss. "Love you."

Minutes after Emma departed, Bryan's six-foot frame filled the door to the den. He stooped to where she sat. "Are you okay?"

She wiped her eyes with her fingertips and started to push herself up. "Yes, just remembering."

With a twinkle in his blue eyes, he gently laid a hand on her shoulder preventing her from standing. "It is a bit sad, isn't it?" He sat next to her just as Emma had done earlier. "We've had a lot of happy times in this house."

"We have." She looped her hand around his sturdy forearm.

He laughed and pointed to the stairs. "Remember the time the toilet tank cracked and water flowed down the stairs?"

She giggled and rested her head on his shoulder, warmed by the memory. "Yes. A real mess. Evan used the stairs as a slip-n-slide."

"I think we used every towel we owned and still didn't

sop up all the water." He fingered the diamond on her left hand and then gazed at Evan's growth markings on the doorframe. "We've been through a lot here."

She nodded. "We've also grown a lot. We're surely not the kids who moved into this house twenty-five years ago."

"Thank God for that." He placed a tender kiss on her forehead.

She wrapped her arms around his bicep. "Remember the first meal I tried to cook on my new electric stove?"

He grinned. "Boy, do I. Nothing like burned beans."

"I can't believe you ate them."

"I didn't want to hurt your feelings." He brushed a kiss on her temple.

Just like Bryan. He always put her feelings before his own. She gently kissed his cheek then ran her hand through the salt and pepper hair gracing his temple. "I love you."

He intertwined his fingers in hers. "I love you too."

"Have the movers gone?" she asked.

"They just pulled away."

"Guess we should head out. They'll be in Baton Rouge tonight and will head to Pecan Pointe to start unloading in the morning."

"Yeah, guess we should." His gaze met hers. "How are we going to get up from here?"

"Speak for yourself." She grinned and hopped up. With an extended hand, she reached toward him. "C'mon ole man, I guess it's time to move on."

A teasing twinkle shone in his eyes. He grabbed her hand, pulled her toward him, and in one swift move, rolled her onto the carpet. After they shared a sweet kiss, he pulled away. "Who are you calling ole man?"

She giggled then wrapped her arms around his neck and kissed him again. "I stand...um...lie corrected."

"Hey." When Evan's deep voice boomed from the doorway, Laney flinched and turned toward the door. "This is something your child shouldn't see. At any age." His lanky six-foot frame filled the opening with Casey, his petite, blonde girlfriend by his side.

Her son's smile tugged the deepest corners of her heart. Respectful, intelligent, and God-loving. What more could a mother want?

A flash of a nurse's sympathetic smile zapped her mind. As soon as the memory appeared, she pressed it back. Crushed it. Letting the past torment served no Godly purpose. But the image prevailed. One so vivid it stole her breath.

A baby sucking his thumb and looking at her with sweet innocent eyes.

On this date.

So long ago.

CHAPTER 5

*L*aney walked from the kitchen to the living room around the multitude of boxes strewn throughout her new home in Pecan Pointe, Louisiana. Her brother-in-law, Eric, who'd come over to help unpack finished his phone call. "Sure, I can be there tomorrow at 9:00 a.m."

She approached just as he hung up and handed him a bottle of water. "I really appreciate your help. I know this is hard work and I can think of a million things I'd rather be doing than this." She laughed. "And this is *my* stuff."

He slipped his cell phone into his pocket and wiped the perspiration from his brow with the sleeve of his T-shirt. "You know I'd do anything for you guys. I'm thrilled to have you living in the same state for a change. Maybe if I get the new job I've got my eye on, I can move closer and spend some time with my nephew."

"He's looking forward to the summer off before graduate school," Laney said. "I know he'd love to spend time with you."

Eric took a large gulp from the bottle and then smiled. "He's grown into a fine young man. You and Bryan should be proud."

She smiled. Proud. No, well, yes. More thankful than anything. Evan had come to them by the grace of God and Laney didn't deserve such a wonderful son. Such a wonderful life.

Not after—

"Hey, are you loafers going to sit there and chat while the rest of us work our fingers to the bone?" Bryan walked into the living room where Laney and Eric stood. He carried a photo of Eric and their father. "Thought you might like to have this. I found it in Dad's things when we cleared out his house."

Eric reached for the photo then bit his bottom lip. A shy grin crawled onto his face. "The ole man. I remember that Boy Scouts camping trip. He taught me how to fly fish. I'll never forget his face when I reeled in that massive trout."

"Yeah, it was all he talked about for weeks." Bryan sipped from his water bottle. "How his youngest son had caught a bigger fish on his first cast than he'd caught in his whole life."

Eric laid the photo on the table. His smile faded. "Wish we could have convinced him to move down South before he died."

"Yeah." Bryan rested his hand on Eric's shoulder. "We tried, Bro. That's all we could do. You know how stubborn he was."

Laney's heart filled for her husband, thankful for the rekindled bond between the brothers. Another reason for her to believe, as Emma said, this move was a *God-incidence*. Since Eric's wife died four years ago, he'd been the object of their prayers. His happiness meant the world to her and Bryan.

"You're right." Eric stood, his pensive gaze replaced by the face of someone wanting to forget. "Well, I guess we need to get back to work."

"Yeah, guess so. Or Sergeant Laney here. . ." Bryan grinned and nodded toward her. ". . . will have us doing push-ups in the wee hours of dawn."

Laney swatted at his arm. "I prefer the title of Supreme Allied House Commander, thank you very much."

Eric and Bryan stood at attention, saluted her, then each brushed a kiss on the top of her head as they walked by to resume the arduous task of unpacking boxes.

She shook her head and gently unwrapped her pottery dishes. God had truly blessed her with a crazy, fun, and loving family. One she certainly didn't deserve.

CHAPTER 6

*M*aggie's pen tapping against the top of the small conference table echoed throughout the room. She waited for the next candidate to enter. Would this interview go well?

After three interviews this morning and several over the past week, she had yet to find the perfect doctor for her clinic. A deep inhale did little to calm the quivering in her stomach, she hated this process. Give her sick babies and she was fine, but hiring another doctor to help treat the patients she'd nurtured all these years seemed a daunting task.

She scanned the resume again. Eric. A nice strong name. Doctor Eric. She could hear the children now. She saw them hugging his neck and his big smile when they did. If only she could erase the image of his face as she left the bar last week. She had to admire his tenacity. He scheduled another appointment. She hadn't scared him away.

A quick glance at the door revealed the reason for the caterpillars crawling in her stomach. Eric's six-foot-three frame filled the doorway. Dressed in navy slacks with a white oxford shirt and striking paisley tie, he made an impressive entrance. When he reached the table, he extended long fingers and a slender hand.

"Shall we start over? I'm Dr. Eric Ellerby."

Okay, she'd play. Maggie stood. "Dr. Ellerby, Dr. Maggie Langston. Nice to meet you." She grasped his hand, shook it, and released it quickly hoping he wouldn't notice the moisture in her palm. She pointed to the side chair.

He lowered into the chair. "Same here. Thanks for meeting with me. Again. Maggie, I'm not sure what happened Friday night. If there's anything I did to upset you—"

She lifted both hands as she returned to her seat. "No. You didn't upset me."

His brows furrowed. "Well, that's good to know. You did seem upset."

She swallowed. "I was. But it wasn't…well, meeting at the bar was a mistake."

Her forced smile, she knew, came across as a wimpy excuse at nonchalance, but she couldn't stop herself.

When his gaze settled on her left hand, his narrowed eyes pierced, the electric blue boring into her.

Why had she deceived him when they first met at the convention last year?

She showed him her ring. "I'm married. I apologize for misleading you. I'll understand if you don't want to work with me." Air rushed from her lungs.

He raised his brow.

She sighed. "I need to be honest with you."

His intense stare morphed into a questioning look. The blue in his eyes flashed. "We spent the whole day together. Toured the art galleries, museums. Had lunch and dinner. There were many opportunities for you to tell me you were married. Why didn't you?"

She drew in a deep breath. "It's a long, painful story, but no excuse. Call it a momentary lapse of reason and good judgment on my part. I assure you, not a mistake I make when dealing with my patients or my practice."

Eric leaned back in his chair and scrutinized—a prolonged assessment making her edgy.

Maggie uncrossed her legs and leaned to the opposite side of her chair.

Could he forgive her for the deception?

After an eternity, she glanced at her watch. "Can we forget about last week and continue with this interview?" While part of her wanted to share why she'd been so shaken last week, a larger part wanted to forget and move forward. She'd know by his response how badly he wanted this job. If he continued half-heartedly then she'd have her answer. She examined the crescent shape of his fingernails before braving a look into his eyes.

He sat up. "Yes, I think that's a great idea. Let's continue."

He gave the perfect answer to all her questions. Deep down, she knew he'd be the right doctor for her clinic.

She twisted her wedding ring with her thumb and glanced at the documents on the table. "According to your resume, you've been in Lake Charles since completing your residency in pediatrics. Why leave the hospital?"

He leaned back in his chair. "Your clinic is the type of environment I want to work in, I can devote my time and efforts to the patients. Get to really know them. Also, I'm tired of hospitals." Tiny creases outlined his blue eyes when he smiled. "My brother and his wife have moved to a small town just a few miles from here called Pecan Pointe. I'd like to spend more time with them. My nephew is starting graduate school in the fall so spending the summer with him would give me a chance to get to know him." He paused then continued. "Also, I believe with a better schedule, I may have a second chance at a family of my own."

Noble response. She nodded and braved meeting Eric's piercing eyes, then quickly averted her gaze.

Her son would be about the same age as his nephew.

She allowed her mind to wander. Would Paul be going to graduate school? Would he have become an architect like his father?

For the next hour, she and Eric discussed his resume. She explained her expectations and listened to his. He answered with energy and excitement. Qualities she admired. Qualities she needed in her clinic.

With each reply, he endeared himself to her. Maybe this might be the one. Maybe she had found someone to help shoulder the privilege and the burden of caring for sick children.

"Eric, I'll be in touch. You should hear something from me by the end of the week." She stood and shook his hand.

"Thank you." He gave her a lasting look. "I'm the right fit for your clinic. I believe we can make a dynamic medical team. If you hire me, I promise, you won't regret it." Before she could respond, he turned and left the room.

#

Animated fish swam across Maggie's monitor as she stared at the screensaver. Usually self-motivated and eager to work, she trudged through her documentation as though working through cane syrup. She hadn't heard back from Captain Jordan and she couldn't decide if this was good or bad. But until he called, she continued to harbor hope that Paul still lived, even if it meant going back to the world of not knowing.

This morning's meeting had zapped her energy. Eric's questioning gaze popped into her mind more than once. Would hiring him be a mistake?

Somehow in the past she'd kept her personal life and work life apart.

Each existing in separate compartments.

Never mingling, never crossing.

But this morning she'd come so close to sharing about Paul. Her fingers trembled as she reached for her mouse. Why was it harder to separate the two now? What if the divider crumbled and the black void encroached on her professional life—the only thing she had left to hold on to. The only thing she did well. What then?

She needed a distraction. Lifting the stack of mail her receptionist had placed on her desk, she flipped through each letter. The brochure for the fall conference in Kansas City caught her attention—the same conference where she'd met Eric a year ago. The self-confidence he'd shown when they shared a table then had come through this morning during their interview. She'd gotten to know a little about him and found she liked him. She'd also felt sorry for him when she'd found out his wife had died.

When she'd entertained the thought of bringing on a partner, she instantly thought of him. But contemplating something more than a professional relationship with him had totally thrown her. Where had that come from? She couldn't believe she'd entertained such a dangerous possibility even for an instant.

An orange fish floated by. His mocking smile seemed to taunt her. She drank from the water bottle on her desk hoping to quench her thirst.

While the interview with Eric tugged at her defenses, a burst of renewed motivation energized her. He was full of new and exciting ideas to improve the clinic and bring fresh treatment methods into the practice. She focused on the thing that had drawn her to Eric—he saw her as a good doctor. Period. Not a poor woman whose irresponsibility had led to the loss of her son. She had stared at the empty door after he left this morning. He would be her new colleague. But instead of rejoicing in her decision, the expanse in her heart grew deeper. Wasn't that how her life progressed?

Nothing but a series of actions. Some as simple as walking through a door. Some as risky as teetering along a moral line. Others as serious as turning a watchful eye for a second.

All simple actions with complex consequences.

Why wait until the end of the week? She already knew.

The position would be filled by Eric Ellerby. As she reached for the phone to call him, the sarcastic smile of the orange fish filled her computer screen.

#

"This will be your office." Maggie opened the door revealing a modest room housing a mahogany wooden desk and overhead shelves. "I thought you might enjoy the view of azaleas along the window."

Eric grinned and nodded. "Not bad. Not that I'll be spending much time in here. Show me the treatment rooms."

She led him down the hall and showed him each of the clinic's six treatment rooms. Her team worked diligently to keep the rooms up to date. The doors sported hand-painted characters from popular children's movies—princesses, superheroes, and smiling animals.

Eric nodded as she opened each door. At the end of the hallway, she paused and showed him her office. As they were walking back to the front, Tara turned the corner and ran into Eric. Her cheeks turned a shade of crimson that Maggie had never seen on Tara before.

Maggie wrapped her arm around Tara's shoulder. "Eric, this is our clinic nurse Tara, she's the backbone of the clinic."

A glint sparkled in Tara's eyes before they narrowed into tiny slits from her broad smile. "I remind her of that fact weekly." She extended her hand. "Dr. Ellerby, welcome aboard. I'm looking forward to working with you. We need new blood around here." She elbowed Maggie's arm. "Someone to keep us on our toes."

Maggie laughed and looked at her watch. "Lunch time. Any plans?"

"Sorry can't. My Bible study group is meeting today," Tara said. "We're having Mexican, my favorite. You may not get much out of me this afternoon."

"How's my schedule look? Any new appointments since this morning?"

"Nope, slow afternoon today."

Maggie glanced toward Eric. "Would you like to grab a bite? There's a small Italian restaurant just down the road. After lunch, you and Tara can review the computer system. She's a much better teacher than I am."

"Sure." He waved to Tara and gave her his megawatt smile. "Nice meeting you. See you this afternoon."

At the restaurant, Eric and Maggie were seated at the last available table—a cozy space with two chairs. When she lowered the menu, Eric's gaze captured hers. "Thank you so much for this job. It means a lot and you won't regret it."

She hoped not. The encompassing warmth showered on her by his dynamic personality was already making her wonder if she'd made a mistake.

"Hey, man." A taller version of Eric stood next to the table. "What're you still doing in town?"

Eric smiled. "Bryan, what's up? You guys getting everything in place?"

"You know Laney. She won't rest until every box is unpacked." Bryan turned toward Maggie with a crease in his brow.

Eric gestured toward her. "This is my colleague, Dr. Margaret Langston. She'll actually be my new boss. This is my brother, Bryan Ellerby."

"New boss? You got the job?" Bryan's questioning gaze zeroed first on Maggie and then on Eric. He slapped Eric's back. "That's awesome."

"It was a surprise I'd planned to share tonight. I'm working just up the road from here at Maggie's clinic. I'm moving to Baton Rouge."

Bryan extended his hand toward Maggie. "Dr. Langston, hello. It's nice to meet you. Are you sure you want to hire this guy?" He flashed a mischievous grin and winked. "Anyone who can put up with him, I admire."

"Please, call me Maggie." She shook hands with him and marveled at how much his smile resembled Eric's. He glanced toward her left hand and when he did something flashed in his eyes. He switched his gaze quickly back to Eric.

She slipped both hands onto her lap. "I hope you enjoy living here."

"Thank you, I'm sure we will." His response was polite, but the sparkle she'd heard earlier was gone.

"Ellerby." A voice from behind the counter called out.

"That's me. My take-out is ready." Bryan smiled at Maggie then tapped Eric on the shoulder. "What time you coming by? We'll throw something on the pit. I'm so ready for a break from unpacking."

Eric creased his brows and shook his head. "Yeah right, so Laney can put *me* to work."

"You know, misery loves company." Bryan shrugged his shoulders and grinned. "See ya."

"I'll be there," Eric called after Bryan.

Once he left, Maggie said, "He seemed excited to have you living close by."

"He and Laney are good people. Since my wife…well, they've felt they needed to look out for me. I'm sure me being in the same town will make it easier for them." His grin held a bit of mystery. "We haven't always gotten along."

Maggie's heart tilted. Family who cared. "It's nice to have family support." She sipped her drink. "And second chances."

"Yes, it is. We lost touch for a few years when we were younger. A misunderstanding. When our dad died we made amends." A veil shrouded the sparkling blue for an instant, but disappeared as quickly. "Bryan pressed the issue of reconciliation and after a while, I knew it was time to put the past behind us. I envy them. They rely on their faith and trust God will lead them."

Maggie pondered his words.

Trust.

Faith.

31

Their meaning fled from her life twenty years ago never to rear their heads anywhere near her again. Now they were empty words to her. Just useless crutches for people who clung to the fantasy of a joyful life—those who believed in happily-ever-after.

CHAPTER 7

*L*aney reached into what seemed like the millionth brown box and retrieved another book to place on the shelves in her living room. She rested her hand on the cover then with her index finger, brushed the tattered edges. She'd read *Goodnight Moon* to Evan every night for three years until he'd turned five and found *Stuart Little*. Many nights she'd cradled him in her arms and read to him. The words would soothe her son to sleep when sleep would not come.

"Pizza's here," Bryan called from the kitchen.

She jumped. His voice brought her back from her sweet memories. "Coming."

"Babe, would you get a couple of plates and some napkins? It's beautiful outside. Let's eat out on our new patio."

Once in the bright kitchen, she reached around her misplaced blender and grabbed a stack of napkins from the holder on the counter. The paper plates sat on the wooden table in the breakfast nook, she grabbed two and then followed him through the French doors off the breakfast area.

Outside the brilliant sun highlighted their backyard

dotted with pink Azalea blooms. The warmer temperatures of spring were a welcome relief. Patches of bare ground in the far corner reminded Laney of the work before her. Bryan sat at the glass table under the twirling ceiling fan. The pizza box remained closed. "Guess who I saw at Luigi's."

"Who?"

"Eric." When he reached for the plates, his raised eyebrow caused her to pause. Had something bad happened?

"Really." She opened the box. "Why didn't you invite him to eat with us?"

"He wasn't alone." Both his brows arched and he pursed his lips.

She ventured, "Was he with a woman?"

"Yes."

"Well, good for him." She slid a pizza slice onto her plate and began to pick off the black olives. "Why don't you seem happy for him?"

"Because she's his boss and she's married."

"Oh. His boss?"

"Yeah, the good news is he got the job he'd mentioned the other day."

"That's wonderful." She did a little clap. "So, what's the bad news?"

"He introduced her as his new boss, but I saw something between them. The way they looked at each other. Maybe it's just friendship, but it seemed to be more."

Laney placed her hand on her husband's burly forearm. "Maybe they're friends. You know how Eric has a way of drawing people in. He makes people feel special and women respond to that."

He shook his head while his lips formed a thin line. "I hope so."

She squeezed his arm. "Honey, please, we're not Eric's judge."

"I know." He placed his hand over hers. "I'm doing it

again, aren't I? Making assumptions."

She smiled and nodded.

"Okay. Maybe you're right. She's just his boss and friend." He bit the tip of his piece of pizza. "I just want him to be happy again. To have what we have." Bryan squeezed Laney's hand.

"I know you do. Give him time."

He nodded.

Laney bit into her pizza and watched the pink blossoms of the Azalea bushes dance in the gentle breeze. Extending grace proved easier for her than for Bryan. Perhaps because she knew first hand the cleansing breath of God's grace. Her past life—before she met Bryan, before she met Christ—and the life she lived now were world's apart. Would her husband be as quick to judge her if he knew?

CHAPTER 8

*M*aggie woke and gasped for air. She bolted upright and swung her legs to the floor. The pounding in her chest matched the rhythm of her labored breathing. She consciously forced slower breaths to temper the adrenaline gushing through her veins.

"Maggie, are you all right?" Craig's soft-spoken words from the other side of the king-sized bed caused every muscle to contract. The soft glow from the lamp at his bedside bathed the darkened room.

"You're home," she said. "I didn't hear you come in." Of course, after the sleeping pills she'd taken a train could have run through their bedroom and she wouldn't have heard it.

He slid over toward her, his voice in her ear. "It's the dream again, isn't it?"

She nodded. The dream always left her feeling as though she'd been beaten up while she slept—tortured then left for dead. A shiver ran along her arms. She ran her hands along the chilled skin.

"Maybe you should see Dr. Elgin. Talk to her again."

Again. Would she ever be free from these nightmares?

Five years ago, work offered a renewed sense of purpose. New babies. No more nightmares. She thought she'd conquered the beast, but this twenty-year mark stirred something in her—awakened the fiend of her nightmares. Maybe Craig was right.

She turned to him. His golden hair and emerald eyes sent her pulse racing while the sharp angle of his jaw and the dimple in his chin reminded her of the photo in her purse. His eyes, his hair, his lips—the haunting features of a toddler grown into a man.

Each distinct trait fueled her nightmare. The body of a child with a man's face. Craig's face. The child stood waist-deep in a rushing river while extending his hand for her to save him from the raging waters. His eyes begged for rescue. The dream ended the same every time. Just as she reached him, he was snatched away by a dark force from the opposite bank. She awoke when the cold rapids engulfed her.

Although Craig's arms wrapped around her, no warmth touched her. The emptiness and loneliness remained.

The next morning, Maggie sipped from the cup of coffee Craig placed before her. The steam tickled her nostrils as she brought the rim to her lips.

"So, have you found your new doctor yet?" He sat in the chair across from her.

She sipped again. "Yes, I think I have. He'll officially start tomorrow." Maggie lowered her cup and stared at Craig. "I got your message last Friday. I also got the call from Captain Jordon. The bones were not Paul's."

"I didn't think they would be." He lowered his gaze and focused on the morning paper folded next to his plate. When he glanced back at her, the sharpness of his jawline increased. His gaze shrouded over and the usual distance grew between them. "Maggie, when are you going to let this go? This guilt is eating you alive. It's been twenty years." He pointed to the entryway. "Paul is not going to walk through our door. You've got to accept that fact."

Again, her filter screened his words, but this time to protect her heart from their brutal honesty. Burning anger inched its way to the surface, birthed by his words and her quiet indignation. How dare he expect her to forget? It was the very thing she struggled so hard not to do. She held on to her brokenness. It sustained her. If she gave it up, she'd be giving up on ever finding Paul.

She exhaled. "That's right. Twenty years and nothing. No word. No body to bury. No closure. Maybe it's easy for you to forget. To move on. This was not some failed business deal. This was our son. Gone. Taken from us. How can I forget? How can *you*?" Her voice quivered.

Craig stood. "You act like you're the only one hurt by this. He was my son, too. But wallowing in self-pity will never bring Paul back."

Anger, mingled with pain, boiled to the surface. "You weren't at the park that day. You didn't turn your gaze for a second. Give the okay for some demented creature to steal our son."

He plopped back into his chair, ran his fingers through his hair, and then leaned toward her. "Maggie, we've been over this a million times. I don't know what to say anymore. Even though I wasn't there, I still live with the anguish. Not only my son, but my wife went missing that day. I live knowing you're right here." He pointed at her. "And there's nothing I can do to bring you back."

He turned his extended finger toward the foyer. "What if, by some miracle, Paul walked through that door? Is this the person, the mother, you want him to see?" His voice softened and his green eyes pleaded when he reached for her hand. "I know it's been hard, but I feel like I've lost both my son *and* my wife."

The bite of cruel reality stung, clamping her throat shut. His last words broke through, unfiltered like a clanging gong. The rage driving her outburst waned leaving an emptiness so vast she craved the anger.

If only, to feel.

They sat in maddening silence. The weight of the wasted years, and their neglected relationship pressed, stifled, as though she was trapped in a grave.

But Craig's words were truth. The very essence of what made her Maggie had indeed disappeared twenty years ago. Stolen, along with her two-year-old son.

CHAPTER 9

*"H*ow many of these do you own?" Eric juggled the paper weight from hand to hand. A glass ball with a small dolphin floated inside.

"I don't know for sure. Probably a hundred or so." Laney reached for the memento. "This one we got in Disney World. Evan was ten."

Eric reached into the box and unwrapped another ball—this one with flowers suspended inside. He handled it like it was a baseball.

She grabbed for it. "Our vacation to the Smoky Mountains."

He handed her the next one a large green globe with tiny stars throughout. "And this one?"

With a slight tremor in her fingers, she reached for it. The translucent globe filled with suspended snowflakes transported her back in time and, for a millisecond, Joseph's face filled her thoughts. She'd forgotten about the gift of long ago. And worked even harder to forget the man who'd given it to her. His memory continued to stab at her heart. When she glanced at her brother-in-law, his eyes roamed from the glass keepsake to hers.

"Well?" He smiled.

Her fingers slid along the smooth glass. "It's a gift from…" She let her thoughts wander to a place and time she'd worked hard to forget. "…from someone I used to know." Laney placed the globe on the shelf behind the others, relegating it to the position of unimportance.

Eric cleared his throat and nodded. He seemed different this afternoon—mired in his own thoughts. He'd almost seemed relieved when she told him Bryan and Evan were off to the local home improvement store. Should she speak to him about Bryan's concerns? *Lord, lead me.*

He held the next keepsake for a moment before slowly peeling the paper away. "Did Bryan tell you he saw me yesterday at Luigi's?" He kept his head lowered.

Once he unveiled the memento—an enameled Aspen leaf from a camping trip to the Rocky Mountains—he handed it to her.

She nodded. "He did."

"Did he tell you I was with someone?"

"Yes." She shifted and reached into the box for another keepsake.

"What did he say?"

She shifted her position and turned to face him. "That you had taken the job here and you were having lunch with your new boss."

"Is that all?" Eric lifted the crinkled paper from around another glass globe—clear with bursts of red, white, and blue within.

"Why?"

"Bryan has a hard time hiding his judgmental nature." He met her gaze with a crooked smile and blue eyes filled with understanding.

She smiled and sighed. How much could she say—should she say—without sounding critical? "He thought the woman was married and she was more than a co-worker." There she'd said exactly what she'd promised herself she wouldn't. "Maybe you should talk to Bryan about this."

"You're easier to talk to than Bryan." He grinned. "I wanted to talk to you first because you're not nearly as critical."

"He wants what's best for you."

He sighed. "I know he does, but Maggie is my new boss. And a friend. He didn't see anything because there was nothing to see."

"I'm sure." Her heart ached with compassion for him. Why couldn't he find the perfect wife?

Eric had been a wonderful husband to Nancy. The memory of his wife's deathbed words gripped her—*Laney, help Eric find someone who'll make him happy.* Laney had never repeated the words to anyone, but had prayed for the right person to cross Eric's path.

Lord, the situation is yours. Reveal yourself to him.

#

Laney stood in the front of the room next to the Associate Pastor of Pecan Pointe Community Church, Andrew Dantin. "Young men and women, this is your new youth leader, Mrs. Ellerby."

"Hello." In unison, female voices echoed from near the door.

"Sorry we're late." A petite brunette rushed to find a seat while her friend, a tall blonde slid into the seat next to her.

"Hello. I'm Laney Ellerby. Your new Youth Director."

The brunette with a cross tattoo on her palm waved toward Laney. "Hi, I'm Christy."

The other teenager smiled. Rings covered her thumb and pinky finger. "Melinda."

"It's nice to meet both of you. I'm looking forward to our time together."

Each of the boys and girls seated on the couches or oversized chairs around the room greeted her with a smile.

Once the associate pastor had directed the teenagers to be respectful, he left the room leaving Laney alone with her charges. She sat on the couch closest to the door. *Guide me, Lord.* "I'd like each of you to tell me about the person to your right. Give me the low-down on them. Tell me three nice things you like about them."

She started with Christy who sat to her right. "Well, to my right is Mel, short for Melinda, my best friend. She's a senior and a cheerleader. The three things I like about her are her strong faith, the way she always encourages me when I'm down, and her never-ending smile."

Melinda shared her smile, surrounded by a beet-red face. When she recovered, she turned to the young man to her right. "This is Brandon Robertson, he's a junior at my high school. Brandon is a champion chess player, he always has nice things to say about everyone, and he has the calmest personality of anyone I know."

The corner of Brandon's lips rose. A tinge of red also covered his face. But as the activity flowed around the room, Laney saw appreciation in the faces of those being introduced. She also saw something in the ones doing the introductions. A new way of looking at one another.

Once all the introductions were complete, she started the week's lesson. She'd chosen 1 Timothy 4:12 as today's verse. She told them the reference and waited while they turned to it. She read the verse to them.

"Can anyone tell me what Paul is saying to Timothy in this passage?" Laney asked. Two girls and a boy raised their hand. "Melinda, what do you think?"

"He's telling Timothy, despite his age, he can be an example of a good Christian by his speech, how he lives, how he loves and by remaining pure."

"Jamie? Do you have anything to add?"

"I think the part about remaining pure is big. So many kids in my school act like you've got the plague if you haven't had sex by your freshman year."

Laney explained to the group what it was like during the Apostle Paul's life. She discussed the immorality of the day and encouraged the group to share their ideas. Many voiced their opinions. About one-third of the group remained silent.

The discussion continued until it was time to go. "Thanks for sharing your thoughts. I want you to remember, just because you're young doesn't mean you can't be a shining example of Christ. If any of you ever need to talk, I'm here." She stood and walked to the small green board and wrote her home and cell numbers. "Anytime, day or night."

Over half the teenagers began typing her numbers into their cell phones. A sign of a world quite different than when she was a teenager. Of course, this conversation would not have occurred in her youth group when she was a teenager.

The teenagers filed out the room and would step back into the world. A world ever-threatening to weaken their resolve, to push them into making decisions they might regret. She knew about regret. She wished someone would have warned her about the wolves lurking and waiting to attack. Waiting to take advantage of the young and unsuspecting. The trusting. She bent over to gather her notes and purse.

"Mrs. Ellerby. Do you have a few minutes?" Tamara, the soft-spoken girl who'd sat in the far corner of the room stood next to the couch. She shifted from one foot to the other.

Laney patted the cushion next to her. "Sure. Have a seat."

Tamara sat with her hands on her thighs. "Um. Ugh." She crossed her legs then uncrossed them.

Laney waited.

Tamara popped up. "It's nothing."

Laney stood facing Tamara. "Honey, what is it?"

Tamara shook her head. "It's nothing. I'll see you next time." She did a quick turn on her heel and rushed out of the room.

Laney followed out into the hallway just as Tamara dashed down the stairs. Her stomach lurched. Should she try to follow her? Laney rushed out the door and just as she reached the parking lot, Tamara entered into a truck with a boy who looked much older. The bumper sticker on the back of the truck read, *Dating me will not make you famous, but I'm a really good kisser.*

Laney sighed and tried to push away the dread twisting in her stomach.

#

The week seemed to crawl at a slug's pace. Laney thought often of Tamara and prayed for her whenever she came to mind. Wednesday night, when the girl didn't show up for Bible study, Laney's concern grew. After class, she got her number from the office and then dialed the girl's cell phone. "Tamara, it's Laney. Is everything all right?"

"Yes, my dad's not feeling well so I didn't have a ride to church."

"Honey, you should have called me. I would have picked you up."

"I didn't want to be a pain. Beside my dad needed me here."

Questions circled Laney's brain. What issue could Tamara be dealing with? She wished the young girl had confided in her when they'd first talked. But Laney knew how hard it was to talk to someone about personal things, especially a stranger. Laney pushed the troubling thoughts from her mind. She didn't want to jump to conclusions without knowing the facts.

"Well, we missed you. I'll see you next week, right?"

"Yes, ma'am. I'll be there."

Laney's heart lifted then sank. She was excited that Tamara would return next week, but so much could happen in a week. If Tamara needed her, it could be so hard to wait that long. "Um…Tamara, you know if you need someone to talk to, I'm here."

"Mrs. Ellerby. I'll remember that." Her voice grew quiet. "Thank you."

Lord, I trust Your will for Tamara's life, if there's something I can do, please show me.

Laney paused hoping she would say more. "You're welcome, honey. I really mean it."

When Laney didn't get a response, she resigned to the obvious—Tamara was not ready to share what was bothering her.

"Okay, I'll see you next week." Laney ended the call and slipped her phone back into her purse. Nagging guilt scratched at her heart. What if, when Laney was a teenager, she had confided in someone besides Aunt Elaine? Would the advice have been different? Would she have listened?

Laney hoped Tamara believed she was serious about having a listening ear. Tamara's shyness and reluctance to talk sent Laney to a time when she'd been just like the young teen. She wished she could tell Tamara and her friends exactly how it feels to live with a rash decision. But she feared, if they knew what lay locked in her heart, she'd lose their respect. How could she begin to tell them how to live a chaste life when that was the last thing she'd done as a teenage girl?

CHAPTER 10

Maggie rested her head against the soft leather of Dr. Elgin's couch. Her two-week wait to get an appointment ended when a regular patient canceled.

Thirty minutes into her session, she'd told Dr. Elgin everything.

"Seems like everywhere I go and everything I hear is a reminder of Paul. A couple of weeks ago at the grocery store, I got a glimpse of a young man who reminded me of Craig. My first thought: would this be what Paul would look like? For some reason this anniversary has hit me harder than the others."

"Could anything else be triggering these feelings?" Maggie soaked in the compassion flowing from Dr. Elgin's gray eyes.

Should she tell her about the near-miss with Eric? "I almost made the second worse mistake of my life—I toyed with the idea of having an affair. But couldn't do it. Couldn't be like my mother."

Dr. Elgin nodded. The chain attached to her reading glasses swayed with the motion. As she smiled at Maggie, the wrinkles around her eyes deepened. "Our actions do bring consequences, don't they?" Dr. Elgin's encouraging nods gave Maggie the comfort to share her heart.

"The dream is back. It's different. This time, instead of a blur, I finally saw his face."

The comfort of speaking with someone who knew her past, spurred her onward. Dr. Elgin knew the difficulty she'd faced.

Once the appointment was over Maggie walked out the door, the familiar heaviness weighed on her heart. The peace she'd anticipated didn't come.

Maggie muddled through the rest of the week and through the weekend. She met with Dr. Elgin twice more over the next week. Once again she needed to work on letting go, and while she hadn't completely accomplished the task, she'd started to move forward a bit. The anniversary and the news story had shaken the small foundation she'd built.

Craig asked about her visits with the therapist and responded with sensitivity. He seemed to care and tried to be there for her each night. He'd even hugged her, giving her a deep goodbye kiss when he'd left this morning for a week-long business trip.

Talking to Dr. Elgin helped open her mind. Although her marriage wasn't perfect, it was comfortable. Something worth holding on to and working to improve. When Craig returned she'd talk to him about joining her in counseling.

As Maggie drove toward her favorite restaurant, the late afternoon sun cast shadows on the hotels lining the highway. She dialed her friend Leslie's number. "Hey girl, care to join me for dinner? My treat."

"I'd love to, but can't. I'm leading the Junior League meeting tonight. You should join. I'll get an application if you'd like."

Her friend never ceased in her efforts to get her to join the non-profit organization, but Maggie didn't want to divide her focus. "I'll pass for now. Work is taking up a lot of my time."

"I'll take a rain check on dinner."

"Sure thing. How about next Tuesday?"

"Deal. I'll meet you at Parrain's."

"See you then." Maggie disconnected the call.

When she walked into her favorite seafood restaurant, a young woman, her hair pulled back into a ponytail, greeted her with a smile. "Dr. Langston. One for dinner?"

"Yes, Priscilla. How are you tonight?" Maggie said.

The hostess pulled a menu. "I'm good. Passed my psychology exam. Your usual table?"

Maggie nodded.

Priscilla motioned toward the dining room. Maggie followed past the booths lining the front of the restaurant to her usual table in the corner near the window. She'd stopped in many times after a long day at the clinic on her way home.

"Thomas will be your waiter tonight."

"Thanks." The young woman left Maggie staring out the window at the traffic zooming along the busy street. Before long Thomas, the stocky young man who was a senior at LSU and had worked here since his freshman year appeared at her table. "Hello, Dr. Langston. How are you?"

"I'm well, thank you. How are your classes going?"

He shrugged. "They're going." He placed a napkin, a set of silverware, and a glass of water on the table before her.

She handed him her menu. "I'll have the Shrimp Remoulade salad and a small cup of seafood gumbo."

"Sure thing. I'll get that in for you right away. Anything to drink?" He waited with his pen poised.

"Water with lemon." Maggie remembered the untouched drink she'd ordered at the bar the night she'd met Eric. That had been over a month ago. The patients and their parents loved him. He fit right in as she'd known he would. Her lighter schedule allowed her to take a day off last week.

When her meal arrived, she ate with the flourish of a woman who'd skipped lunch. The gumbo's thick rich roux and the tasty shrimp slowly satisfied her hunger. Once she'd finished eating and paid her check, she prepared to leave.

"Thank you, Dr. Langston." Thomas picked up the small black folder. "See you next week?"

She laughed. "You know me too well. Yep, I'll be here." With her purse hanging off her shoulder, she stood. "Study hard. I expect to hear you aced your exams this week."

Thomas nodded. "Sure thing."

Maggie retraced the route back to the front door, as she passed the last booth along the windows, the sound of a familiar voice reached her ears. A quick glance toward the booth confirmed her suspicion. Eric. Another voice drifted from across the table and for a fleeting moment, plucked a chord of recognition within her. Eric looked up as she walked by. "Maggie, hello. I took your advice and decided to eat here." He sat across from a young couple and waved her over. "Come here, I'd like you to meet my nephew and his girlfriend."

Maggie moved closer to the booth.

Eric slid out of the booth and stood next to the seat. "Maggie, this is my nephew, Evan and his girlfriend, Casey."

The young man unfolded from the bench seat and stood next to Eric. When she met his gaze, her dinner churned in her stomach and burned like acid. She stared into the face of a stranger, but one she knew intimately. One who haunted her dreams and plagued her days. Evan had every feature she saw every day. The tall lanky physique. The arresting emerald eyes. The brown hair. The small cowlick tilting his hair toward the left. His stance. The way he protruded his hip and settled his weight on his back leg. Even the way he arched his brow.

His traits grew in her vision as though she looked through a magnifying glass until they filled her view.

Everything about this young man was the same as Craig. Not just a resemblance, but a clone of her husband.

A certainty rising from the depths of her soul exploded past the doubt.

She knew.

This young man, the one who stood before her with the handsome eyes and awkward stance, was her son, Paul.

Blood pooled into her legs and the room twirled around her. Paul's face came in and out of focus. Glimpses of the questioning gaze in his green eyes opened the door to the deepest recesses of her heart—the place a mother reserves only for her children.

CHAPTER 11

*L*aney stood on her patio, portable phone to her ear. "Emma, it's been so nice talking with you. I'm glad you called and can't wait for you to get here."

"Just a week away."

Laney smiled at the high pitch of Emma's voice. "See you then."

She ended the call and cradled the phone to her chest. Gratitude swelled her heart.

"Laney, I'm home."

"I'm on the patio," she called.

Bryan strolled through the back door and kissed her cheek. "Hey, sweetie. Where's Evan?"

"Eric took him and Casey out to dinner. They're trying to spend as much time as possible together before he starts school in the fall. So you and I are on our own."

"Have you fixed dinner?"

"Chicken casserole."

"Why don't we keep it for tomorrow? Let's go out tonight. I found this great little Mexican restaurant close to the office."

One thing Laney learned in her years living with

Bryan—be flexible. He loved spontaneity. She loved that about him. She transferred the casserole into another dish and popped it into the refrigerator. "Let me change my shoes and I'll be ready."

He grabbed her hand and pulled her toward him. Her heart dissolved every time he showered his smile on her. When their lips met, Laney closed her eyes and melted into the accepting warmth of her husband's kiss.

An hour later, they slid into the cozy booth in the small restaurant. Both sitting on the same bench. Bryan had been right—it was just the kind of place she'd like. The gentle strains of Spanish music drifted through the hidden speakers. After they ordered, Bryan turned to Laney. "Do you know how much I love you?"

She faced him. "I think I have an idea."

Before long their meal appeared and they began eating. Stopping only to share the details of each other's day.

Bryan's phone chirped. He peered at the LED screen.

"Work?" Laney asked.

"No, it's Eric." He tapped the screen. "Hey, bro. What's going—"

Laney lowered the second taco she was getting ready to bite into.

"Evan? Where's Eric?" Bryan's words sent her pulse racing. Her gut twisted at the concern in her husband's voice. The taco she'd just eaten grew like a sponge in her stomach, and the booth in the brick-lined corner of the restaurant felt like a cell. Something was wrong.

The crease in Bryan's brow deepened.

"Okay, we're on our way." He returned his phone to his belt clip.

"What's wrong?" She searched his face for a clue. The tightening of his jaw caused an icy chill to flow through her.

"Eric wants to meet with us at his house. Evan and Casey are with him."

"Are they all right?"

"Yes, but he wouldn't go into details. He said it's important." He reached into his back pocket for his wallet.

She sipped from her water glass in an attempt to douse the dry, parchment lining her throat then slid out the booth. She sighed. What in the world would cause Eric to be so theatrical. She'd never known him to...except when he'd told them about Nancy's cancer. Could Eric be sick?

CHAPTER 12

Eric's voice drifted to Maggie as though he spoke through a filter. "Maggie, are you all right?"

As she blinked, the blur cleared to individual faces. With one face in the forefront. Etched forever in her mind.

Paul's.

Questions volleying through her brain screamed for answers. She closed her eyes again. Was this another dream? "Paul?"

"Maggie, c'mon. What are you talking about? Here have a seat." With a gentle touch he led her to the bench where he'd been sitting. "This is my nephew, Evan." Eric waited for her to move over then slid into the booth next to her.

Each of the faces stared at her. But there was only one she locked her gaze upon.

"No. It's Paul, my son." She reached toward the young man who now sported Craig's furrowed brows. Her fingers trembled. "You look just like your father."

"Maggie this is insane." Eric shifted his gaze from Evan then back to Maggie in search of another answer. "What son?"

"The one kidnapped twenty years ago."

She turned toward Paul. "How old are you?"

"Um...Uncle Eric? I-I-I'm not sure what to do here." The younger version of Craig shifted his weight from one foot to the other, the same way Craig did when uncomfortable.

Eric glanced around the restaurant. "We're going to my house and talk about this. Tell me why you think Evan is your son Paul."

"There's nothing to talk about. He is my son."

He motioned for Evan to sit. "You've got to see how strange this seems. You're saying you think Evan is your abducted son?"

She nodded. Hearing Eric say the words stressed how outlandish her accusation sounded. But...she knew. She knew the young man seated across from her with panic-stricken eyes was her son. She hated the suspicion she met in his gaze. One thing propelled her forward—the insistent yearning to know the truth. "Eric, is Evan your brother and sister-in-law's natural child?"

Eric bit the corner of his bottom lip. He met her stare. His Adam's apple bobbed up then down. "No." He averted his gaze. "He was adopted."

CHAPTER 13

*M*aggie faced out the window to where elegant houses dotted the road to Eric's townhouse.

"You have to realize how far-fetched this sounds." Eric glanced away from the road toward Maggie. He'd insisted she ride with him.

"I know." Maggie knew how ridiculous it sounded, but it didn't matter. Paul followed behind in his truck with his girlfriend.

Had the heavens shown mercy on her? Craig's words rang through her mind. *If by some miracle Paul walks through that door, is this the woman you want him to see?* Her chest tightened. Did her son think she was a lunatic?

"Maggie, I'm not sure how Bryan and Laney are going to react to this."

"I'm just looking for the truth. I want to know what happened to Paul." Had Eric's brother and his wife kidnapped him? How could they possibly explain this?

"Surely, you can't believe my brother and his wife are kidnappers."

"I don't know." She ran her thumb along the smooth leather of her purse strap. "Now that I've finally found Paul, maybe the truth will come to light."

"I have a feeling it won't be that easy." Eric turned into his driveway.

"It has to be easier than living the past years without knowing anything." At least now she knew he was alive. If only she could hold him, run her fingers through his hair as she'd often done, but those things were not possible. He was a grown man now. At least she could tell him how much she loved him and missed him. Had he been told she'd given him away? The thought twisted her heart. And her stomach.

He turned the key in his ignition. An ominous silence filled the interior. Eric turned to her. The intensity of his gaze caused her to pause. "Maggie, you know this is insane. Evan is not Paul."

No. She wouldn't go there. Wouldn't allow her mind to entertain such a heart-shredding possibility. Would fate dangle the possibility of reuniting with Paul only to immediately snatch it away again?

CHAPTER 14

*L*aney held her hands in her lap and tried to imagine every possible scenario while Bryan headed to the interstate and then sped through the Baton Rouge streets to Eric's place. With a tight jaw, his eyes never left the road. His thumbs tapped on the steering wheel.

Please Lord, let Eric be okay. Let Evan and Casey not be hurt. Although Eric had told Bryan they were all fine. Something wasn't right. "What do you suppose could be so serious Eric has us going to his house?"

"I don't know." He shook his head, but not in the finite way of a person who's sure of the answer. He did so in a slow thoughtful way as though there were more to say. Fear seeped through her and held her in its haunting grip. Did Bryan know more than he was saying?

Once in Eric's driveway, they parked behind Evan's pickup truck. Bryan shifted the car into park and turned toward Laney. He reached for her hand then kissed her fingertips. "Honey, I'm sure this is nothing to be upset about." His voice softened. "I trust both Eric and Evan."

His words offered little comfort. Something was wrong. Bryan's actions on the drive over betrayed his words. She slid from the car and rushed toward the door.

When Bryan pushed the doorbell, her legs weakened from the overwhelming dread coursing through her. She felt that once the door opened as the proverbial Pandora's Box, whatever waited inside, could never be closed again. *Breathe.* She inhaled a sharp deep breath.

As the door swung open, she released the breath she held when Evan stood in the doorway. Tall, unharmed, but her relief was short-lived when she saw his pale face and questioning gaze.

"Are you all right?" She ran to him.

"Yes, Mom. I'm fine." He reached down and hugged her. When they separated, she searched his eyes for a clue to what was going on. He pressed her hand into his. "Uncle Eric's in the living room." His short response magnified her troubling fear.

As she and Bryan followed Evan through Eric's small, neat kitchen, Laney willed her feet to move forward and not relent to the temptation to squeeze Evan's hand, turn and run. Her Mexican food churned in her stomach. This would not be good.

Her brother-in-law sat on the couch. A woman with dark brown, shoulder-length hair and striking amber eyes sat next to him. Was this the woman Bryan had seen with Eric? His new colleague? Why was she here? And why was Evan involved? Mascara smudged the corners of her drooping, red-rimmed eyes. Her gaze fixed on Laney.

Eric stood when they entered the room.

Bryan walked directly to his brother. "What's going on? Eric, why the theatrics?"

"Please, have a seat."

"Tell us." Bryan remained standing with a tight jaw and pursed lips.

Eric exhaled and glanced toward Laney. His blue-eyes veiled an unidentified emotion sending deeper fear through Laney.

She'd seen that look before. Once in the eyes of the

surgeon who'd delivered the news her mother had died during surgery. Then again, when her doctor had told her she could never have children. What could Eric possibly have to say to cause him to look at her this way?

He turned toward Maggie. "Bryan you remember Maggie, my co-worker. Laney this is the woman I told you about, Dr. Maggie Langston. Maggie, this is Laney, Evan's mother."

Maggie glanced toward Eric at the mention of Evan then hooked her gaze back to Laney. "Hello."

"Hi." Laney responded to Maggie's reluctant greeting.

Eric pointed to a set of matching armchairs facing the couch. "Please sit." His firm voice left little room but to do as he commanded.

Bryan exhaled and guided Laney toward the chairs. He sat on the edge of the chair then said, "What is going on? Tell us now." His voice resonated through the room and seemed to bounce from the walls to strike Eric.

He lowered his head, exhaled, then stared at Laney. "Maggie's son, Paul, was abducted twenty years ago."

Laney turned to Maggie. She stared at the floor. The poor woman. What a horrible thing to live with. Laney's own familiar loss churned to the surface, but she quickly stuffed the pain in the well-worn spot she always did. She glanced back at Eric.

He continued. "Maggie believes Evan is her son, Paul."

Eric's words sailed through the air like a spear aimed at her heart. They pierced through and left a trail of scorched flesh in their wake. Evan, her son. Not possible. Laney shook her head. "What? No…we adopted Evan through a reputable attorney."

Bryan reached across the chairs and lifted her hand. "This is ridiculous." Laney searched his eyes for the conviction she needed while Bryan's penetrating gaze shifted toward Maggie. "That's insane. Why would you think such a thing?"

Maggie's chin jutted forward. "Evan is the exact image

of my husband. His eyes are the same as my Paul's." Maggie stared at Evan who stood behind Bryan's chair. When Laney saw how Maggie looked at Evan, an unfamiliar streak of jealousy rose in her. But, another emotion reigned supreme—pain for her son. His furrowed brows twitched her heart. Why should he be in the middle of something so absurd? Bryan needed to fix this. Now.

Bryan shifted in his seat and released Laney's hand. He shook his head and turned to Eric. "You called us over here because Evan resembles her husband? Come on." He lifted both hands and exhaled. "People resemble other people all the time."

Maggie sat upright. The desperation in her eyes stabbed Laney's heart. "Mr. Ellerby, I know what this sounds like, but I didn't say Evan resembles my husband. Evan is the exact image of my husband. Even his mannerisms are the same." She reached into her purse and retrieved the age-progressed photo of Paul. "Here, this is what the police believe Paul would look like at twenty-two." She handed the photo to Bryan.

The photo lay in his palm a second before he examined the likeness. He cast a glance at her then exhaled. "Mrs. Langston, my son looking like your husband or this photo doesn't convince me he's your son. Like my wife said, we adopted Evan through reputable channels. I don't see the need to continue this conversation."

Laney caught a glimpse of the picture and restrained a gasp when she saw just how much the image resembled Evan. But a fictional photo didn't mean anything. Evan was hers. She glanced at her stoic son. He stared at the photo as well. What was he thinking?

Bryan handed the photo to Maggie then stood and extended his hand for Laney to do the same. Maggie's eyes widened and she leaned forward. Laney sensed her despair.

Maggie popped up from the couch. "Was Evan about two years old when you adopted him?"

Bryan paused then shook his head. "We're not

discussing this." His mouth clamped into a thin line and, by the straightening of his shoulders, Laney knew his patience wore thin.

Maggie walked toward Laney. Their eyes connected and, in them, Laney saw her longing for the truth. She also saw pain too deep to understand. Yet, somehow, she did understand. She also saw vestiges of something else—hope.

How could she sympathize with someone trying to take her son? "I'm sorry for your loss. Really I am, but Evan is our son. He is not Paul."

Maggie said, "If there was a blood test or DNA—"

"Absolutely, not." Bryan's resolve crumbled. "He's our son and that's all there is to it." He wrapped his arm around Laney's waist and propelled her toward the door. "Evan, you and Casey can follow us home."

Evan stood next to Casey. Their arms around one another throughout the entire meeting. Neither said a word. The confusion etched on his face cut her strength. Even though he was twenty-two he was still her son, and she wanted to protect him from such an outrageous claim.

Bryan shot a darting glare toward Eric. "I can't believe you called us here for this. Do you support this woman's accusations? She's so desperate and jealous she'd cause doubt in the first happy family she sees. What kind of sick person does that?"

Her husband's caustic words burned in her ears. Had she heard him correctly? Bryan had never spoken so harshly to anyone before. Of course, no one had ever claimed his son as their own before..

CHAPTER 15

*M*aggie stared at Bryan and Laney, dumbfounded. Why wouldn't they want to know the truth? Bryan's comment stung, but she tried to put herself in his position. How would she react if some stranger had laid claim to her child?

Evan's gaze swept from her to his parents then back again, seemingly in search of an easy answer. A confused young man striving to draw his own conclusions. He shifted from one foot to the other. The action tore Maggie to pieces. Craig did the same thing.

At his anxiety, regret seized preventing her from falling to Bryan and Laney's feet and begging them to do what they could to release her from her twenty-year agony. The thought of hurting Evan more proved the stronger restraining hand. Her heart ached to know him as her son, but also to protect him. As Bryan and Laney walked through the door followed by Casey, Evan lingered behind, his hands in his pockets.

"Uncle Eric, I'm sorry about all this. My dad only wants the best for me. He's always looked out for me. Don't be angry with him. You don't know how excited he was you're back in his life." Again, he shifted his weight from one foot then to the next. "And Dr. Langston, I'm sorry your son was taken from you, but I don't feel any connection. Surely, I'd feel something. Wouldn't I?"

When their eyes met, a flicker of determination flashed. A challenge of beliefs. She'd seen that look many times with her husband when he had made up his mind about something. A stabbing pain pierced.

"You can get a court order for my blood or DNA if you want and I'll follow the order, but know this, I'm not doing it voluntarily." His gaze drifted toward the door. "My parents just walked out the door and no test result will ever change who they are to me." He turned to Eric. "I've got to go, they're waiting." With his long strides, he crossed the kitchen and slipped out the door before Maggie could respond. She started to run after him. To stop him from leaving her sight. As long as she saw him, heard him, she soaked in the comfort he was real. A living breathing person. Alive. But if he left. . .

An indiscernible wall restrained her. Held her back from telling this young man what her mind screamed. Although Evan didn't *feel* their relationship, she did. Every part of her mind and soul and especially, her heart cried out. *You are my son.* Because, a mother knew. As she stared at the closed door, reality hammered loud and brutal.

She'd found her son and he didn't want her.

"I'm at a loss for words about all this." Eric, with his hair askew, plopped into the leather couch. He removed the knot from his tie and slid it from around his neck.

"I'm sorry. The last thing I want is to cause trouble for you." Maggie legs were anchored to the floor.

Eric rolled the silk tie into a cinnamon roll like circle. His concentrated effort to keep the edges aligned seemed a ploy to avoid eye contact with her. "Is it possible this twenty-year anniversary is stirring emotions in you? Maybe causing you to see things ..."

Her legs, innervated by the rush of adrenaline earlier,

refused to hold her any longer. She collapsed into the nearby chair. How could she tell him about the gaping hole where her heart should be? About the constant pain— numbing, yet scarring, every part of her all these years? How could she tell him she was not imagining things? How could he understand?

"I'm sorry. I know this seems bizarre." She exhaled, suddenly exhausted.

"It's been twenty years..." He shifted on the couch and placed the rolled tie on top the end table. "How can you be so sure?"

"Because he is my son. I know deep down I'm right about this. I just know."

His compassionate gaze caressed her with warmth and understanding. Did she see a glimpse of pity there?

"Bryan's right you know, there are people who look like someone we know all the time." His words broke the connection his eyes had created. He didn't believe her and as much as she wanted him to, there was nothing she could say to change his mind. Her focus in life had switched in the course of an instant the same way a mere instant had changed things twenty years ago. She would have to prove to him and the Ellerby's she was right.

She ran her hand along the leather of the chair. Moments ago, Laney Ellerby had sat here. Maggie sensed a connection with the woman. There was something in Laney's compassionate look that drew Maggie to her—to the woman given the awesome privilege of mothering her son.

Strengthened by her resolve, Maggie stood. "Please take me back to my car. I'm going home to do some research. I *will* discover the truth."

His eyes bore into her as he stood. "Be careful. The truth is not always freedom."

"I'll keep that in mind."

As he drove her back to her car, Eric's words played through her mind. Truth. She needed truth whether it provided freedom or not. She'd been living this nightmare far too long. Imprisoned by her guilt and the past. It was time to wake up. Tonight a long-closed door had finally opened and she intended to walk through it.

CHAPTER 16

*H*ouses peeked behind ancient oaks lining the street as Bryan drove Laney home. The warm glow of cozy lights spilled from antique windows creating the illusion of perfection. Telling the world all within was good and right. Just moments ago, Laney's world had been just as cozy, as secure. Now, an instant later, things had spun in a different direction. She thought of Job's lament, *Shall we accept good from God and not trouble…?*

"Can you believe that crazy woman?" Bryan's right hand gripped the wheel while his left elbow rested on the door. The lines around his eyes deepened, casting tiny shadows in the creases. And his hair, usually neat and in place, spiked out in random directions. A result of repeatedly running his hands through it during the night.

Maggie's pain haunted Laney. As a mother, she understood. Her throat tightened. Just when she thought she could forget her past, reminders like canon balls came barreling toward her pinning her in their grip. Not that she ever wanted to truly forget. "What would doing a DNA or blood test hurt?"

Bryan whipped his head toward Laney. "Are you

serious? You want to play into this woman's delusion?"

"No, but if it will put her mind at ease, couldn't we at least consider it?"

Forty minutes later, he steered into their driveway and pushed the garage door button. His lips set into a thin-pressed line. As the door lifted, several unpacked boxes came into view. Another reminder to Laney of their unsettled life.

Evan had been unusually quiet during the meeting and Laney's heart broke for him. He didn't like being the center of attention and she knew how difficult this whole episode must have been for him.

As they walked from the garage to the back door, Evan's headlights illuminated the garage casting shadows on the boxes. Laney stood with Bryan at the back door and waited.

Evan, alone, exited his truck and met Laney and Bryan at the door. He remained silent until they'd entered the house and settled around the kitchen table. When he spoke, his voice held quiet resolve. "I think she really believes I'm her son."

Bryan ran his hand once again through his disheveled hair. "Your parents and brother were killed in a fire and there were no other relatives. So there's no way you're her son. Don't let her wild accusations cause trouble for this family."

He stood with slumped shoulders, as though he held the weight of the evening. "I'm not giving my blood or DNA. As far as I'm concerned you're my parents and that's all I need." He turned and left the kitchen before Laney could respond.

She glanced at her husband. The glow from the kitchen made the wrinkles around his eyes more pronounced. Laney pushed down the lump of compassion swelling in her. Bryan adored Evan. From the first day they'd seen him—a two-year-old who came to live with them. He'd attached to Bryan immediately.

"Come on, Laney." He flipped the light switch. "Let's try

to get some sleep."

"Sure, but Bryan." She followed him into the bedroom. "I can sympathize with this woman. She just wants an answer. Some type of closure. Can't you understand that?"

He exhaled through tight lips and turned revealing sad deep-set eyes. "Yes, I feel for her, but we can't allow her to disrupt Evan's life like this. He's got a good future. I don't want anyone to create any doubts or confusion for him."

She removed her rings and placed them in the tray on top the dresser. "I'd say that's already happened.".

CHAPTER 17

Maggie typed into Google's search box. Sites touting information about Bryan Ellerby filled her screen. As she scrolled through the entries, she found what she searched for—his former address and phone number in Mobile, Alabama. Enough to give a private investigator a start. Of course, the person she had in mind could work wonders with this basic information.

Maggie mapped her plan. She needed to know who was responsible for stealing her life and future. For creating the agony she lived daily.

Tomorrow she'd make an appointment with an attorney. She wanted to know what legal options remained. Also, she'd call on the woman who had raised her son. Perhaps Laney would be generous enough to give her the name of the attorney who handled the adoption.

As Maggie lathered her face during her nightly ritual, her body responded to the day's events. The weight of her aching muscles pressed on her and begged for attention. She popped a couple of Ibuprofen then headed for bed. Maybe tonight, she'd sleep through the night.

As she dosed off, the images of Evan's confused

expression, Bryan's set jaw, and Laney's compassionate eyes filled her thoughts. Along with an empty sandbox.

CHAPTER 18

*L*aney rolled toward the alarm clock. 3:00 a.m. She and Bryan had gone to bed at eleven, but sleep eluded her. Haunting thoughts whirled through her mind. What if Maggie's claims were true? Could the blessing Laney received have caused another woman such pain? Guilt poured in and with it, came her past, crashing through the concrete wall she'd built around her heart. *Why, Lord? If this is true, how could You allow for such a blessing for me to be so painful to Maggie?*

She slipped out of bed and strolled through the darkened living room. An eerie green glow from a nightlight illuminated the oak floor path to the kitchen. She circled the barstools then headed for the refrigerator. As she poured milk into her glass, she allowed the torment to take her where she'd resisted for so long. Back to that day twenty-eight years ago, two years before she met Bryan.

She'd been nineteen at the time and at the end of her sophomore year at Colorado State University. Her aunt lived in Fort Collins and had insisted she come to live with her while attending school. Laney's dad had been delighted. Her scholarship had only covered tuition and her family's limited budget couldn't stretch any further. So she'd packed up and moved in with Aunt Elaine—her mom's older sister and Laney's namesake.

Aunt Elaine's face scrunched into her old maiden's sneer was the face she saw tonight. Her words accompanied the vision. *It's the best thing for everyone involved, Elaine Marie.* Laney shivered at the thought of her aunt's nasal, high-pitched voice. Since that time in her life, she'd had everyone call her Laney. No more Elaine. No more memories.

Her aunt's no-nonsense way of handling things had intimidated Laney. But then again, Aunt Elaine had not forced the decision on her, it had been entirely Laney's— one she'd had to live with all these years. Would things have been easier had the decision been made for her? If there'd been someone else to blame?

Maggie's grief-stricken face came to mind. She could sympathize with Maggie on losing her child, but couldn't imagine the anguish of having her child stolen.

She leaned over the cool marble of the center island. *Lord, help me to let go. You've forgiven me, help me forgive myself.*

"Honey, are you all right?" Bryan's whispered words floated from the edge of the hallway.

Startled, Laney lifted her head. "Yes, just thinking."

He extended his hand. "Come back to bed."

She downed the last of the cold milk, letting it wash down her throat and soothe the constriction there. If only her thoughts could be cleansed as easily. "I'm coming."

Bryan waited. When she neared, he wrapped his arm around her shoulder and kissed the top of her head. "That bed is too big without you in it next to me."

She allowed him to lead her back to the bedroom. As she lay next to him, her head on his chest, she listened to the steady rhythm of his heartbeat.

Bryan grasped her hand. "Sweetie, don't worry. Evan is our son. Nothing will change that."

She sighed. "I know." The truth could change many things. Could crack the foundation of their world. But Evan was not the only child who filled her worried thoughts.

CHAPTER 19

*D*uring the past two nights, Maggie spent endless hours scouring the Internet in search of legal answers. Her days were filled with patients so it was easy to avoid Eric.

When Craig called, she burned to tell him about Evan, but something inside stopped her. This needed to be told in person. Maybe by Friday, when he returned, she'd know the truth.

Yesterday, after work, she'd driven to Sunset Park. This time the children playing brought joy, not the sorrow usually marking her trip.

Today, Maggie had taken an extended lunch and met with her business attorney, Jason Burrows. He adjusted his bow tie and leaned forward after listening to her story.

"What are my legal options here?"

He gave her the legalese on the felony then leaned back into his leather chair. "Do you think the Ellerby's may have been directly involved?"

Maggie shook her head. "I don't think so, but who knows? They claim they used a reputable attorney who specialized in private adoptions."

He wrinkled his pointed nose then nodded. "We can

petition for a court-ordered DNA test."

"No, not yet. I don't want to go that route unless I have no other alternative." She shifted in her seat. Evan's words flooded her thoughts—*You can get a court order for my blood or DNA if you want and I'll follow the order, but know this, I'm not doing it voluntarily.*

"Well, finding their attorney may help get to the truth. Can you get a name?"

"I think so." She thought of Laney's eyes. Maybe…just maybe. "I'm meeting later today with a private investigator."

His green eyes narrowed. "Maggie, advise him this may not be an isolated case, he may be investigating a black-market ring. It could be dangerous."

She hadn't considered other children may have met the same fate as her son. Her gut twisted. Children sold as a commodity. Disgusting.

She swallowed past the rising lump in her throat. "I'll do that. Thanks for the advice, I'll keep you posted."

"Anything, you need, let me know. I'll help in any way possible." His smile reached the corners of his eyes making them crease. "I'm not the most qualified in this area, but I can give you names of attorneys, if you need them." He rose from his desk and extended his hand.

She shook it and thanked him again. As she walked to her car, her stomach coiled like a rubber band twisted to its limit. Children sold on the black market like wares to the highest bidder—bile rose in her throat.

Alone in her office, she dialed the number she retrieved from Eric's personnel file—Bryan Ellerby's number. With each ring, her heart pumped faster. She breathed in and out in an effort to control her rising pulse. When the soft hello came across the line, her hand trembled.

She took a deep breath. "Laney, this is Maggie Langston. I know you've had a terrible shock and I'm sorry. I don't want to put Pau—er…Evan through any type of court-mandated tests, but I have to know the truth. Could you give me the name of your attorney?" She finally paused for a breath. Silence filled the gap. Had Laney hung up?

A sigh came through the line. "I've been waiting for your call."

"Waiting? Why?"

"Because if the situation were reversed, it's what I'd do."

Maggie bit her bottom lip to keep the sob rising in her throat from escaping. "Will you help me find the truth?"

"I wish it were that simple. I have other people to consider. If I help you, I'll be going against my husband and my son's wishes. What would you do if you were in my place?"

Maggie's heart melted. She wanted to say she'd go against her husband and son to help the woman who wanted to lay claim to her child. But when she thought about what she asked of Laney, she couldn't. The sinking weight in her stomach grew heavier. She couldn't count on Laney for the attorney's name. Why did Laney have to be so nice? It would have been much easier if she were mean or vicious.

"I guess I'd be loyal to my family." The soft-spoken words left her painfully aware that she'd reached a dead-end.

"I'm sorry, Maggie." Laney paused.

Maggie waited. Was that all she had to say?

"Maggie?"

"Yes."

"His office is in New Orleans."

The silly fish on Maggie's computer monitor became a blur of orange and blue as tears marred her vision. She knew what it took for Laney to share the information.

She whispered into the phone, "Thank you."

CHAPTER 20

*L*aney clutched the phone to her chest after she hung up. What had she done?

Given a desperate woman a way to the truth. Once Maggie realized Evan was not her son, she would leave Laney and her family alone. They could all move on, get past this chaos. Yes, that's what she'd done—opened the door to freedom.

Evan had said very little over the weekend. He'd spent time with Casey and when they'd left Sunday after church for the lake, he'd simply repeated what he'd said Friday night about believing she and Bryan were his parents and that was enough for him. Bryan voiced the same belief. Why then was it not enough for her?

Evan's birth certificate, in her safety deposit box, stated he was Nicholas Johnson, a two-year-old whose parents and older brother were killed in a house fire in Oklahoma. According to Mouchaux, their attorney, little Nicholas had been found roaming near the back door. They were told the bruise on his forehead when they'd met him was because of falling debris. Her heart had shredded when she'd seen him for the first time. A ragamuffin sitting on the couch in their attorney's office. Dirt covered the bottom of his tennis shoes and his hair lay matted to his head. Those frightened green eyes had drilled a hole in her heart.

As she replaced the phone handset on the charger, Evan walked through the side door into the kitchen. "Hi, Mom." A mature version of those green eyes enveloped her.

The sight of his tall, lanky frame and tousled hair made her smile. She wanted to spend as much time with him as she could. Before long, he'd be busy with school and friends. "How about leftovers?"

"Fine with me. You know me, I'll eat most anything." He smiled.

He'd always been an agreeable child. Guilt speared her heart. Traitor. She'd given Maggie information which would encourage her to continue this madness. *Please, Lord, let the truth be revealed.*

****

"Looks like you're in tip-top shape." Maggie closed the chart of her last patient of the day—a young girl who needed a physical to participate in a community gymnastics class.

"Thanks, Dr. Maggie. I can't wait to start. Will you come to my meet?"

"Let me know when it is and I'll do my best to be there."

The freckle-faced, pre-teen bounced out of her office. Her mother, shaking her head and smiling, followed close behind. "Few things in life are as exciting for her."

"Until she discovers boys," Maggie laughed and used the chart to pat her patient's back.

In her office, she quickly updated her charts and glanced toward the clock on her computer screen. Almost four. Her appointment with Clancy, the investigator was in a little over an hour. Would she have enough information for him to find the truth? Each bit of data she'd collected since Friday had gone into the folder she planned to give him.

"Maggie, have you got a minute?" Eric stood at her doorway.

Her stomach clenched. She'd planned to slip out the office before he'd finished his caseload. She didn't want to talk to him. Not today. She glanced back at the clock. "I have an appointment at four. I have to go."

He stood at her door. "We have to talk about this."

No they didn't. She said all she intended to say to him.

"I want to talk about what happened." He entered her office and sat in the visitor chair. "I know you've been avoiding me. How are you doing?"

A glance his way revealed his concerned gaze. Not at all what she'd expected. He was torn by this, but could he really be fair to both sides? "I'm fine."

CHAPTER 21

Laney tossed fresh greens of a Spring Mix salad. Just as she finished, the melodious chimes of her doorbell brought a smile. Emma.

She rushed to the door and flung it open. Emma greeted her with a dazzling white smile, her thick black hair was gathered in a half ponytail. Curls cascaded around her shoulders. She extended a bouquet of daisies. Big beautiful and fresh.

"Hello, friend." Laney took the flowers. "Thank you. These are lovely." She placed them on the antique sewing machine table near her door and then embraced her best friend.

"Laney, girl." Emma's south Alabama accent came through with just those words. "I've missed you so much. What's been goin' on here?"

She melted in the warmth of Emma's voice and the comfort of her hug. Both brought back soothing memories of the home she'd left. The friendships she'd left. And the peaceful life she'd left.

Although she'd been working hard to make the Baton Rouge house a home, it still missed the mark. She didn't have Emma next door.

"Come in. Lunch is waiting." She picked up the flowers then led Emma into the kitchen.

"Wow, your place looks wonderful. Did you hire an interior decorator?" Emma rotated in a circle looking at each wall.

"No." Laney lifted her eyebrow at Emma. "I did it myself."

"C'mon Laney, you can tell me the truth."

"I am telling the truth."

"Well, I'm impressed. You did a great job. I knew you had a special talent. You just needed a reason to use it. With Evan grown you can concentrate your efforts on others things besides being the perfect mom."

Laney exhaled a deep sigh. "Honey, there's no such thing as a perfect mom. I can't wait to tell you what's happened."

Emma's brows arched. "Really. Well, spit it out. I'm all ears."

"We can talk after lunch."

"Now you know, I'm not gonna be able to eat in peace. You've got to tell me what God is up to." Her dark eyes twinkled.

Laney pointed to the table and the large salad. "Start serving. There's grilled chicken in the covered dish on the table."

Emma plopped mounds of salad and grilled chicken onto their plates while Laney filled a purple vase with water.

"Your salad is ready. Time to eat *and* talk." Emma poured sweet tea from the pitcher on the table.

Laney arranged the flowers in the vase allowing the long stalks to splay from the opening. "Thanks for the flowers, these are beautiful." She laughed, knowing how much her procrastination irked Emma. A game they'd often played. Her heart warmed. Would she find such a friend here in Baton Rouge? *Lord, would you send me a friend here. One like Emma?*

"Laney, I'm waiting."

"All right, already. I see you've not improved in the patience department."

Emma laughed. "Yeah, funny thing, I keep praying for more patience, but it's not happenin'."

Laney joined in Emma's laughter. They both knew patience came one way—through challenges. She placed the flowers in the center of the table and sat across from her friend. Emma's rich voice asked for blessings over the food.

Between bites, Laney told Emma about Maggie Langston and the turmoil she'd created in Laney's perfect world. She rolled a grape tomato along the ridges of her plate. "I feel for her. A part of me wants to help her so she can find the truth. So she can leave us alone. Then there's a part that doesn't want to see this woman hurt any more than she already has."

Emma brushed her fingers along Laney's hand. "Awww, honey, you have such a tender and generous heart."

"No, I don't. It's not generosity spurring my feelings. It's selfishness. I want my world back." She paused. A thought she'd not dared speak before rolled through her brain. "What if … what if she's right and Evan really is her son?" She swallowed through her constricted throat.

Emma's gentle gaze touched Laney's heart in the place where she needed comfort the most.

"Laney, even if by some strange twist of fate, that woman gave birth to Evan, you raised him, you taught him right from wrong, you showed him a stable home. He's not a child anymore, he's a man who can make his own choices. And I know, if given the choice, he'd choose you. Because you are his mother. Hear me?" Emma leaned closer, a twitch of a smile played at the corners of her lips. "You, Laney Ellerby, super mom, are Evan Ellerby's mother. Got it?"

Laney smiled. "Now I know why I missed you so much."

Emma didn't return her smile. "Laney, I can't help feeling there's more to this story than you're telling me."

Laney sighed. "Seeing Maggie's torment over losing her son has awakened past demons." It had peeled back the layers to her past she'd worked so hard to forget. "Some things I can't let go."

"Sounds like God has a mighty plan brewin' through all this."

"I hope so. Sometimes the truth is a scary thing to face."

Emma grinned. "Not when it's faced with God's truth. But remember my sweet friend, be careful what you pray for. It might come to pass."

Laney sighed and remembered her recent prayer, that the truth be revealed. The twist in her stomach told her she may have to remember Emma's words one day soon.

CHAPTER 22

*"H*ere's all the information I have." Maggie sat across from Clancy Chauvin as she handed him the folder over his cluttered desk. It contained everything she'd found since seeing Evan. She'd filled him in on the situation including the concerns Jason brought up about the black market ring. His beefy hand with a wedding ring embedded on his chubby ring finger grasped the folder.

Clancy's large lips chomped on the end of a fat unlit cigar. "I know a lot of people in N' Awlins'. If he had false records created in the 1990s, I'll find him. Only a few people could have done that." The dark of his eyes deepened and he nodded toward her. "Thanks for thinking of me for this job."

"Please call me when you find out anything. Oh, and Mr. Chauvin, I want to meet this man. I want to look into the eyes of the man who stole twenty years of my life."

He blinked a few times. "You want to meet him?"

She tightened her jaw. "Yes."

"Sure." He shrugged his shoulders. "Whatever you want, you're payin' my salary. I'll call with updates."

"Thanks. Is there any way to predict how long this will

take?"

He shook his head and his jowls jiggled with the motion. "Not really. I'll leave in a couple of hours. I could have something for you as early as tomorrow or it could take several weeks. It's hard to say. I'll know more by tomorrow night."

Craig would return home tomorrow. Maybe she'd have great news for him. But the logical part of her knew that likelihood was bleak at best. She shook Clancy's massive hand and left his tiny office tucked in a strip mall in the old part of town.

On the drive home, she played her favorite 70's playlist music a little louder and actually sang out loud to the tunes. A feeling she'd not known in a long time filled her. Hope. Maybe her life finally moved in the direction it needed to go. But what if Clancy found this guy and she met him? What would she say? What would one say to the person responsible for twenty years of agony?

The next morning she went into work early to catch up on her documentation. The first inkling of light in the eastern sky streamed into her office window promising a hot and brilliant day. A tilt of her empty travel mug prompted her to head for the break room to make a fresh pot of coffee. When she turned the corner and entered the room, her breath caught. Eric poured water into the coffee maker.

He turned toward her and his lips barely spread. "Maggie, hello."

"Eric." He was the last person she wanted or expected to see.

"What brings you out so early?" He poured coffee into the filter and turned on the machine.

"Needed to catch up on a few things." She set her coffee mug on the counter.

Coffee splashed into the glass carafe as its heady aroma filled the room. The smell usually tantalized Maggie's taste buds, but this morning the scent punched her like too much perfume in a stuffy elevator.

He took a step closer. "We need to talk."

She slid the metal chair from the table, sat, and then gestured for him to do the same.

He did. "I'm concerned about the impact your claim will have on my nephew. He's starting graduate school in the fall and he doesn't need doubts stirred in his life."

"Eric." She sighed and crossed her arms. "For the first time in over twenty years, there's a clue to what happened to my son. I'm not going to let this door close without following through."

He nodded. "I understand your need to know, but haven't you thought about what this will do to Evan?"

She rolled her bottom lip between her teeth. "I have. I'm not going to get a court order for DNA or blood."

He drummed four fingers on the laminate top of the table. When he looked up, she saw something akin to relief in his eyes. "You're going to drop this?"

"I didn't say I would drop this." She arched her brows. "I'll not pursue court action out of concern for Evan, but I'll investigate this as far as it takes me."

His fingers stopped in midair. "Regardless, of what this does to the Ellerby's?"

"I deserve to know. They should know the truth also." All the reunion visions she'd imagined never came close to the reality she now lived. Then again, she'd learned a long time ago dreams never did.

His quiet gaze rested on her. "I hope you understand what you're doing. Promise me, before you take the next step you'll think about this. There is more at stake here than knowing the truth." He stood and walked out the door. His empty coffee cup still on the counter.

She understood his concern for his family, but he would never understand what she'd been through. He'd never understand her burning need for the truth. While she was grateful for his honesty and friendship, his retreating back filled her with remorse. Two feelings she knew could be on the same edge of a sharp sword.

As she left the break room, empty coffee cup in hand, the gurgling sound of the coffee pot followed her. Was she wrong for wanting to pursue the truth?

CHAPTER 23

*M*aggie glanced toward the LCD screen of her office phone. *Memorial Hospital.* A slight tremor shook her hand as she reached for the receiver. Why would she get a call from a hospital? As the handset reached her ears, she heard Clancy's voice. "Hold on. Hold on, I can't—"

This could be it. A moment of truth she'd waited twenty years to hear. "Hello." She raised her voice to compete with Clancy's booming words.

"Maggie, Clancy here. Listen, Henri Mouchoux, the attorney who set up the adoption is dead. But—owwww, Jarrett take it easy. Sorry, Maggie, I got bad news. I broke my leg yesterday, it's a long story. I had surgery last night and they're keeping me in the hospital a few more days. Then they're shipping me off to some rehab place. My cousin is taking this opportunity to repay all the torture I inflicted on him during our younger days."

An arrow to Maggie's heart would not have seared any deeper. She coiled the cord around her finger. "Clancy, I'm so sorry about your leg. You said the attorney is dead?"

"Yeah, and I won't be able to meet with the secretary until I get out."

"Secretary? What secretary?"

"The attorney's secretary. I got her name. She lives in the old office in N'awlins'. Somewhere near the quarta'. Same woman who worked with him the whole time. Supposedly pretty loyal…"

A moan crept into her throat. She struggled to keep it there. So close… Her heart ached, it could be weeks before Clancy recovered.

What if she went to New Orleans and spoke to the secretary? But would Eric be willing to handle her caseload for a few days?

Clancy's voice droned on, "…so turned the office into a Bed & Breakfast. It's called Hazel's Bed & Breakfast."

Maggie scribbled the name on her blotter.

Clancy rambled. "People I talk to said she must be close to a hundred years old, but she still runs the place—"

"What's her last name?"

"Oh, it's a very common Cajun name. Sorry, Doc, I'm on these heavy duty drugs for the pain. I jus' can't remember." He paused. And she thought she heard a sniffle.

The regret in his voice touched her heart. The burly, tough guy had a soft side after all. Or had the drugs just spoken? "Clancy, you concentrate on getting better and don't worry about the case. I might just call Hazel's Bed & Breakfast myself."

"Don't forget to ask her—oops gotta go, the nurse is here. The good-looking one. Bye."

"Ask what?" Silence followed a click. What could he have wanted her to ask the secretary?

She smiled, despite the news, then dialed the number of her friend, Adele who owned the Pecan Pointe Florist. Even burly, tough guys needed get-well flowers. With the phone cradled to her ear, she gave Adele her credit card number. "Thanks, Adele. I know you'll make it special."

After she completed the order, she typed in *Hazel's Bed and Breakfast—New Orleans* into her search engine. The first entry gave the phone number and address. She quickly dialed Hazel's number.

"This is Hazel." A raspy voice tinged with age continued. "How can I help ya?"

Maggie froze. She hadn't given any thought to this. She couldn't discuss this over the phone.

"Hello, anybody there?"

"Yes, um...I'd like to make a reservation." Maggie clicked to her calendar. Craig left again on Sunday around noon. She could drive over after he left.

"When?"

"Sunday night." Would she have the nerve to tell Craig before she left? This time she knew he'd think she was crazy, think she'd finally crossed into the realm of insanity.

"This Sunday?"

"Yes."

"Well, honey, it's your lucky day. Someone just called about ten minutes ago to cancel. It's a room with a double bed and a day bed, the only one I have left. How many nights?"

"I'm not sure. Book it for three."

She read the numbers from her credit card to Hazel. Would the woman on the other end answer the most important questions of her life? Could she?

Now to clear her schedule for next week. She walked down to her receptionists desk and told her to remove her name from the schedule for the beginning of next week. *Now for the hard part.* She walked down the hall to Eric's office. What would she tell him? She couldn't very well tell him the truth. Could she?

When she reached his door he was dictating a chart update. She sat in his visitor's chair and waited for him to finish.

"Eric, something has come up and I need to take off the first part of next week."

He dropped his pen and leaned back in his chair. "Why do I feel this has something to do with Evan?"

She averted her gaze. "Can you cover for me?"

He hadn't moved since she'd walked it. His scrutiny unnerved her, but she held her ground.

After a while, he answered, "Yes. I can." He leaned forward. "Why do I have a strong feeling I'm going to regret this?"

She smiled. "Thanks, I owe you."

"Yes, you do and don't you forget it." He narrowed his eyes and pointed at her. "Maggie?"

She bit her lower lip and waited.

"Be careful." His voice softened. "There are a lot of people involved that could be hurt. Including you. Whatever you discover, remember that."

"I will. I don't want anyone hurt. You know, I'm only searching for the truth, but I will be careful. Thanks for covering for me. It means a lot."

He smiled. "No problem. That's what partners do."

She knew bringing Eric on board had been the right choice. Hopefully, she wouldn't need much time, just enough to prove Evan was Paul.

Hope ignited her heart with excitement. It felt good to finally be moving away from her twenty-year prison. Could she be days from having proof? The thought propelled her onward. Eric's warning rang through her brain. And once she found proof? What would she do then?

She'd tackle that obstacle when she crossed it.

CHAPTER 24

"*L*et's get a cup of coffee." Laney linked her arm through Emma's and guided her into the coffee shop.

"Sounds, great. My feet need a break." Emma transferred her shopping bags to her left hand. "And so do my arms."

On Emma's last day of her two-day stay, Laney drove Emma to several plantation homes along the river road. They strolled through the anti-bellum homes and imagined what life would have been like when the homes were first built.

They browsed the gift shops admiring the hand-painted dishes, Junior league cookbooks, but the handmade children's clothing brought a sparkle in Emma's eyes.

"Amy is gonna love the little dress I bought her. Every little girl needs a tatted dress. It should fit her by next Easter." Emma laughed. "At least I hope so."

"I'm sure it will. You're such a great grandma. I can't wait until I'm a grandmother." Laney envisioned Evan coming home to visit with kids of his own. The thought warmed her heart and triggered a smile.

"Oh, girl, it's the best thing. I can spoil them, love on

them, feed them all the things they like..." She grinned and arched her right eyebrow. "many of which they shouldn't have, then send them home to mama. I love it."

While holding a cream-topped, frozen coffee, Laney followed Emma to the tall ceilinged, front porch of the well-known home. She pointed to a corner table with a view of the river. "There's the perfect table." Once seated, Laney sipped on her drink and enjoyed the cool reprieve from the afternoon heat.

Emma lifted the straw tip so the end rested in the whipped cream then sucked in. She leaned back in her chair. "So how's Evan holding up to all this controversy?"

"So far, good. He's not saying much. He and Casey are spending as much time together as possible. She's been good for him." Laney sipped her coffee. "I've accepted we no longer have him to ourselves." Her thoughts drifted to Maggie and the turmoil her allegations had caused. If what Maggie claimed was true, she may be sharing Evan with more than Casey.

Emma smiled. "It's hard to let go. That's why God gives us grandchildren. As a reward for letting go."

"I think I'll like being a grandmother. I remember what it was like having Evan running around the house and I have to admit, I miss having a little one under foot."

"When the timing is right, you'll be the best grandma ever. I wouldn't expect anything less from the best mom ever." Emma slurped the last of her drink then squeezed her eyes shut. "I think I'm gettin' a brain freeze."

Laney laughed with her friend, but the underlying squeeze in her heart reminded her no matter how hard she tried or what anyone thought of her, she'd never be the best mom. Never.

The afternoon flew by and Laney was painfully aware that Emma would be leaving tomorrow. They gathered their bags and headed for the door.

"I've got to stop at the cleaners on the way home, I hope you don't mind." Laney wrapped her arm around Emma's shoulders. "Bryan has a meeting tomorrow and needs his suit."

"On Saturday?"

"The company owner is flying in tonight and wanted to meet his newest manager, so he lined up a seminar and luncheon for the region's managers. Evidently, tomorrow worked best for him." Laney got into her car then rolled down the windows to release the stifling heat.

Emma slid into the passenger seat and adjusted the air conditioner vents. "So what are you going to do tomorrow?"

"Who knows? I haven't made any plans. Whatever the day brings, I guess."

The days with Emma provided just what Laney needed—a reprieve from her troubling thoughts.

"I'll just be a minute." Laney parked at the dry cleaners and slid out of the car. She stopped on the sidewalk and fished through her purse for the claim ticket. The smaller purse she'd purchased didn't work to alleviate the clutter she managed to amass.

Someone approached the door from the other direction. Finally, the white ticket with a staple on the end, appeared. She loosened it from its surroundings then looked up to see a tall gentleman holding the door for her.

When her eyes met his, she gasped. She knew those eyes. With the recognition, the foundation of her world cracked along the fissure recently created by Maggie Langston.

For twenty years she'd looked into those eyes. She'd worked to straighten the stubborn cowlick.

His smile crept into her heart and spread into the special places reserved for her son. Daily she embraced the lopsided spreading of his lips. Craved it. But not today. Not now. It didn't comfort. Didn't soothe. Didn't belong.

Her muscles, strong from workouts and long walks, melted into a mass of quivering putty unable to support her shaking frame. A strong, slender hand reached out to steady her, its shape larger, but dangerously similar to one she'd held on the first school day. "Are you okay?"

His voice. So similar. Her pulse sprinted. She swallowed.

"Um . . ."

Words jammed in her throat, refusing to flow through her mouth. She pointed to the opened door encouraging him to walk in and then turned toward her car. Before she could convince her obstinate legs to move, Emma's comforting hand steadied her.

"Did you see...?"

"I did." Emma reached for the ticket. "Let me get your clothes."

Laney held firm to the receipt as though it was her ticket to the future. "No, I have to know." She entered and approached the counter, Emma by her side.

"Are you sure?" Emma whispered.

Laney fixed her gaze on the tall lanky physique of the stranger. "Yes."

A young dark-haired clerk handed plastic-wrapped laundry across the counter. "Here you are, Mr. Langston, see you next time."

The name singed Laney's ears. One she'd not known weeks ago. But now. The name had entered her life and shattered the framework of her world.

This man had to be Maggie's husband.

Could he also be her son's father?

She willed her throat muscles to relax and approached the familiar figure. Could she trust her voice?

She inhaled and pressed on. "Excuse me. Are you Craig Langston?"

CHAPTER 25

*M*aggie clicked the log-off icon on her computer then gathered her purse. Friday afternoons usually held a buzz of anticipation in the clinic, but she'd never shared the excitement before today. For the first time in twenty years, she looked forward to the weekend and her time off next week. Her plans to meet with Hazel held the promise of long-awaited answers. Could the barred door holding her captive for so long finally open? Could truth restore what fate had stolen from her?

As she locked the clinic door, the non-descript warble of her cell phone sounded. No fancy ring, favorite song, or cute jingle for her. "Hello."

"I'm home. I've picked up the dry cleaning. You won't have to stop there."

Maggie smiled. One less thing on her to-do list. Her chest clenched. Craig was a good man—too good to have stayed by her side all these years. She didn't deserve him.

"Thank you. How was your flight?"

"Good. We got another investor on board so I think the project will start sooner than expected."

As she walked toward her car, the humid air swamped

her. "Great."

"Oh, I met a friend of yours at the drycleaners."

She reached her car. "Really, who?"

"Laney Ellerby."

CHAPTER 26

*M*aggie's feet cemented to the pavement while her pulse raced. She adjusted the phone closer to her ear. "Did you say Laney Ellerby?"

"I did. She seemed real nice. A bit nervous, but nice."

Maggie leaned against the fender and instantly jumped back as the heat scorched her leg. Had Laney told Craig? Surely, he wouldn't be as calm if she had. "So, what did she have to say?"

"She said she'd be calling you soon."

Sweat dripped from her palms and her breath caught as she gulped in the steamy air. "Is that it?"

"Yeah, that's it."

She exhaled, long and hard. "I'll pick up a couple of steaks for dinner."

"Sounds good. I'll fire up the grill."

The remainder of her conversation with Craig progressed in a blur. Her pulse pounded and her focus remained on one thing—Laney had seen Craig. She'd witnessed the older replica of the boy she called her son. What would she say?

Now would she be willing to convince Evan to undergo

a blood test?

Maggie's heart ached. Simply knowing Evan was her son was not enough any more. She yearned to know how Paul became Evan. To understand the sequence of events leading to her path of loneliness and Laney's path of motherhood.

Perhaps, Hazel held the answer.

Should Maggie tell Craig about her suspicions? The answer lay buried almost as deep as the truth.

****

Laney stood next to Emma's car and hugged her friend one last time. Emma's tiny frame transferred strength and assurance. She clung tighter and longer than usual, letting go meant breaking the bond and losing the connection supporting her today.

Emma whispered into her ear. "I can stay. I don't have to leave just yet."

Stay pushed at the back of her lips begging to be unleashed. She wanted to scream the word. But couldn't. Even in her most selfish moments, she couldn't imagine causing Emma to miss her granddaughter's first birthday party. Instead she backed from Emma's embrace and forced a smile through quivering lips. "I'll be fine. Bryan will be here soon and we'll talk."

Emma glanced at her watch. "Are you sure?"

She nodded. "I'm sure. You need to get home to your grandbaby."

"If you're sure, then I'll go. I'll be praying for you, dear friend. All the way home."

"Thanks, Emma." She released. "You be safe."

Emma slid behind the wheel and looked up. "Laney, God has amazing plans for you. This may seem like a hard pill to swallow, but I know He'll work something good out of this. Something beyond anything you can imagine."

Laney choked back a sob. "My head understands what you're saying, but my breaking heart needs a little convincing."

Emma squeezed her hand. "I know, sweetie, you'll have to trust Him like you've never trusted Him before."

As Emma drove away, Laney realized the depth of what lay ahead and the opportunity she had to show her Lord how much she trusted Him. She'd never laid her heart on the line this way, she'd never risked exposing the deep truths tucked away in the far recesses of her heart, and she'd never had a more compelling reason to trust than she did today.

Laney absorbed the words from the Psalm she'd often turned to throughout the years. The words of David always brought a soothing calm to her spirit. But today they didn't quiet the raging storm within.

A jingle of the lock grabbed her attention. Bryan.

"I'm home."

"I'm in the den." She closed her Bible and returned it to the basket next to her chair.

He approached, bent over and kissed her cheek. "Hey, honey. How was your day?"

"Bryan, we need to talk." She hesitated. The saturated tissue she held refused to absorb any more of the dripping perspiration from her palms. She had rehearsed how to tell Bryan about Craig, but words couldn't accurately define what she'd seen today. And how it made her feel. Could anything she say convince her husband to investigate the truth?

He sat in the recliner next to hers and faced her. "Babe, what's up. Is it that Langston woman again?"

The sting of tears pierced behind her eyes. She blinked and took a deep breath. "Not the woman. The husband. I saw him today."

Bryan shook his head and drew his brows together. The action gripped her. "You saw her husband?"

"Yes. Craig Langston." She met his gaze head on. "Evan looks just like him."

Bryan exhaled. "C'mon Laney, not you, too? People resemble other people all the time. I don't want to go down this road." He reached for the television remote control.

She placed her hand over his. His eyes held a hint of irritation when he met her gaze. "It's more than a resemblance. His mannerisms are like Evan's. Same eyes, same color hair, down to the cowlick."

Bryan shifted in his chair and avoided looking at her. "It doesn't matter. Evan's ours."

"It does matter."

"It shouldn't. Why are you going down this path? Leave it alone." He rubbed the bridge of his nose. "You're opening a can of worms that's best left closed."

Her pulsed quickened. His refusal to make eye contact twisted her belly. He shifted from side to side and tapped his right foot. All signs she couldn't read from her husband. Something didn't add up. Her racing pulse sent more sweat to her palms. This was not normal for Bryan. Warning bells tolled through her head.

"Bryan…?" She crossed her arms and glared.

Reluctantly, he lifted his eyes to hers. "You do know I love you, right?"

"Yes." She swallowed hard. "Bryan? What have you done?"

He exhaled and replaced the remote on the table. "I had no idea it would lead to this."

"You're scaring me." Her hand shook as she brushed a stray lock of hair from her eyes.

He stared at the floor.

"Bryan?" Her insides trembled as possibilities rolled through her mind.

With his head lowered, he raked fingers from both hands through his hair then looked up again. Tears moistened his pain-filled eyes. "I paid our attorney extra to make the adoption happen."

"You did what?"

"Trust me, I thought the extra was to move us ahead in line for the next child. That's it."

"How much?"

He pressed his lips together and continued to stare at the floor.

"How much?" When she raised her quivering voice it echoed in the large living room.

"Ten thousand."

Before she could question where he'd gotten the additional funds, her heart exploded. *Please God, no. Not Evan.*

The truth turned into a double-edged sword, slicing through her no matter where she turned. Could her husband have encouraged the kidnapping of an innocent child? All for the sake of making her happy? Tears blurred her vision and the distorted image of her husband's tormented face left an indelible mark in her mind.

CHAPTER 27

*M*aggie flipped two saucer-sized pancakes, grateful for the time alone while Craig slept in. The question of whether or not to tell him about Evan volleyed through her mind. Should she? Or not? His flight to South Carolina left at noon tomorrow and he wouldn't be back for two weeks. Maybe when he returned she'd be able to tell him the truth and not risk the humiliation of him thinking she had finally gone over the edge.

"Good morning." Craig walked in with a clean-shaven face, perfectly combed hair along with khaki pants and a pressed polo shirt. Maggie still wore the oversized t-shirt she'd slept in and her fuzzy gorilla face slippers. Her long hair still tangled from tossing and turning throughout the night.

An unlikely couple. Each had handled their grief in unexpected ways. Craig had become the neat-freak workaholic. Maggie had become the sloppy workaholic.

"Good morning. Grab a plate. These pancakes are about ready." She slid the flexible spatula under the fluffy batter.

Before Craig reached the cupboard, the ding of the doorbell sounded. He glanced toward her slippers. "I'll get it."

Maggie filled Craig's plate and placed it on the table.

"Maggie, there's someone here to see you."

Who could be here at 9:00 a.m. on a Saturday? "Who is it?"

"It's your friend Laney. She's in the living room."

She froze. Laney here? Now? "Be there in a minute."

Maggie scurried into the bedroom, flipped off the slippers then yanked off the oversized shirt. A simple sundress hung near the closet door. She yanked it off the hanger and wiggled into it. On her way out, she stepped into a pair of sandals while tying her hair into a messy bun. When she entered the living room, Laney sat on her couch. Craig carried a cup of coffee to her.

He handed the cup to Laney then said, "I'll leave you ladies to visit while I finish breakfast." He stepped out as Maggie sat next to Laney.

Laney turned toward Maggie. "You haven't told him?"

Maggie shook her head. "No."

Laney lowered her voice. "I just came by to give you the name of the attorney."

She shook her head. "I already have it." Should she tell Laney the attorney was dead? "Laney, look, I'm leaving for New Orleans tomorrow. The attorney has passed away and the only person left is his secretary."

"Hazel?"

"Yes."

"I can't believe she's still alive." Laney stood. "Well, it seems you already have the information I'd planned to give you."

Maggie stood and walked with Laney toward the door. "Why the change of heart?"

Laney stopped at the door then turned back toward Maggie. "I want to know the truth."

"Why now and not last week?"

"It's a bit of a long story. One I could share with you on the way to New Orleans if you'll have me."

No way. If this woman thought she could tag along and sabotage this search, she had better think again. "You want to come with me? Why?"

"To help uncover the truth." Laney's eyes glistened.

Did she really want to know the truth or keep it hidden from Maggie? She scrambled to process what Laney's coming here meant. Had she known something all along and her guilt propelled her?

There was something about Laney. Something keeping Maggie from believing the worst. Perhaps, she'd found out more details about the adoption. Whatever the case, and regardless of Maggie's reservations, could she say no? "Are you sure about this? I'm not sure this is a good idea."

"Maggie, I believe it's what I have to do. I'm going to New Orleans whether I go with you or not. Besides, Hazel knows me. She'll talk to me."

Laney had a point. She could be helpful. "Why would you want to go with me?"

"Because I feel your pain. I can only imagine the torment you've endured. I've got more information that may help us find the truth. But I want to be part of finding it. We can get more answers together than apart."

Maggie vacillated between wanting to trust her and not trusting a word she said. But when she looked into Laney's eyes, the compassion she saw there prompted her to be less suspicious, to take the chance.

"We leave at noon tomorrow. I'll pick you up. I've got reservations at Hazel's Bed & Breakfast for three days. You can share my room."

What had she done? Invited the woman who may have been involved in kidnapping her son to share a room. What was she thinking?

"I'll be ready," Laney said.

****

"I'm going." Laney pitched another blouse into her suitcase.

Bryan stood in the doorway of their bedroom still

wearing his business suit. His commanding presence filled the frame. "This is crazy. I can't believe you're going to New Orleans with that woman. What do you hope to gain by doing this?"

She stopped folding clothes and stared into the half-packed suitcase. Her husband didn't understand the pain of losing a child, he couldn't sympathize with Maggie the way Laney could. He also didn't understand her need for answers. God had been generous to her and she'd thanked him everyday since becoming a Christian. There had to be a reason she and Maggie had crossed paths. "The truth," she said.

"And where will that lead?" He raised his voice.

Her glare lasered into Bryan. "I don't know, but now that I know there's a possibility Evan is really Maggie's son...I can't ignore this."

"Even at the expense of our happiness?" His blue eyes held the shroud of betrayal.

She lowered her voice. "Bryan, I need to do this. Try to understand. Always wondering would rob us of any future happiness. Maybe if you'd thought about the—"

He crossed his arms and exhaled long and hard. "Don't Laney. Don't you dare. I only thought of us. Of you. You wanted a child and I did what I thought would get us a child. I never thought in a million years there was a possibility of illegal actions. I'm sorry. If you feel you have to do this, I'll support you. But, Laney, I really think you're making a huge mistake."

"I believe the huge mistake was made twenty years ago." She folded a pair of white slacks and laid them in her suitcase. A yellow cotton shirt followed—the last item before she zipped the cover closed and hoisted the suitcase from the bed.

He approached her and placed his palm on her shoulder. "Can you ever forgive me?"

"Oh, Bryan." She turned to face him and brushed her fingertips on his cheek. "I already have. I know where your heart is now and where it was back then. I'm not doing this because I'm angry with you. I need to know the truth so our family can move forward."

"I never dreamed he'd kidnap a child. Never. I pray that he hadn't. I could never forgive myself." His eyes misted.

"I've prayed for revelation, now maybe we should pray for strength to handle whatever the truth may be."

He nodded. "What should I tell Evan when he gets back from Gulf Shores?"

"Maybe you could start with being honest." Once she voiced the sentiment, her stomach rolled. Who was she to be spouting off about honesty? She had no right to feel betrayed by Bryan. Hadn't she kept her own secret from him? Could her family handle more than one revelation right now? *I'll tell him when I get back.*

"Tell Evan I've gone with Maggie to research his adoption."

CHAPTER 28

*"I'*ll see you in two weeks." Maggie planted a kiss on Craig's cheek before he left for the airport.

As she waved goodbye, a tug on her heart made her wince. She hated keeping her plans from him, but she needed facts before she told him. She couldn't let this be a reason for him to question her sanity. But of utmost importance, she wanted to give him back his son. Then maybe, if she could allow her heart to heal, she could also give him back his wife.

Maggie gathered her luggage then loaded her car. She dialed Laney's number as she went through the house locking all the doors and making sure the lamp timers were set. "I'm on my way."

"I'm ready."

She jotted down the directions then headed for her car. The first step of a journey filled with the promise of bringing light into the unknown darkness binding her all these years. Truth. Dreams of this day filled many of her waking moments. But those images never included another woman as her son's mother.

When she turned into the Ellerby's driveway, Eric's car

loomed before her perched like a predator at the top of the drive. Laney stood at the door and waved her in. *Great*. Not exactly what she'd planned to encounter on the first leg of their journey.

"I'm sorry. Bryan has something he'd like to say before we leave. Parting words to see us off." Laney curled her index and middle fingers of both hands in the air as quotation marks.

"I'm not too sure about this." Maggie paused at the spacious entry.

"Come in." Laney cupped Maggie's elbow and guided her forward. "It's all right."

Maggie picked up one foot and willed the other to follow.

"Okay. . ."

Bryan and Eric rose from the warm brown couch when she entered the room. Rich earth-tone decorations welcomed. "Maggie." Bryan nodded toward her while Eric's familiar gaze unnerved her. This was not at all how she expected this trip to start. Why had she allowed Laney to come with her?

Bryan removed an oversized pillow from the chair closest to Maggie. "Please, have a seat."

She lowered into the chair, sat upright, crossed her right ankle over her left, and braced herself for the upcoming conversation.

Both Bryan and Eric sat while Laney stood next to Maggie's chair. Her presence beside felt surprisingly comfortable as though she were a friend supporting her.

Bryan took in a deep breath. "I wanted to say..." He leaned forward and shifted more toward her. "I'm sorry about how I acted and the things I said to you at Eric's house."

Had she heard him correctly? An apology.

His drooping eyes spoke to her. Was he willing to support this investigation? How could she harbor ill toward him?

She willed the word to move past her lips. "Accepted." She paused. Not sure why. Maybe to allow her acceptance to sink in or to allow her next words time to build then flow. "I know my accusations had to be a shock." She leaned back into the chair. The breath she'd held for a moment released in a deliberate rush. The encounter wasn't what she expected.

"They were." He leaned back as well and glanced toward Laney, while his words continued to be directed toward Maggie. "I can't say I'm in total agreement of this fishing expedition you and my wife are embarking upon, but I am praying for safety during your travels and God's will be done in this whole matter."

Maggie drew in a deep breath. Another unexpected turn. God's will? She simply nodded.

He pointed toward Eric. "I'm sure you're wondering what Eric's doing here. I've asked him to come so he can hear what I have to tell you." Bryan shifted in his chair and took a deep breath. Seemingly, to gather strength.

"When Laney and I met with Henri Mouchaux, the attorney who arranged Evan's adoption, he told us he had approximately twenty couples ahead of us. It would take about two years to get an infant, but if we would be willing to take an older child the wait time would be less." Bryan paused and turned to Eric. "The next day, I called Mr. Mouchaux and asked what I could do to reduce the wait time. He said an additional ten thousand would put us at the top of the second list for the older child or twenty-five thousand would move us at the top of the first list." He exhaled. "That should have been my first clue not to trust him."

Maggie uncrossed her leg and inched to the edge of her seat. Her pulse raced, eager to hear more.

The ruffle of leather filled the room as Eric shifted on the couch.

Bryan's Adams apple slid up and down. "I sold some of the stock I'd inherited from my grandpa." He squeezed his lips together and glanced toward Eric. "And paid him the ten grand. I couldn't come up with twenty-five without Laney knowing. Certainly a foolish thing to do, but all I cared about was her happiness. And I couldn't bear to see her wait any longer to be a mother." His eyes glistened when he reached for Laney. She moved toward him, small steps with an outstretched hand.

Bryan continued. "Dr. Langston, if my actions prompted your son's kidnapping, it's a burden I will have for the rest of my life. And should you and my wife discover that's what happened, I ask, in advance, for your forgiveness."

Maggie blinked back burning tears. What could she say? Words could not capture the bevy of emotions swirling through her. A shaft of light beamed from the door she'd banged on for twenty years. This was more than she had imagined.

His words, like soaking rain, penetrated the driest part of her heart. Emotions—ones she'd suppressed—toiled within and threatened to release in the midst of this family.

Where was the anger she expected? Could she forgive this man for stealing her life?

But one emotion rose above the others taking her by surprise.

Gratitude.

Her son had been raised by this compassionate man and understanding woman. He'd been protected. Loved. Suddenly finding the truth, though still important, paled next to the reality of the here and now.

Maggie cleared her throat. "I don't know what to say. For twenty years, all I've thought about was finding my son. Agonizing over whether he was still alive, if so where he lived, who he lived with, and were they good to him. It's changed me in ways I'm not proud of. Because I couldn't let go. Something t-t-to—" A sob constricted her throat. She lowered her head. "I'm sorry."

A gentle touch rested on her arm. "It's okay." Laney's emotion-laced voice drifted near her. "We've all done things we're not proud of."

Maggie accepted the tissue in Bryan's outstretched hand.

Bryan cleared his throat. "Dr. Langston."

Maggie lifted her head and met his gaze. "Call me Maggie."

"Maggie...please don't hurt my son." Tears glistened in his eyes.

"Even if you discover he is the boy you gave birth to."

CHAPTER 29

Maggie gripped the steering wheel and peered through the hammering rain. The unexpected storm started fifteen minutes after they'd left Laney's house. Sheets of water spattered the windshield making the wipers struggle in their futile effort to keep her view clear. Each intense splatter matched the intensity of her heartbeat. Finally, she was on the path to discovery. Even if she did have to compete with nature to get there.

"Are you okay to drive in this weather?" Laney wiped the interior of the windshield with an extra fast food napkin she'd found in the glove box.

"Yes, I'm ready to get to New Orleans to hear what Hazel has to say." She stole a quick glace toward Laney. "Where was Evan today?"

"He's spending the week in Gulf Shores. He won't be home until next Sunday."

Maggie had hoped to see him again. To look into his eyes. To deepen the bond started the night of their first encounter—not at a restaurant but in a hospital room twenty-two years ago.

"Bryan is worried isn't he?" Maggie peered through the

sheets of rain.

"He loves Evan and doesn't want his world disturbed. . ." Laney's words hung in the air.

Maggie waited for more, but sensed Laney couldn't give more, couldn't betray her husband.

The swish of the wipers provided a rhythmic backbeat to their spoken and . . . unspoken words. The rain drilling the roof increased in intensity making soft-spoken words impossible. Maggie leaned forward as though the motion could make her a better driver, increase her focus, or simply make her hold tighter to the wheel.

An eighteen-wheeler zoomed by splashing water onto her windshield. She curled each finger tighter around the wheel. For the next twenty miles, the sound of pounding rain and the slapping of windshield wipers filled the car.

CHAPTER 30

Laney stared at images of pine trees blurred by torrents of water. Thoughts of Bryan and his unconditional love crept in. She didn't deserve such a loving husband. Why had she kept her past from him? He deserved a wife who trusted him—trusted that he would understand. Regret squeezed tight in her chest. So simple. Why couldn't she summon the courage to tell him? To have faith in him? Yet, hadn't he done the same thing to her? What type of Christians were they if they couldn't be honest with each other?

Laney leaned against the headrest as the plummeting rain dissolved into a slow drizzle. Images materialized. The green and brown of the pine trees and grass along the interstate became clearer. The view infused a newfound courage in Laney—confidence that she could accept whatever their journey unveiled.

"Looks like the worst of the storm is past us." Laney's voice, no longer competing with the pounding rain, boomed in the car. "Sorry, I didn't mean to be so loud."

Maggie laughed. "No worries. Let's hope the worst is behind us."

Had Maggie meant the weather? An overwhelming urge

gripped her. Could she tell this woman why they could relate? And why she'd taken the risk of losing her beloved son's devotion, and the life she'd built, by joining her on this quest.

"Can I tell you something?" Maybe if she spoke the words today, repeating them later to Bryan might be easier.

"Sure."

"I gave up a son when I was nineteen." The secret she harbored for twenty-eight years broke free. Nine simple words. But, why Maggie? How could she share this with someone she barely knew and someone who threatened to take away the bit of normalcy she currently had? Yet, not with her husband. But if anyone could understand, it was Maggie.

Maggie remained silent.

Laney focused on a minivan with a bumper sticker touting the academic performance of the driver's child.

"Complications during the birth prevented me from having another child. It's why we adopted Evan." The steady drizzle ceased, giving way to clear skies and a rainbow stretching across the sky. The vivid colors reminded Laney of God's promise to Noah and of his faithfulness. If only she had such faith.

"I'm sorry." Maggie glanced away from the road and for an instant, their eyes met. "Is that why you're helping me?"

"Partly."

"And the other part?"

"I can't live with another unanswered question. I'd always wonder if Evan was Paul."

"Another question?"

Laney stared at the rainbow. "Every day of my life I wonder what happened to my first son."

"Have you tried to find him?"

"No, I didn't feel like I had the right."

"Why not? He's your son."

"Because I chose to give him away and because I didn't know how Bryan would feel about me having a son."

"He doesn't know?" Maggie glanced toward Laney.

"No."

High humidity and the car's air-conditioning fogged the windows. With one hand, Maggie swiped the condensation forming on the windshield. She switched on the de-fogger then turned to Laney. "I'm sorry Laney. I'm sure that was a tough decision."

"It was. I'm not sure I was old enough to really understand the consequences. All I wanted was for the baby to have a family and the adoption would solve my current problem."

Maggie nodded. "What about the father?"

"He lived by his own set of irrational rules. A handful of cash for an abortion turned out to be his idea of solving the problem. Taking responsibility for getting his English lit student pregnant was not in his plans. Nor was letting his wife know."

"Oh."

Laney sensed Maggie searched for something more to say, but the silence hanging in the car offered an enveloping comfort. A blanket she savored. It was as though telling Maggie allowed her the freedom of sharing without laying her burden on a friend to keep her secret. Oddly enough, she trusted Maggie and didn't totally understand why. Maybe they were more alike than either of them wanted to admit.

As they traveled east, the landscape changed. Subtle changes. From tall skinny pines to water and swamp on an elevated road then to a tangled mass of houses as they neared the city. "The exit for the Bed and Breakfast is just ahead, right past the cemetery," Maggie said.

Weathered and battered tombs stood as silent overseers to the generations of changes and people inhabiting the city. She suspected that they housed families as deep rooted in the city as the mighty oaks whose limbs cast shadows on the whitewashed stone.

Maggie followed the GPS directions through the

crowded streets of the city.

Laney pointed past an old grocery store with a rusted sign. "I think the building is just at the end of the street. This looks a bit familiar."

A small parking lot, valuable land in the city, was adjacent to a two-story building supported by Old Chicago bricks.

Maggie maneuvered in through the narrow gate and secured a parking space identified by a sign: *For Hazel's Guests Only.*

"We're here." Maggie put the car into park and stared at the building.

"Yeah, we are. The building hasn't changed very much." Did this old building house the answers to years of secrets? Stabbed by a bolt of fear, Laney remembered the last time she'd been here. Joy had followed her home. She feared that wouldn't be the case this time.

CHAPTER 31

*M*aggie released the trunk latch and met Laney behind the car. Bags in hand, they walked toward the building. A wrought iron balcony adorned the top floor. Bright red gardenias spilled from terra cotta pots and bougainvillea cascaded from hanging containers attached to the top of the roof. A cheerful place. Did its façade act as a romantic veil hiding horrid events orchestrated here years ago?

A small sign with curly letters along the porch greeted: *Welcome to Hazel's Bed & Breakfast.*

Irony, slapped with cruel mockery. Would she finally get answers to her tormenting questions from such a welcoming cheerful place?

"Wow, I can't believe she's turned this old place into a B and B." Laney lugged her suitcase up the cement steps.

Maggie craned her head back and gazed to the tops of skyscrapers sharing the space with Hazel. "A cozy retreat right in the center of town."

Sirens blared and the buzz of traffic circled. Hopefully, the old building was well-insulated and blocked the sounds of the city.

When Maggie turned the iron doorknob and opened the

heavy oak door, the hinges creaked. A cherry desk as old as the door stood across the foyer with a modern sign encouraging guest to *Check In Here.*

An elderly African-American woman sat behind the desk. The deep lines on her face spread thin when she smiled. "Hello, ladies. Welcome to Hazel's. It's good to have ya here. I'm Elois Badeaux." She flipped through the pages of a worn guestbook. "Your names?"

"The reservation is under Maggie Langston."

She ran a thick finger down a handwritten list. "Langston. Hmm. Yeah, right here." She looked up toward Laney. "And you are?"

"I'm Laney Ellerby."

Elois turned back toward Maggie. "Didn't know you'd have another guest with you. I'll git more towels."

"We'll pay extra."

Elois shook her head. "No need." She turned the guest register and Maggie signed it. "You ladies are in the Mardi Gras Suite. French doors open to the north balcony. It faces the garden. Real pretty at night. There's a couple of rockers out there."

Laney smiled. "A garden?"

Maggie handed Elois her credit card. "In the middle of the city?"

"Yep, Hazel turned part of the property into a garden. Developers didn't like dat too much. They was salivatin' for dat land."

Elois used a small manual machine to make an imprint of the card then filed the carbon copies in a metal four-by-six box. She handed the card back to Maggie then pointed toward the ornate, wooden stairway curving up to the second floor. "Right up those stairs and turn left. It'll be the door at da end of da hallway. There's a dumb waiter just under the stairs for your luggage. Open the door, put your suitcases inside, and when you get up da stairs there's a pulley you pull on it to lift dem up. Real easy."

Maggie returned her card to her purse. "Is Hazel in this

afternoon?"

"Nah, she went down da bayou to visit her sister. She should be back late tonight or sometime tomorrow."

"Thank you." Maggie nodded then grabbed her bag.

Laney pulled her suitcase toward the stairs and placed it inside the dumb waiter. Maggie followed and did the same. "This is unique."

Laney headed up the stairs. "Brings a whole new meaning to the word bellhop."

The drumming of their heels on the wooden stairs echoed against the plaster walls. At the top and just to the right, another door greeted them. Maggie opened the door and tugged on the cable. The action moved the elevator car, bringing their luggage up to them.

When the cart arrived, Maggie retrieved her bag and then Laney's. "Wow, wonder how many kids tried to ride in here."

"Evan would have tried . . ." Laney paused.

Maggie stopped. The image of her two-year-old son squatted inside the cart filled her mind. A pang of jealousy drilled through her, sharp and quick. This woman knew her flesh and blood better than she did. Whether Paul would have tried to ride in the dumb waiter had never entered her mind. Was that the thought of a good mother? Or just someone who had been a mother? How much more inadequate could she feel?

"Maggie, I'm sorry."

She raised her hand in what seemed like slow motion. As much as her self-pity pulled her to wallow in the emotion, she couldn't let Laney stop talking about Paul. Although it hurt to hear about his childhood, it was excruciatingly more painful not to. "It's okay."

She looked into Laney's eyes. For an instant and for the first time in twenty years, she felt someone understood her pain. But why did it have to be the woman who had raised her son? What kind of twisted fate was this? She rolled her bag left toward the end of the hall and the Mardi Gras room.

Laney followed. "Look," she said. "There's a ceramic purple mask on the door."

Maggie remained silent. A mask—how appropriate.

The Mardi Gras room boasted a canopy bed to the east side and a wrought iron daybed to the west. Laney rolled her luggage toward the daybed.

"You're welcome to the larger bed." Maggie said.

"You take it. The daybed is fine. Also, I want to pay for half the room."

"Not necessary." Maggie dropped her suitcase on the floor next to the canopied bed. Decorative netting hung from the ceiling and cascaded over its purple paisley bed covering. Laney's bed was covered with a gold version of the same cover. Posters of every combination of purple, green, and gold covered the walls.

The French doors and the city sounds beckoned. Maggie turned the glass doorknob and stepped out. The warm April air greeted her.

Laney followed close behind. "Wow, I can't believe I'm in the middle of New Orleans." She peered over the wrought iron railing teeming with climbing ivy and budding night-blooming jasmine. "There's a fountain in the garden below. It's some type of courtyard."

Maggie soaked it in. She'd been to New Orleans many times and appreciated all the city had to offer—the good and bad. But never, had she been more at ease and relaxed here than she felt right now. The balcony held pots filled with bougainvillea. Their fuchsia flowers flowed from the branches like vibrant waterfalls. Large leaves of Boston ferns spilled from hanging pots creating a tropical-like haven.

"This is amazing." Maggie plopped into one of the antique wooden rockers then kicked off her shoes. She leaned back and rubbed her hand along the smooth arm then closed her eyelids. The gentle motion of the rocker took away the anxiety of the treacherous drive and the uncertainty of the very reason she sat here.

Could she finally get the answers she craved? She shivered, despite the warm afternoon air. Would the answers end the nightmare? Would knowing change anything? New questions loomed. She'd come this way thinking all would be well if she only knew. But would all be well? Years of emotions churned inside her, some she'd stuffed so far down, she wasn't sure what they'd look like when they finally surfaced.

"I think I'll freshen up and unpack." Laney's soft voice floated across the flower scented balcony coaxing Maggie back to the present. This was where she needed to focus. Today a new path dawned.

"Any ideas where we can have dinner?" Laney asked. "My treat since you won't take anything for my half of the room."

"I don't know," Maggie answered with her eyes still closed. "We can take a cab to the quarter and see what strikes our fancy."

Laney's laughter drew Maggie's attention.

"I have an idea. Let me make a phone call." Laney stood near the hanging fern.

In that moment, with the sunlight beaming around her, she looked like a character right out of a Tennessee Williams play. So elegant, yet carefree.

Could Maggie ever be described as carefree? "I'm game."

How could Laney look so endearing considering the reason they were here? Envy snaked along Maggie's heart and threatened to slither in. Laney had it all, her son, a caring husband, and could just enjoy things for what they were. Of course, she hadn't had her son taken from her years ago. Then Maggie remembered. Laney had lost a son. She had past demons of her own. Maybe worse than the ones Maggie battled.

As Laney walked past Maggie and opened the French doors, a blast of cool air from the room brushed along

Maggie's bare arms. She reached for Laney's hand. "I'm really sorry about your son. I think I can somewhat understand the torment you've dealt with all these years. Thanks for confiding in me. Also, thanks for searching for the truth with me."

Laney blinked, the joie de vivre present earlier drifted away and a glimpse of sadness replaced the liveliness. "I believe you do understand." Laney gave Maggie's hand a gentle squeeze and then walked into the room.

The hum of traffic, the occasional dings of the streetcars, and the blast of the distant tug boat horns blended into one steady chorus. Easy to ignore in the beauty of Hazel's garden. Maggie stood and peered over the railing. The cement fountain Laney had mentioned dominated the tiny courtyard and a brass plaque sat at its base. She squinted to read the words but was too far away. Must be a dedication of some sort.

A cement walkway circled the fountain and concrete benches dotted the path. The vision of a peaceful resting place. She'd have to take a stroll later this evening.

She glanced at her watch. Almost five. She inhaled and allowed her lungs to take in the thick moist air. Not a cleansing breath. Just a surviving one.

****

Laney dabbed the new shade of pink onto her lips. She'd finally found a color that worked on her fair complexion. She was a stark contrast to many of the Louisiana woman she'd met. Once the final touches were applied, she puckered her lips, kissed a napkin, then headed back toward the bedroom, pulling the bathroom door closed behind her. Maggie stood next to the balcony doors.

"I didn't hear you come in."

"I thought it was time I got ready for dinner."

Laney paused. "I want you to know..." She placed her hand on the iron frame of the bed. "...how much I appreciate what you said out there. And I'm sorry about your son as well. And if...if Evan...if it turns out Evan is

Paul, please know I'll still be sorry. I can't imagine what you've endured and I wouldn't want to be the cause of such horrific pain."

She stared at the tapestry of the worn Oriental rug partially covering the bare oak flooring.

Had Laney said too much? She continued to observe the rug, afraid to look into Maggie's eyes. Afraid the pain there could transfer into her own heart. Afraid she wouldn't know what to say or do.

Lord, give me Your words. Guide me. Take her pain and disbelief. Laney braved a glance toward her roommate.

Maggie stood near the door, her hand still on the glass doorknob. She stared at the floor, probably at the same markings on the rug Laney had studied. She allowed the latch to click, resounding throughout the room as a final say-so and then lowered onto the edge of the bed. She ran her fingers along the stitching of a hand-made, double wedding ring quilt of purple, green, and gold draped at the foot of her bed.

"Thank you." She lifted her eyes and met Laney's patient gaze. "I don't know how to handle this situation. I find myself vacillating between being grateful you're here to being angry and jealous you had the privilege that should have rightfully been mine. You got to raise my son. You knew he would have tried the dumb waiter." She drew in a deep breath then exhaled slowly.

"I thought I had felt all the emotions possible, but this…this place has raised emotions I never knew I could feel. To be honest, I don't know how to handle them. This…this situation we're in. What if we find out he is my son? Or that he isn't? Where do we go from there? Just being here for this reason has changed us. Do you realize we'll never be the same regardless of the outcome?"

Laney absorbed the words and allowed them to seep to the deep recesses of her heart where the fears she'd refused to acknowledge lived. The very fears Maggie voiced.

"Yes. I know." Laney whispered, unsure of her ability to

keep her voice from wavering. She knew the night at Eric's house had inexplicably changed her life forever. What she didn't know was why. The Lord had obviously brought her to Louisiana for a reason. But to shake things up in her life in such a big way? Why? "I can't say I understand what's happening, but I know there's a reason. I've found there's always a reason."

Maggie's left eyebrow darted up. "A reason. What possible reason could there be?"

Laney bowed her head. *Lord, give me the words.* "I don't know, but I do know whatever the reason, you and I will be stronger for having done this."

"Maybe you're right. I don't know." Maggie grabbed her leather toiletries bag and headed toward the bathroom. At the threshold she turned. "Laney, I'm not sure I'd be here if I was in your shoes. You're a better person than I am." She walked into the bathroom and closed the door.

Laney stared at the closed door trying to make a whole of all the pieces thrown her way the last few weeks. If the circumstances were different, she and Maggie could be friends. But how could they be a solid support system to each other through this? It would be like rooting for your archrival. If either one found a comforting answer, it would mean the other would suffer.

CHAPTER 32

*M*aggie waited at the curb of the Bed and Breakfast while Laney paid the cab fare. "I'm stuffed. I don't think I've eaten that much in years. The food—it's the thing I love *and* hate about Louisiana."

Laney straightened and stood next to her. "The seafood was wonderful. I remembered a friend telling me about *Ralph and Kacoos*."

Maggie paused while Laney walked ahead. She looked up at the building, the place where her two-year-old son came and left with a new set of parents. Probably done in a matter of minutes. How many other children were exchanged here? Somehow the beauty of the place morphed into a grievous atrocity. Could the building ever be redeemed?

"Aren't you coming in?"

Maggie stepped forward and focused on Laney. This must be as hard for her. "Sure." She followed Laney into the building. The floor creaked and moaned under their footsteps. Elois sat behind the desk thumbing through a magazine. "Ladies, Hazel axed me to tell you she's in the parla if you'd like to go in and meet her." She flipped over the *People* magazine and pointed to the left of the stairway. "Right there."

Maggie's sandals echoed on the hardwood floor. She peered around the opening. A Duncan Phyfe couch provided an elegant focal point to the richly decorated room—a stately regal room, unlike the elderly woman who sat in one of two wingback chairs covered with blues, greens, and burgundy. She pushed up from the chair and then waddled toward Laney when they entered. "Mrs. Ellerby, it's so good to see you again. It's been a long time. You still live in Alabama?"

Laney bent to kiss her cheek. "Mrs. LeBlanc, it's good to see you. No, we just moved to Louisiana. Maggie," Laney swept her hand along Maggie's arm. "I'd like you to meet Hazel LeBlanc."

Maggie walked forward and extended her hand to the woman who barely reached five feet. No doubt, the slight curve of her back shaved a few inches from her height. When they touched hands, warmth spread through Maggie. It's presence powerful—jolting.

"So happy to meet you," Hazel said. "And I'm so glad we had a cancellation. I hope you're enjoyin' da place. I'm so sorry I wasn't here yestaday. I went to see my sister in Pecan Pointe."

Maggie nodded unable to speak. Hazel looked like every image Maggie had seen of Mrs. Claus. The stark white of her hair. Her sparkling kind eyes—like sapphires. She also looked a lot like Rosamie Chabert. The well-known owner of Rosie's Restaurant in Pecan Pointe.

Maggie peered into the blue gems and smiled. "Y-y-yes. It's quite lovely here. "Is Rosie your sister?"

"She is! You know my Rosie? Please have a seat." She pointed toward the couch near the set of chairs. Her eyes twinkled.

"Yes, my husband and I have enjoyed many a meal at her place. Her restaurant is only a couple of miles from my house."

Hazel beamed. "Well, well, imagine that. Such a small world here. And you, Mrs. Ellerby, you live in Pecan Pointe, too?

"I do."

"Do y'all go to Rosie's Bible study?"

Both Maggie and Laney shook their heads.

"Well, it seems my sista's got a nice little group of women gettin' together every Wednesday night to study God's word. They doin' some powerful prayin'. Give her a call when y'all get back."

Hazel tapped her head with her index finger. "Now where are my manners? Can I get y'all somethin' to drink? Tea, perhaps? Or how about a cup of my N'awlins blend coffee?"

Maggie lowered onto the couch. "No thanks. I'm still stuffed from dinner."

"Not for me," Laney said.

"Elois said you ladies wanted to talk to me about somethin'."

Laney sat in the opposite chair from Hazel. "Mrs. LeBlanc—"

"Please, call me Hazel." Hazel leaned back and intertwined her fingers over her ample belly.

"Hazel…" Laney took a deep breath and cast a glance toward Maggie. She nodded. "Do the records from my son, Evan's adoption still exist. There's a question as to whether Evan is really who Mr. Mouchaux said he was."

Hazel's wrinkled face twisted and her knitted brow gave her the appearance of a wrung out dishtowel. Maggie straightened her posture and noticed Laney sat a little taller as well.

"Mr. Mouchaux, bless his soul, tried the best he could to bring happiness to folks who couldn't have children. It was the part of my job I adored. But I have to say, there were some dealin's I wondered about. Of course, he never told me anything. Those were always between him and Mr. Salter."

Hazel's eyes narrowed and she shook her head. "Never did like that fella. Mr. Mouchaux used him for certain cases needin' investigation. The man kinda reminded me of a marsh hen—ya know, skinny and beady-eyed. Never quite trusted him and couldn't understand why an upstandin' citizen like Mr. Mouchaux would do business with him." Hazel's face returned to its former, kinder pleated self.

The question hovered on the edge of Maggie's tongue. Had Mr. Salter been involved in Evan's adoption and was the man still alive?

Laney spoke before Maggie could organize her words. "I don't remember a Mr. Salter. Was he involved in Evan's adoption?"

"Hmm." Hazel paused with her lips puckered. "I don't remember. You wouldn't have met Johnny Salter. Mr. Mouchaux never let his clients near that man. Rightly so because he'd scare any decent person out the door."

Laney glanced toward Maggie. "Mrs. Le…Hazel, do you still have Mr. Mouchaux's records?"

"Most of the boxes are in the attic." Hazel turned to Maggie. "You know this used to be his office before I turned it into a Bed and Breakfast. Serves a much better purpose. Don't you think?"

"It does," Maggie said. "You've done a wonderful job with the place. About those records, do you suppose Laney and I could look through them?"

Hazel beamed. "You ask Mrs. Ellerby here, she can tell you what this place looked like before." She glanced from Maggie to Laney then back to Maggie. "Why would ya want to look through those dust and bug-infested files?

Laney piped in. "Yes, Hazel, it's amazing what you've done. I hardly recognized the place. Now, about those files. We're searching for my son's records. There's a possibility his real parents are still alive."

Hazel gasped. "Oh my, that would be tragic. But if I remember correctly your son's family was killed in an automobile accident in Oklahoma."

"A fire is what we were told, but I have reason to believe there may have been a mix up and the only way I can know for sure is by looking through those records."

"By all means, honey, if looking through Mr. Mouchaux's files will put your mind at ease, you have my permission to do so. I know how hard this must be for you." Hazel reached over and patted Laney's hand. "To think your son may not be who Mr. Mouchaux said..." She shook her head. "That would be jus' awful."

She withdrew her hand from Laney's and pointed her finger in the air. "But I can assure you, Mr. Mouchaux would never have made that mistake." The sparkle in her eyes dimmed.

Had Hazel LeBlanc been in love with her boss?

"Will you be here tomorrow to show us where the documents are?" Maggie wanted to make sure they wasted no time in getting the information they came for.

"I won't be here in the morning, but they're not hard to find. There's a staircase next to the dumbwaiter upstairs. Go up those stairs and turn right into the attic." She pointed above her head. "The boxes are all stacked on the attic floor above this room."

"Thank you." Laney stood. "We'll let you get to bed. I know you've had a long day."

Hazel stood then flipped her hand in an awe-it's-nothing gesture. "Visitin' with Rosie makes me happy. But I do hate that drive. I keep tryin' to get her to move up here to the city, but she won't have it. She says God has her just where she's suppose ta be. That woman has more faith than any other person I know."

Maggie rose from her seat. "Thanks Hazel. I know Laney will be grateful to know the truth."

Hazel patted Maggie's shoulder. "You're a good friend to want to help her like this. Not many times a woman has another woman she can count on. Actually, that's kinda why Rosie does those Bible studies. To bring women together. You should call her. I mean it, you'll be blessed

I'm sure. I think her next study is something about showing wives how to fall in love wit their husbands again." She laced her fingers together. "Well, I hope you ladies enjoy your visit here in the Big Easy and you find what you're looking for."

Maggie's cell phone chirped and she scrambled to retrieve her purse from the floor. She reached for the phone sticking out a side pocket. "Hazel, thanks again."

She darted out the room, took a few steps to the left and then stood in a small room off the parlor. It had glass walls and served as a green house of sorts. A solitary white wicker chair competed for space with an overabundance of plants.

She glanced at the screen. Speaking of husbands. "Hello, Craig."

"Hey, I just wanted to say I made it to South Carolina. If you need to reach me and can't get through on my cell, I'm staying at the Marriott. I've forwarded my itinerary to your email address. Are you out shopping?"

As much as she and Craig's relationship had deteriorated over the years, she had never lied to him. She'd withheld telling him how she felt about things, but never lied. Now she stood at a crossroads. She couldn't tell him the truth. He'd never understand. Yet, she couldn't lie.

"No. Just coming in from dinner. I had dinner with Laney, the lady you met the other day."

"Oh yes, I remember. She seemed nice enough. Maggie, it's good to see you forming new friendships."

"She is nice. I've enjoyed her company."

"Good for you. When I get home, maybe we can have Laney and her husband over for dinner."

"Ahhh…ummm…they've just moved into town. Maybe we can hold off a while to let them get settled."

Craig's delayed response caused her to pause. She needed to change the conversation and quickly, but to what? That's the problem with a relationship on the brink of non-existence, there's nothing to discuss. "I hope things go well for you this week."

"Me too, I think it will. The investors are meeting in the morning and then later this week I'll present the proposal to the development company. So, it looks like my two-week trip will be for one week only."

"I know you'll do great. See you Friday night?"

"Yes, my flight comes in at seven. Well, I hope you have a good night. And Maggie, I've noticed a change. I'm not sure what caused it, but I'm grateful for it. See you when I get home."

"G'night, Craig." She disconnected the call and cupped the phone in her palm. Change? She hadn't changed. But there was a change. Now there was real hope. Something missing from her life for too many years.

****

Laney stretched back in the rocker. The moon rising from behind the tall building adjacent to the Bed & Breakfast cast a blue glow on the garden below.

The creaking of the wooden floor and Maggie's voice floated from the bedroom. "Laney, you out there?"

"Yes, I'm on the balcony. C'mon out. It's really nice."

"In a few. I'm going to change."

In the distance, the horn of a tugboat blasted and the *swoosh-swoosh* from the stream of traffic soothed.

Maggie strolled through the French doors. "Wow, what a beautiful moon."

"Full. And bright."

Maggie descended into the other rocker. "Craig called."

"I talked to Bryan earlier. He wanted to know if we'd found anything yet. He's chomping at the bit to know."

"I didn't tell Craig. Keeping this from him bothers me."

"Wish I could give you advice, but who am I. Right? I'm the one who hasn't told her husband the biggest secret of all." She turned toward Maggie. "Want to know the funny thing? I thought we had a great marriage. Ha, what kind of marriage starts out with secrets and continues that way? This jolt to our life has brought revelations I'd obviously refused to see. Maybe I should consider Rosie's Bible study."

"Yeah, there's a lot I've refused to see as well. Craig said something to me tonight that's shaken me up." She glanced out toward the courtyard.

"Want to talk about it?" Laney waited.

Maggie crossed her feet and relaxed her head against the rocker. "He said I'd changed in the last few weeks and, regardless of what caused it, he liked it."

How could Maggie have changed for the better in this turmoil? Laney had not been her best during the past weeks. In fact, she'd felt horrible because she'd not relied on her Christian values as much as she should have.

Maggie continued, "The only thing I can figure is now there's hope that I'll get some answers after all this time. Before I didn't have anything."

Laney let the words seep in. What gave Maggie hope sapped it from Laney. Despite her own emotions, her heart wept for Maggie. Twenty years of not knowing was a long time to let your imagination torment and a long time to allow those torments to destroy. Although Laney had given up hope of ever seeing her own son, it had been her choice. Not something inflicted upon her. She couldn't imagine the same thing happening to her. Of course, she hoped that if it had, her faith would have sustained her. But Maggie…Maggie didn't have faith. Laney tried to imagine the hopelessness Maggie must have felt.

She stared at the full moon and let the delicious memories it invoked wrap around her heart. Let it cushion the blow of reality. Could she share this with Maggie? Would it bring happiness or pain?

Lord, lead me. After a moment, peace settled and she knew she'd want to know if she were Maggie. "Want to hear a story about Evan?"

Maggie remained silent, her eyes closed. The moonbeams played on the features of her face, sharpening the angles and giving her a structured appearance. Like a painting with too much depth. Finally, her lips spread and she said, "Please."

"When he was about six or seven, can't remember exactly, we went camping in the Rockies. One night we sat around the campfire and there was a full moon like tonight."

Laney lifted one leg into the chair and turned sideways. "Evan looked up into the sky and said, 'there's got to be a gazillion stars out there, but look there's only one moon. Guess what my Sunday school teacher said about the moon? It has no light. But Mom, look it's shining so bright. It too, has light.' I explained to him how the light is a reflection of the sun."

Laney smiled at the memory. "He laughed and said, 'that's what Mrs. Crumby said. She said we should all be moons.' When I asked why, he said, 'so we can reflect the Son's light. S-o-n get it Mom? Not s-u-n.' That became our family's code words whenever we wanted to remind each other of being a good Christian. Be a moon. It sounds so corny now, but back then it was a huge revelation for Evan."

Maggie's broadened smile gave Laney peace. She leaned back and enjoyed the view of the moon-lit garden. Memories of special family times flooded her mind. Twenty years of laughter and love. Of course, there were moments of tears, but their family had been close. Her heart grieved for Maggie. She'd been robbed of that. Yet, a twinge of regret pierced. Could the reason she had been blessed with the memories was because Maggie had been robbed of them? How could life be so cruel?

Maggie's gentle words drifted through the night air searing Laney's thoughts. "Thank you, Laney."

Laney breathed out long and slow. *Thank you, Lord. Give her peace Father so she can know hope no matter what happens. The hope that only comes from You.*

"Thank you, for giving my son a warm caring home to grow up in. That's more than I ever had and for twenty years I've wondered if I could have given that to him." Her face remained emotionless. "I've never told anyone that. Not even my therapist. Some things hurt too much to acknowledge."

"Maggie, you would have given Paul everything he needed and more, because you loved him. What woman would hold onto the possibility of ever seeing her son again after all this time if she didn't love him? It's what makes us mothers."

Maggie remained motionless, eyes closed. "Not all mothers are good. Not all mothers love their children."

Laney suspected the sentiment came from a place of significant pain. She waited, giving Maggie time to share more. Or allowing her the space to be comfortable with what she'd already shared.

Maggie opened her eyes and leaned her elbow on the large arms of the chair and stared at the garden. "Laney, what was your mother like?"

"From what I remember, she was a good mother. She sacrificed for me and my brother. She died when I was eleven so I missed out on having her for my teenage years. I loved her and I know she loved me."

Maggie didn't move. Her words were spoken toward the rising moon. "You had a good role model. You're lucky. Casandra Thomason, my mother, only loved one thing— herself. She ran my dad off when I was six. From that point, my life turned into a living hell. My father moved from Florida to California and started a new life with a new family. For the first few years he called for birthdays and sent gifts at Christmas, but as the years progressed the calls and gifts became fewer and fewer until they ceased altogether. I'd call him whenever my mother allowed me to use the phone. Usually when she wanted something from my father. Typically money. By the time I was nine my father was completely out of my life and my mother had replaced him with a string of sugar daddies."

Maggie rolled her bottom lip between her teeth and then

exhaled. She kept her focus on the moon. "Whatever man paid her bills and kept her in fancy dresses got to live in our house, or sometimes we lived in his and she'd rent out our house."

Maggie lowered her head into her hands. Minutes passed before she continued. "Our house guest not only got my mother, but me too."

Laney sighed. Her heart ached for Maggie. She couldn't imagine the life Maggie described. How could this beautiful, well-respected, and successful woman have had such a horrid childhood? But now, she understood why Maggie had been so tormented and mired in the past.

"I can't imagine what you went through," she said.

"A lot of it, I suppressed. Just didn't remember. It was easier that way. Then, when Paul was kidnapped, it all came back. The more I dealt with the kidnapping the more I remembered the past and the more I felt like a total failure. Like trash. I don't know why Craig stayed with me all these years. I've not been a loving wife. I can't seem to open up to anyone." She paused still staring at the garden. "I can't believe I'm sharing this. I've always feared that once I opened the gate the floods would overwhelm bringing more bad than good."

Laney blinked. What could she possibly say to Maggie? Her heart ached with compassion for her. *Lord, heal this poor woman. Let her know You care and You've not abandoned her.*

She leaned across the chair and rubbed Maggie's shoulder. "Maggie, there are no words I can say to tell you how sorry I am. And I'm sure there are no words I can say that'll make you feel better. Would you mind if I prayed for you?"

Maggie shrugged her shoulders. "Why?"

"It's all I have."

"No one's ever prayed for me before. Laney, you have to know I don't believe prayers can help. Where was God when those men had their way with me and where was God when Paul was abducted?"

Laney bit her bottom lip. Those were hard questions. Ones she didn't have answers for. She was never good at explaining God to anyone. What could she possibly say to let Maggie see that bad things happened and God could still be found in the midst of them?

She bowed her head and kept her hand on Maggie's shoulder. "Dear Lord, show Yourself to Maggie. Let her come to know Your will for her life and to know You intimately so You can give her revelation. Heal her from the past. Remove the demons tormenting her present and cast a new light toward her. Father, I ask you to cradle my new friend in Your healing arms and remind her she is worthy of all the blessings You have for her. In the name of your son, Jesus. Amen."

In the moon glow, Maggie slid her fingertips beneath her right eye. The lingering *swoosh-swoosh* of the traffic filled the silence on the balcony. The lonely whistle from a distant tugboat set the tone. Laney slid her hand from Maggie's shoulder and crossed her arms. The light shafts danced through the limbs as a gentle breeze blew through the garden making the shadows shift in response. The prayer she had prayed before she left Mobile came to mind, she asked God to send her a friend. And, he had sent Maggie. A woman, despite the reason for their meeting, she felt comfortable calling a friend.

Maggie finally turned toward Laney. Her eyes glistened in the moonlight. "You called me your new friend. Did you mean that?"

"Yes."

"Do you think you'll still feel the same after we go through those records?"

Would she? Laney inhaled deeply then slowly exhaled. She swallowed to keep the rising ball of emotion from choking her. "Yes."

"Why?"

A calming peace enveloped Laney and she knew that

God had brought her to this moment for many reasons, but the one she knew at this moment was that she'd had the wonderful privilege of being Evan's mother and nothing could change that.

"Because nothing in those records will change the past. Regardless of what we discover, I've been Evan's mother for twenty years. You gave birth to Paul and was his mother for two years. I don't know what the future holds, but if Evan is indeed Paul, I know Evan is a great enough guy to share his love with another mother if he wants to. And I'm okay with that."

Maggie's gaze locked on Laney. "I envy you."

"Don't. There's nothing about me that's so great."

"Your faith. I envy your faith. And the twenty years with my son."

Laney's heart hammered in her chest. Maggie envied her faith. She certainly wasn't a model Christian. *Give me the words.*

She reached for Maggie's hand and squeezed. "You don't have to envy my faith. It's something you can have too. The years with Evan, I can't change. If it makes you feel any better, I love Evan. I don't think I could love him more if he was my biological child. But we still don't know for sure he's Paul."

"He is. I can feel it in my gut."

"Only a good mother would have such conviction."

Maggie grinned. "If only I could believe that."

"It's the truth…" Laney met her gaze and smiled. "…it's what we came here to find."

CHAPTER 33

*M*aggie looked up when Laney announced she was going to bed. She still held onto Laney's hand. "G'night, Laney. Sleep well."

"You too." She walked into the room leaving Maggie alone with the shadows in the garden below. The light reflecting off the fountain made it shine brightly in the night.

Be a moon.

Maggie tried to imagine her son at seven saying those words. Tried to imagine the direction his wide green eyes and puffy cheeks would have taken in five years. She let the moist breeze blow through her hair and Laney's words seep through her brain and heart. The woman had actually prayed for her.

Two figures appeared in the garden, moonbeams reflected from the blonde hair of a woman. She strolled next to a tall thin man whose arm draped over her shoulder. When they reached the fountain, the man dug through his pockets and handed the woman something. She pitched the object into the fountain and then walked into the man's outstretched arms. They shared a long, passionate kiss.

Maggie sighed. If wishes were gold, she'd be a rich woman. There were so many things she wished for, longed for. But tonight more than anything, she wished right along with the woman as she cast the coin. She wished she could find the evidence to prove Evan was Paul. Not to steal anything from Laney. Like Laney said, nothing would take away the years she'd had. But Maggie wished to end the decades-old question.

Whatever the future held would depend on Evan, but at least Maggie would be free of several tormenting demons. And maybe, she could move on. Her marriage might have a chance. Another thing she wished, that Craig could kiss her the way the man in the garden had kissed the woman. Could the hope churning in her heart where Paul was concerned spill over to her marriage? Dare she hope that her marriage could be revived?

#

The next morning in the sweltering attic, Maggie swiped her forehead with the sleeve of her T-shirt. "It's like a sauna in here."

"No doubt. Maybe we can slide these boxes closer to the stairs where it's cooler." Laney flipped through a dust-covered manila folder tilting it toward the sparse light shining through the single dusty window. An incandescent bulb hung from a tattered wire near the door, providing the only lighting.

Maggie glanced around the room at the stacks of boxes. "There's no way we can go through all these files and survive this heat and lack of lighting. There must be another way."

"It would take forever at this rate." Laney sneezed, scattering a cloud of dust motes.

"Excuse me ladies, Miss Hazel sent me up here to see if I can help," a husky male voice called from the bottom of the stairs.

Laney glanced toward Maggie. "Maybe we can find the box with files from nineteen ninety-four and look through those on the balcony of our room."

"Good idea." Maggie shifted and walked toward the door. "Yes, we can use some help. If you'll help us find a certain year's files we'd appreciate it if you'd carry it to our room."

"Will do." A tall young man wearing a worn T-shirt and faded blue jeans entered the attic and hunched over to avoid hitting his head on the attic beams. "Hello, I'm Justin. I do odd jobs for Miss Hazel." His muscled bare arms glistened in the dim lighting of the attic. "What year are we looking for?"

"Nineteen ninety-four."

Maggie shoved the box nearest her foot over to the side. Red marks covered the side, nineteen ninety-five was scrawled along the side.

Justin and Laney slid each box so all the dates faced outward. After forty minutes, Justin lifted his head. "Ladies, I'm afraid the year you're looking for is not here. The earliest is nineteen ninety-five."

Maggie met Laney's forlorn gaze. Her blonde hair formed little curls around her forehead and perspiration dripped from her temples. "We'll take that one for now. Would you carry it onto the balcony of the Mardi Gras room?"

Justin lifted the heavy box as though it was empty. His biceps bulged from the effort. "Ladies you go down first, I'll be right behind."

Once in their room, they freshened up and then sat on the balcony with the file box and glasses of iced tea sent up by Hazel, Maggie turned to Laney. "Although this isn't the year of Evan's adoption, maybe we'll find something here to send us in the right direction."

"Maybe." Laney wiped off the remaining layer of dust not removed by Justin's fingerprints from the top of the box. She withdrew the first five folders and handed them to Maggie then took the next one.

Maggie opened the first folder, a completed application

form sat on top, the ink faded from time and the heat of the attic. But she was still able to read the name, Arceneaux, Adrien. The first paragraph outlined Adrien and Barbara Arceneaux's desire to adopt a child. The front page detailed personal information about how long they'd been married, their financial ability to pay for the adoption, and a general synopsis of their medical history. Maggie flipped the page to see nothing but first and last names with cities and state names filling every line except for the name Arceneaux on the bottom line. "This is strange. Does your file have a dossier of the adoptive parents then a random list on the next page?"

Laney flipped through the top folder. "Yes, do you suppose these are the names of children eligible for adoption?"

Maggie shook her head. "It's hard to tell. Maybe we can research these names. I brought my laptop. Let's try. I think Hazel said there was wireless internet here." Maggie popped back into the bathroom. While the soap and water washed the grime from her hands, she glanced into the mirror. Had she changed as Craig mentioned? Her hair, like Laney's, curled around her face in the high humidity, her eyes had a smudge of mascara underneath, and her nose seemed a little too big for her liking. Yet, she looked different. Not the haggard woman of her past.

She retrieved her laptop, turned it on then typed the code Hazel had given her. A few seconds later, she had an internet connection. "We're in."

She Googled the first name on her list, Tommy Paimer. Within minutes, a face appeared. Tommy's face was found on a website tracking missing and exploited children. She typed in the other name, but not every name brought up a picture. Had all these names been of children reported missing?

She'd never thought to Google Paul's name. The temptation proved too strong. She typed her son's name into the missing children's database. Nothing. Had his abduction happened too long ago? Just one year before this child's. Maggie's shoulders slumped. Was she doomed to hit brick walls at every turn?

She typed in the Arcenaux's name and got their latest address and phone number. A quick scan toward the end of the folder revealed they had adopted a girl, Misty Brownstone. The name didn't match any on the second page list. Mouchaux had probably changed the names. "I vote we call this couple and see if their child matches any of the photos on this website." Maggie reached for a pad and pen.

CHAPTER 34

*L*aney stopped looking through the file. "Maggie." She paused waiting for Maggie to look her way. "Do you think that's the best way to handle this? I can't imagine getting a phone call from some stranger after all this time telling me my adopted child had been kidnapped. I know how hard it was to hear it from Eric. I can't do this."

Maggie's hand flew to her mouth. "Oh, my goodness, you're right. What was I thinking? Guess I only thought about the women who had lost their children."

Laney closed the folder and let out a long sigh. She pushed back the bile burning her throat. "Understandable, but I can't help thinking about the adoptive parents. This breaks my heart."

Maggie tucked a wayward strand of brown hair behind her ear. Her soft words broke through Laney's jumbled thoughts. "What should we do?"

"I don't know." Her heart hammered. So many folders. So many children. Justice after all these years would bring so much pain, yet much needed relief as well. As hard as this would be, she knew what the right thing was. She pushed the words past her lips. "We should call the police."

Laney scanned another folder. The list of names matched the first two. Seems Mr. Mouchaux had a ready-made list of children to match with possible clients. Had these children already been abducted? Or were they part of his "hit" list of possibilities?

Despite the heat, the thought shimmied a quiver through her. "I can't believe the same man I met was responsible for this. He was charming. The perfect gentleman. But this…this is despicable. How could Hazel have such respect for him?"

Maggie approached with slow deliberate steps. She placed her hand on Laney's arm. With a tender squeeze, Maggie said, "Laney, I don't like this either. It's hard regardless of which side you're on. But, please know, I appreciate how brave you've been and your willingness to help find the truth. That takes a lot of courage. Thank you." She slid her fingers along the top of Laney's forearm.

For a moment, silence dominated the room. Maggie's words seemed to hang in the air like a comforting blanket flicked outward and frozen in its fully stretched position, suspended in midair.

Waiting to cover.

Waiting to comfort.

Waiting to provide a place to rest.

Laney longed to grasp those words and let them seep in. Let them do what she knew Maggie intended. To comfort.

She and Bryan had been taken. Not by a stolen credit card scheme or even identity theft. They'd been deceived about the most important thing in their lives.

Their son.

Unseen claws raked through Laney's heart. What about Evan? How would he feel when the truth came out? No, she couldn't go there. Couldn't imagine how he'd feel.

Wait.

They hadn't found anything to prove this same practice was applied when they'd adopted him. Maybe Mr. Mouchaux had been legitimate before and when the demand for children became too great, he reverted to dishonesty. Maybe.

Laney placed her hand over Maggie's and nodded. If she spoke, the emotional avalanche she had barricaded might break through and she'd be helpless to regain her composure. She avoided Maggie's eyes. "We've got to find the nineteen ninety-four file box."

Maggie sighed. "I'll go downstairs. Ask Hazel. Maybe they stored the files somewhere else. She may remember."

Laney nodded then stared at the door as it closed behind Maggie. She ran her hand over the list of names. *Dear Lord, protect everyone involved. Including us.*

In the past few weeks, she'd ridden a roller coaster of emotions where Maggie was concerned. The woman had become her foe, rival, object of pity, confidant, and friend. How could this be? By all reason, they shouldn't be friends. Had God sent Maggie to her to test her faith? If so, it was a cruel test. One she wasn't sure she'd pass.

CHAPTER 35

Maggie stepped into the hallway and inhaled. But instead of fresh air, the musty scent of old wood and long-held secrets filled her nostrils and added to the rolling in her stomach. The elegance of the antique hall table covered by a crocheted doily lost its beauty, as did the other furnishings. Their loveliness marred by the revelations she and Laney discovered. This place had been the starting point for a journey of a thousand pains. Would Hazel remember? Or had she chosen not to?

In the kitchen, Maggie found Hazel, Elois, and Justin engaged in a baking project of sorts. Flour, sugar, and banana peels covered the cultured marble counter top. Hazel had spared no expense in designing the kitchen. Had the money come from the dozens of families searching for a child?

She swallowed the cotton ball lodged in her throat.

"Hello, Mrs. Maggie." Justin smiled. "You need me to get another box from the attic?"

"Not yet." Maggie slid onto the vacant barstool next to the counter. Hazel and Elois turned their attention from the flour-covered dough ball to Maggie.

"Can I get you anything, Mrs. Langston?" Hazel wiped her brow with the back of her chubby wrist. Flour snowed to the counter.

"Are any of Mr. Mouchaux's files anywhere else in the house?"

Hazel's faced scrunched up into its raisin imitation. "Not that I remember. He did use a storage facility near the river in the early days, but I thought we brought all the files to the office when he bought this building."

"Do you remember the name of the storage building?"

"Store-all or All store, or You store. Something along those lines." She turned to Justin. "Do you remember?"

His eyebrows drew together. "It was a small warehouse near the river. His cousin owned it and he rented a room in the back of the building. I can take you there if you want to see it."

"We're looking for the files from nineteen ninety-four and earlier. The oldest box in the attic was ninety-five. Do you think the older files may still be there?"

Hazel shook her head while her thick hands kneaded the dough. "I doubt it. That area got hit pretty hard by Katrina. But it wouldn't hurt to look." She turned her gaze toward Justin then nodded toward the back corner of the kitchen. "Use my van. The keys are on the buffet table."

Maggie slipped from the stool. "When can you take us?"

Justin glanced at the clock above the sink. "How about in an hour?"

Maggie struggled with telling Hazel what they found. The elderly woman with flour covering her cheeks melted Maggie's heart. She would wait. At least until they checked the warehouse. She followed Justin's glance. It was 10:00 a.m. "Perfect. Maybe you can show us a great place for lunch. My treat."

Justin grinned. "You got a deal. I know jus' the place."

A couple of hours later Maggie surveyed the warehouse from the back seat of Hazel's van. Laney, sat in the front passenger seat.

"This doesn't look good," Laney said.

Clumps of dried mud, twigs, branches, Styrofoam cups, dirty plastic milk jugs, and a variety of gravel and trash contributed to the pile stacked against the warehouse walls.

"Is this warehouse still in use?" Maggie asked Justin as he pulled into what could barely be defined as a driveway. Large potholes made Maggie sit back and grip her seat to keep from hitting her head on the back of Justin's seat.

"I'm not sure," Justin said. "My guess would be it's not." He parked and got out of the van.

Maggie and Laney got out and waited next to the van. As Justin walked around the building, he peered into the windows where there wasn't as much debris. When he came to the side personnel door, he turned the knob. The door opened.

He shouted toward Laney and Maggie. "It's opened. Wait here until I check it out, there's no telling what has taken to living in here."

Justin disappeared into the building leaving Laney and Maggie standing in the muddy driveway. Maggie leaned against the van's fender and, when the heat from the engine penetrated her thigh, she slid toward the door.

Should she go in after Justin? The thought of what lurked in there kept her from charging in. She pointed to a line about ten feet above the ground. "If that's the water mark, then anything left in this warehouse was destroyed by the flood. If those records survived, I'll be surprised."

Her last words floated on the dense air as a whisper. Would she ever find evidence to prove Evan was Paul? Knowing in her heart worked for her, but it wouldn't work for the Ellerby's and certainly not for Craig. There needed to be something concrete to connect Evan to Maggie and Craig.

Once Craig saw Evan, he'd believe even without proof especially once these other cases came to light. But she knew him, he'd probably want DNA or blood testing, just to be sure. That would be a problem. Evan would not consent. Maybe, when they returned to Pecan Pointe and shared with Evan what they discovered he would agree to testing. Maggie hoped the news would be enough.

Justin appeared at the door and waved for them to come forward. "C'mon, no animals."

Maggie led the way, trying to avoid parts of the sludge that sucked at her shoes. A few pieces of wood provided the perfect stepping stones to get to the warehouse door. Justin called to them. "Walk closer to the right. The mud is drier there."

As Maggie stepped onto a piece of plywood, watery muck swished over the sides of her new loafers. Great. She'd never get the mud out of the stitching. *It's for a good cause. This may be where you'll finally find the truth.* How ironic she may find proof here in this dilapidated and abandoned warehouse?

Laney followed close behind. "Are we by any chance getting closer to solid ground?"

"Almost. There's a cement slab just a few yards away. It leads to the door." Maggie took a few more cautious steps putting her onto the cement. Her sole slid on the thin film of mud covering the platform. Laney supported her from behind and kept her from landing on her rear. While Justin grabbed her arm and kept her from falling forward.

"Ladies, be warned. It smells nasty in there." Justin pushed the door open. Its hinges groaned in resistance. The acrid aroma of rotting wood and wet mud assaulted as Maggie crossed the threshold. She slid the crew neck of her shirt over her mouth and nose.

"Eww, no kidding. This place reeks." Laney's voice drifted from close behind.

Maggie stopped and waited for Laney and Justin. When they stood next to her, she asked, "Where to?"

He pointed toward a room across the expanse of the warehouse. "Over there, that's where the files were stored." He kicked aside a pile of debris, yogurt containers, plastic coke bottles, and an array of unidentifiable trash scattered in the mud leaving a semi-cleared path.

Maggie followed Justin. She took a step onto the path and paused before shifting her weight forward. Confident she wouldn't slip on the muck, she slid her left foot forward. She lowered her shirt from her mouth. "Laney, how are you doing back there?"

"I'm good. Right behind you."

Maggie lifted her collar back over her mouth and repeated Justin's stepping pattern. She cringed at the thought of falling onto the slimy floor.

Light filtered in from opaque overhead panels every four feet, illuminating the path and the rug of debris. Justin scraped his boots on the floor as he walked, to clear the way for her and Laney. Maggie shifted her gaze from the floor to where they were headed. A wide shaft of light shone through an opening at the far corner where a tree limb poked a hole in the roof.

"Ladies, please be careful."

Maggie slid the top of her shirt off her nose once again. "Justin, aren't we trespassing?" She held her arms out to keep her balance. She hoped Laney did the same. It would be nasty to fall in this stuff. Yuck. Germs everywhere. She really hadn't thought this through very well. She slipped her shirt back over her mouth and nose.

"It's okay." Justin's raspy voice echoed in the empty warehouse. "I know the owner. He doesn't live in New Orleans anymore which is why this warehouse hasn't been cleaned. I don't think he's come back since the hurricane. The rain we got a couple of nights ago soaked everything."

"Do you think the files are still in there?" Laney voiced Maggie's question.

"It's hard to say. I remember hauling the boxes to the office building in the afternoons after school. Keep going we're almost there."

Mud covered Maggie's soles. She stopped next to some type of rusted car part and scraped off the bottoms of her shoes.

Laney came up next to her and offered her arm. "Here lean on me." The words filtered through her shirt. Muffled, but discernable.

"Thanks." Maggie held on to Laney.

Once done, Maggie nodded for Laney to go ahead of her. Her trek behind Laney was easier with firmer gripping soles.

Justin reached the room and turned the doorknob. He placed both hands and pushed against the door, but it wouldn't open.

Laney stood next to him. "Is it locked?"

"I don't think so. There's something pressed against the door." He settled his hip against the old door and pushed. It inched open allowing daylight to seep through the slit. "This doesn't look good." He heaved his weight onto the door again causing the slit to spread into a two-foot wide opening.

Justin poked his head through the opening. "Just what I was afraid of." He moved aside. "Take a peek."

Maggie inched forward. "I'm not too sure about this." When she peered through the opening, she gasped. Twisted metal, tree limbs, and other debris stacked about a foot high pressed against the door. Branches from trees nestled around the warehouse served as the ceiling of the building. The largest part of a gigantic downed tree rested inside the room. The room didn't have an eastern or southern wall. Trees surrounded the area hiding the damage.

"No," she whispered, more to herself than to anyone around her. The truth seemed right at her fingertips just minutes ago. Now, lost to her forever. Taken away by an abominable force of nature affecting lives years after its landfall. Affecting lives not even living any where near New Orleans. Would the full affect of this devastation ever be known? At this point, it didn't really matter. Maggie hung her head then pulled back to face Laney. "It's no use. Everything is gone."

Laney ducked into the opening and gasped. When she

turned to Maggie, her eyes misted. "I'm sorry, Maggie. I know how badly you wanted this. I wanted it too."

CHAPTER 36

*L*aney stretched her leg along the edge of the oriental rug. She sat on the floor leaning against her bed surrounded by folders. "This is tiring work."

After they'd returned from the warehouse and lunch at the mom and pop restaurant where Laney had eaten the best shrimp po-boy she'd had in a very long time, Justin had removed all the boxes from the attic. She and Maggie had removed the files from the cardboard file boxes, brushed the cobwebs and dust from the folders, and then brought them into their room.

Stacks of green folders sat on the oak floor surrounding them. Each one held the same setup. Adoptive parents application followed by a list of children's names on the next page. When Maggie typed the names into her laptop, several showed up as missing children.

Maggie exhaled. "How could this man have gotten away with such horrific crimes?" She glanced toward Laney who focused on the last folder.

"Those poor families." Realizing what she said, a stabbing revelation pierced her heart. She and Bryan were probably one of *those poor families.*

"It upsets me to know the cases prior to ninety-five won't be brought to light," Maggie said.

Laney sat on the back of her feet still on the floor next to Maggie's bed. "Yeah, but it's not as many as you think. Mouchaux had only been doing adoptions for a year when we met him. So the earliest would be the spring of ninety-three. According to the patterns in these files, I'd say, as word got out, he increased the number of adoptions he did per month. But it's still sad to think some people will never know the truth. Maybe if the children's pictures were here, the authorities could post them. Maybe do a national television show."

Maggie stared at her. "Why didn't we think of that before? The truth was staring us in the face the whole time."

"Maggie, don't you have a picture of Paul just before he was kidnapped?"

Maggie paused. "Talk about not seeing the obvious when it smacks you in the face. At home. I didn't bring it with me."

"I was so excited when he came to live with me, I took hundreds of photos. Videos too." Laney stood and reached for her purse. Maybe she had one there.

A quick flip through her wallet produced one picture—Evan's graduation picture. She slid it toward Maggie.

Maggie reached for the photo and then gently squeezed Laney's hand. "You are a special lady."

Laney placed her other hand over Maggie's. "So are you."

Why had exchanging photos not been their first thought before going on this wild goose chase? Would they have been as willing to exchange photos had this journey not happened? Probably not. And would the evidence they'd unearthed have ever come to light? Had God sent them here to accomplish more than knowing the truth about Evan?

Maggie winked at Laney then smiled—the first time she'd seen Maggie really smile. "Who do we call first?"

"The police." Laney paused. What were they doing? She imagined all the families torn apart by what they contemplated. And what if she had heard about the attorney on TV, would she have pursued the truth?

One thing she did know, sheer curiosity would have lured her to the website. Once she'd seen her son's picture there, she would be doing just what she's doing now. Somehow, a calming peace settled through her. "I'd like to pray about this. Pray for all the people about to be affected by what we're going to do."

Maggie nodded. "That's a good idea."

Laney's heart flipped. Good idea? Was Maggie's heart softening? Laney returned to her knees and locked fingers with Maggie. "Dear Father, we come to You today to ask for Your wisdom and guidance in handling the information You allowed us to uncover. Father, we know many lives will be affected and we ask You to place Your hand upon all touched by the revelations to come. Father, give them peace to know truth can bring a healing bond to reunited families. To bring answers to long-held questions and even to the ones given up on. Lord, I ask you to draw each of these families to You and show Yourself to them in amazing ways. Lord, we ask this in the name of Your precious son, Jesus. Amen."

Before she released Maggie's hand, a tender tug of Maggie's fingers in hers warmed her. She silently thanked God their paths had crossed. Regardless of why.

****

Maggie slipped her hand from Laney's and met her gaze. "Thank you."

Laney smiled. "Are you going to call the police?"

Maggie sighed. "Yes, I'll call."

"But first I think we should tell Hazel." Laney sighed. "She'll be crushed when we tell her this."

Maggie nodded. "She will."

Laney stood. "I'll tell her while you call the police."

As Laney slipped from the room, Maggie looked up the

number for the New Orleans Police Department. How could she explain this?

She dialed the number and waited. A female voice answered. Maggie said, "I'd like to report a series of crimes. They happened over a period of ten years and started over twenty years ago."

"Twenty years?"

"Yes. Kidnapping and extortion."

"Hold please." The voice had a distinct accent, but it wasn't like the other Cajun accents This woman sounded as though she hailed from New Jersey. Or was it Chalmette?

Before long, a male voice filled her ears. "Sergeant, Nelson. How can I help you?"

Maggie paused. She hadn't thought about what she'd say. "Yes…my name is Dr. Margaret Langston, and I need to report a series of crimes." She exhaled after the first sentence then proceeded to explain the entire situation. After which, the policeman asked her to hold for a moment.

Maggie glanced out the French doors and into the garden below. Laney and Hazel sat at the wrought iron table near the Mimosa tree. China cups sat on the table in front of them.

"Dr. Langston. I can send someone to see you. What's your address?"

She gave him the address and then hung up.

****

Laney sipped the bold aromatic brew from the Blue Willow china cup. There were things about Louisiana she was starting to like. Coffee was one.

Hazel lowered her cup. "Let me get this straight." She lifted both hands, palms facing Laney. "You think Mr. Mouchaux may have kidnapped the children he placed with adoptive parents?"

Laney nodded.

"That's not possible. Mr. Mouchaux was a kind, generous man. He would never have done dat."

Laney explained about the pictures on the internet and

the names in the folders.

Hazel shook her head. "I can't believe it." Her eyes moistened and thick emotion edged her voice.

Looking into Hazel's tear-filled eyes broke Laney's heart. She took a long sip and slowly lowered her cup. "Hazel." Laney embraced Hazel's hand and met her confused gaze straight on. "Maggie and I are here because she believes Evan, the son I adopted through Mr. Mouchaux, is her son, Paul who was kidnapped shortly before we got Evan."

"Oh, Laney. I'm so sorry." Hazel's grip tightened. "Maggie seems like a nice woman. I can't believe she'd make such a horrible accusation."

"I'm starting to believe her accusation may be the truth." Laney extracted her hand from Hazel's and took another sip. A glance upstairs revealed Maggie standing on the balcony. Seems calling the police had been the easier task. "Maggie has called the police so they can conduct an official investigation."

Hazel pulled her hands away from Laney. Her eyes narrowed and she shook her head. "You can't do that. He's dead and gone. Why would you disrespect his memory?"

Laney straightened in her chair and drew in a deep breath. "It's not about disrespecting his memory, it's about justice. It's about righting horrific wrongs."

"Are you sure this is the right thing to do?"

"Yes. I'm sure."

"What about your life? And your son's?"

"We're willing to work things out."

"Your son is an adult, he can understand things and make his own decision. What about the adopted children who are underage and still living with the adoptive parents? What will happen to them and how will revealing this damage their lives?"

"Oh, Hazel. I don't know, but we can't just pretend this didn't happened. There are families out there who don't know if their children are still alive. Can't you imagine how they feel? Maggie has lived with guilt and pain for two decades not knowing what happened to her son. We just want the truth. Surely, you can understand that, can't you?"

"But Mr. Mouchaux's good name will be ruined." Hazel used her napkin to wipe at the corners of her eyes.

Laney found her compassion waning. Mr. Mouchaux's good name? Really? Children were in established homes with parents, they were not orphans who needed homes. He didn't save those children. He used them for his own gain. "Well, if the truth proves he was innocent then his good name will stand."

"I hope so. I thought he was getting orphaned children. He kept me out of that end of the adoption. He brought me in once the children were identified and he had their paperwork. But…" Hazel's voice softened and she paused.

"Hazel, what? Did you remember something?"

"Nothing specific, but I overheard an argument between Mr. Mouchaux and Johnny Salter. Johnny raved about Mr. Mouchaux's hands being clean, but if anything bad came to him, Johnny that is, he said he would take Mr. Mouchaux down with him. I didn't pay much mind to it because I didn't like Johnny and thought he was just waggin' his tongue."

"Would you be willing to speak to the police?" Laney shifted on the wrought iron chair and leaned closer to Hazel.

Hazel remained silent. She stared into her cup as though she expected the answers in the small circle of coffee grounds at the bottom. When she finally met Laney's gaze, her eyes drooped at the corners and the moisture in them glistened in the afternoon sun. "Talking to them would feel like I'm betraying Henri, destroying his memory."

Had Hazel loved Henri Mouchaux? A gentle breeze ruffled the branches of the Mimosa tree causing a few flowers to drift to their table.

Laney patted Hazel's hand. "You do what you're comfortable doing."

Hazel nodded causing the pooling tears to flow.

Laney's heart swelled. Hazel *had* loved him. And Laney bet he probably didn't return the sentiment. Would Hazel's heart be broken again when she found out the man she'd given her heart to for many years was not who she thought he was?

Laney found it hard to remember Henri Mouchoux with warmth. His actions had damaged many lives and the far-reaching effects had yet to be discovered.

The cell phone in her pocket chirped. She glanced at the screen. Bryan. "Excuse me," She said then answered the phone.

"Laney, how are things going?" Bryan's voice filled her with both comfort and dread. She loved hearing him, yet knew what she had to tell him would be devastating.

"We haven't found the actual proof we're looking for, but we've found so much more."

"Really? Are you okay?" Compassion covered his words.

She gulped around the lump blocking her words. "Yes...I am."

"Honey, I just got a very strange phone call from your cousin in Colorado."

Laney's pulse quickened. "Aunt Elaine's son?" The aunt she'd been estranged from since her son's adoption. She hadn't seen nor heard from either her cousin Mark nor her Aunt Elaine in over twenty-seven years.

"Yes. He said your aunt is very ill and is asking to see you. He'd like you to call him."

CHAPTER 37

Maggie sat on the canopy bed. The police would be here soon. Had Laney prepared Hazel for the encounter?

With her index finger, she traced the hand-stitching on one of the double-ring patterns of the quilt. The deep purple, green, and gold blurred together.

Other families would have proof. She wouldn't. She hadn't come here to rescue those other children, she'd come here to find the truth about her son. But...something in her warmed when she thought of all the mothers, like her, who would finally have answers. Could they finally have peace knowing their children were alive? The thought made her smile—a bittersweet smile.

The adopted children appeared to have gone to gentle loving families who wanted them. Families who'd paid handsomely to have them.

She and Laney would exchange photographs when they returned to Louisiana. She'd told Eric she'd be out until Thursday. Now all she wanted was to head back home.

A timid knock on the door grabbed her attention. "Miss Maggie, the police are here. They said you called." Elois' voice filtered through the closed door.

It had only been a half hour since she called. She hadn't expected such quick response. A slow day at the New Orleans Police Department? Was there such a thing? The opened door revealed a wide-eyed Elois. "Thank you. I'll get my shoes on and be right down."

As Maggie descended the stairway, voices rose from the parlor. Why did she feel she had opened the proverbial Pandora's box? Once made public, there would be no stopping the inevitable chain of events set in motion.

Laney's prayer came to mind. If Maggie ever wished she could pray and believe those prayers would be answered, it was right now. She planted her foot on the last step of the stairs and drew in a deep breath.

As she came around the corner, the silhouette of a tall, thin man stood next to the window. The burgundy, velvet drapes contrasted sharply with his navy sports coat and gray slacks. His concentrated gaze and the way he'd crossed the room in two strides to shake Maggie's hand made him seem ill at ease among the crocheted doilies and Duncan Phyfe furniture.

"Detective, Carroll Thibodeaux NOPD." He handed her a business card.

Just as Maggie extended her hand and began to give him her name, Hazel and Laney strolled into the room.

"Carroll, it's nice to see you. How's your mama?" Hazel patted his forearm and tilted her head back to see his face. Her five-foot height made her seem like a child standing against Detective Thibodeaux's six-foot-plus stance.

"Miss Hazel, it's good to see you too. Mama's not so good these days. Ate up with arthritis, but you know mama, she keeps going. Walks to mass every morning."

"I'm sorry to hear dat, but I know if anyone can be a shinin' light in the middle of personal tragedy, it's your mama. She inspired me to keep going more times than I can remember."

"Thank you, ma'am, now about some kidnapping charges?" He turned back toward Maggie.

She extended her hand again. "Dr. Margaret Langston and this is my friend, Laney Ellerby."

"Detective…?" Laney grasped the narrow, long-fingered hand Detective Thibodeaux offered.

"Oh sorry, Carroll Thibodeaux."

Hazel spread her short chubby arm toward the furnishings of the Victorian clad parlor. "Why don't we have a seat?"

Detective Thibodeaux glanced at the formal couch and chairs. He angled his body toward the couch, but then changed direction and sat on the wingback chair next to a marble-topped table with a lyre base. His knees came above his hips making him seem like an adult sitting in a child's chair. The parlor's furnishings were more about looks than function.

"Um…Mrs…um…Dr. Langston? I believe you called the station. I came right over when I recognized Hazel's address. Please tell me what this is about." He retrieved a wire-bound notebook from his jacket then leaned back and crossed his right ankle onto his left knee. He flipped a few pages. With pen poised he turned his intense gaze toward Maggie.

She relayed the information she and Laney had discovered. Laney interjected when Maggie missed an important point. When they finished, the detective remained silent. Hazel shifted in the opposite chair and looked at her hands in her lap.

After a few moments, Detective Thibodeaux spoke. "About how many of these adoptions took place between…" He drew his eyebrows together. "…nineteen ninety-three and nineteen ninety-eight?" He turned to Hazel. "Is that when Mr. Mouchaux retired?"

"Yes, and when he moved to Pensacola, Florida."

Had Hazel's voice quivered when she mentioned the Florida town? So he'd left her here when he retired. Did she still harbor the pain of unrequited love?

Detective Thibodeaux continued, "Six years of

adoptions and many of those children were abducted?"

Maggie nodded. "We're not sure of the total number. Somewhere around one-hundred fifty. We don't know if all of them dealt with abducted children, but we believe the majority did." She sat on the edge of the couch. "We have the records from nineteen ninety-five through ninety-eight. The earlier years ninety-three and ninety-four, we believe, were destroyed by Katrina."

He twitched his lips together. "Not surprising. Katrina took a lot from this city." He turned toward Hazel. "Do I have permission to gather these records?"

Hazel paused. Was she contemplating saying no? Performing a last ditch effort to save Mr. Mouchaux's reputation? She looked up and glanced toward Laney who nodded. Hazel turned toward Maggie—uncertainty shrouded her pained expression. The room fell silent. Would Hazel consent? Maggie held her breath. *Oh, please say yes.*

Hazel exhaled then nodded.

Detective Thibodeaux tilted his head again in Hazel's direction. "Is that a yes?"

"Yes. I'll have Justin begin hauling the boxes downstairs."

"That won't be necessary. Our men can pick them up from wherever they are."

Laney said, "Two of the boxes are on the balcony and the rest are in our room."

He lifted a cell phone from the holder on his belt. Within minutes, he'd given the request to have the records removed.

Maggie said, "Oh, one more thing. Hazel told us about a man who had dealings with Mr. Mouchaux. His name is Johnny Salter."

He turned toward Hazel. "Is that right?"

"Yes, he did investigations for Henri."

The detective's eyes narrowed and his lips drew into a thin line. "Figures."

He jotted a few things in his notebook then got Maggie and Laney's telephone numbers. "I'll be in touch if I need any more information." He stood then walked toward the door. "You never told me how you two came to be rifling through those records. Any reason why you're digging up adoption records from the early nineties?"

Laney shot a glance toward Maggie. Her brow arched. Maggie read the action as questioning if it was okay to tell him the truth. She nodded.

Laney cleared her throat then told the detective about Evan. A flash of compassion crossed his face. His gaze encompassed both Maggie and Laney. "I'm sorry to hear that. I'm sure if what you say is correct, there will be a lot of families impacted by this."

Hazel stood next to Maggie. "More than you know." She walked toward the detective. "Let me see you out."

When Hazel and Detective Thibodeaux left the room, Maggie blew a stream of air through pursed lips. "Thank goodness that's over."

Laney flopped back onto the couch. "I have a feeling it's only just begun."

****

Laney closed her eyes for a moment and tried to ignore the voices rolling through her mind. Her aunt wanted to see her. What could she possibly have to say from her deathbed? An apology for convincing her to give her first-born away?

She needed to call Bryan again. He'd be worried about what was happening here. She'd ended their call when Elois had told them the Detective had arrived. He'd also be curious about why her cousin had called. Would every aspect of her life be exposed and turned upside down at the same time? She'd never gotten a phone call from her relatives in Colorado. Had she even told Bryan she had an aunt in Colorado?

Maggie lifted her right knee onto the couch and angled her body toward Laney. "Are you all right?"

Laney paused. Should she tell Maggie? "I'm not sure. I got a strange call from Bryan earlier. My cousin from Colorado called."

"Really." Maggie paused.

"I need to call him. Honestly, I'm a little leery. It's been years since I've heard from my relatives."

Maggie brushed a strand of hair away from her eyes. "Including your aunt?"

"Yes. Evidently, she's ill and wants to see me. Guess I should get this over with." Laney stood and fished her phone from her back pocket.

"Sounds intriguing." Maggie rose also. "I'm going to take a shower, those dusty files have me feeling pretty grimy."

"I'm coming up too. I'll call Bryan from the balcony. I know what you mean about the files, but I'm not sure if I feel dirty so much from the dust on the outside or the filth on the inside."

Maggie put her arm around Laney's shoulders. "I think it's more the nastiness on the inside."

"I think you're right." Laney squeezed Maggie's hand then walked toward the staircase.

Laney clutched her cell phone for a moment. She needed to call Bryan. As she dialed, she formulated the words. When he answered, she filled him in on all the events of the last few days in New Orleans. He assured her, if she wanted to fly out to Fort Collins to see her aunt he would do whatever he could to get off work to be with her. That was Bryan. Always looking out for her. Even to his detriment. That's what had gotten them into this mess, he'd wanted to give her the desire of her heart.

If she decided to go to Colorado, Bryan couldn't come with her. Not without knowing what her aunt had to say. Would she be able to do this alone? She'd have to. Maybe this was the opportunity she needed to finally deal with her past.

She dialed the number Bryan gave her and pushed back

on the rocker. After several rings, a man answered.

"Hello, Mark is that you?"

"Laney?"

"Yeah, my husband said you called. What's up?"

"I did. Mother is at Poudre Valley Hospital. She's not doing well. Congestive heart failure. The doctor's have done everything they can, but it's progressed and with her diabetes...it looks like her time is near. They're talking about sending her home with hospice." His voice was barely more than a whisper with his last words.

Laney pushed the floor with her foot to start the back and forth motion of the rocker. "I'm sorry to hear that."

"She's been asking to see you."

"Me? Why?" The traffic noise from the balcony melded with the patter of her heartbeat.

"I don't know. She won't say."

Mark had been away at college in California when Laney lived with his mother, so even though they were close in age, he had not known about the baby or the adoption. "Laney, please try to come. I've never seen her so adamant or distraught. I don't know if it's the drugs she's taking, but every time I walk in she asks for you. She's begged me to get you up here. Said to buy your ticket and one for anyone you wanted to bring with you."

Would going up there solve anything? Maybe her aunt had information about her son. But how could she? It had been a closed adoption which meant even Aunt Elaine wouldn't know who had adopted her son.

"Another thing. She's in so much pain. I can't understand what keeps her alive, but I have a strange feeling she's holding on until she can talk to you."

The wall she'd built around her heart where her aunt was concerned crumbled. How could she deny a dying women's request?

"I'll come." Would she regret saying those simple words?

"Good. Let me know your schedule and I'll make the

reservations."

"I'll call you back in a bit."

"Laney, thanks."

She sighed and disconnected the call.

"Laney, are you out there?" Maggie's voice drifted to the balcony from the room.

"I'm here."

Maggie, with her hair wrapped in a towel, spread the French doors and walked onto the balcony. "What's wrong?"

Laney shook her head. "It's my aunt." She shared the details with Maggie.

"Are you flying up? Is Bryan going with you?"

"I can't let him come. Not yet. I need to know what she has to say first. He doesn't know about the adoption and this would be a horrible way for him to find out."

"Maybe you could tell him before."

"No, I want to tell him when I'm home and can explain all the details. Besides, he can't take off work this soon after getting this job. It wouldn't be a good idea."

"You're going alone?" Maggie sat in the rocker next to Laney.

"As much as I hate the thought, I will. My curiosity is piqued. Maybe she has information about my first son. This may be the last opportunity to know what happened to my baby."

Maggie stopped rocking and turned to Laney. "I can honestly say I understand how you feel. Would you like some company? There's nothing more we can do here. The police will start the investigation soon. I still have two days off." She grinned.

"You'd do that for me?" Laney's throat tightened. "I'd love to have you."

"Are you kidding? You've lived all these years not knowing what happened to your child. I know what that's like. I thank you for coming out here with me. Although we didn't find exactly what we were looking for, we're much closer to the truth. You've been a big help. I'd like to return the favor."

"Looks like we're going to Ft. Collins, Colorado." Had she only met Maggie a couple of weeks ago? Her heart warmed toward Maggie. *Thank you, Lord. You sent the friend I prayed for.* Emma's sweet words came to her—*Be careful what you pray for, you just might get it.*

CHAPTER 38

Maggie leaned against the plane's window and stared at the ground below. Circles of browns dotted the landscape as the plane headed north to Denver. The earthen quilt changed to a multitude of lush greens. Laney flipped through a magazine in the seat next to her.

Doubts rose to strangle the freedom she'd felt just a few hours ago. Why had she volunteered to accompany Laney? Here she was helping find someone else's child, when she still hadn't discovered the truth about her own. But, something drew her to Laney. Something about the woman's gentle nature and caring spirit made her want to be around her.

Maggie couldn't understand her feelings where Laney was concerned. One thing rose above all else: Laney was a good person—that and more.

Maggie wanted to be a better person when around Laney. Her son had grown up with an amazing example of a mother. Could she have been as good a mother to Paul? More doubts surfaced to steal her peace. Had Paul been better off living with the Ellerby's?

Stop. No good came from such thoughts and she

couldn't go where they'd take her.

"We should go to one of these conferences sometime. Look there's one in Dallas in August." Laney folded the magazine and handed it to Maggie. The page highlighted a Women Of Faith Conference. *A religious conference?* The only ones she'd attended were for medical professionals.

She handed the magazine back to Laney. "I'm not sure religion is my thing. I don't think this would be something I'd like."

"Think about it. Emma and I attended one in Mobile and it was amazing." She peered into Maggie's eyes. "It's not about religion. It's about praising and worshiping God with other women. There's something about hearing thousands of women's voices singing out to God. There's nothing like it. It gives me chill bumps." She rubbed the tops of her forearms. "It binds us together in a common heritage, as daughters of a mighty God."

Not sure how to answer, Maggie simply nodded. This seemed just like the invitation from Elizabeth and Hazel to attend a regular class at Rosie's. She didn't want to offend Laney by telling her she wasn't interested. But, despite her quick-to-deny attitude, the thought of bonding with other women whose faith was the cornerstone of their lives sparked a tiny flame of interest. Being around other women was something she'd always avoided.

Women had children.

Women talked about their children.

Women reminded Maggie her child was gone.

It was easier to be around men who discussed sports and other non-threatening topics. Safe topics that didn't send her into a pit of depression.

Laney returned to the magazine. Maggie turned to the view out the window. Each patchwork of earth seemed so perfectly edged as if carved out by the grand master. A jigsaw puzzle of sorts. But Maggie knew those land plots were not perfectly sized and as neat as they appeared from a distance.

Like her life.

She and Craig appeared to be the perfect couple. Great jobs, great home, nice cars. But within the façade, much was missing. Would he be angry with her for not telling him about the trip to New Orleans? Maybe she could at least tell him about this trip. She'd gone to help a friend. He would like that. How often had he encouraged her to forge friendships with other women? Only to have her tell him he didn't understand. Maybe he understood more than she gave him credit for.

****

Laney flipped the blinker of the rental car and steered out of the Denver airport and into the flow of traffic on E-470. In an hour or so, they'd be in Fort Collins. Could she handle being back in the city? She'd left after her baby was born and never returned. The town held memories too harsh to explore and feelings too cutting to dwell on. Had she written her son off because she couldn't deal with her emotions when she thought about him? Maggie never stopped looking for Paul. It's what she admired about her new friend. She'd never stopped believing he still lived. Laney had replaced her biological son by adopting someone else's.

The full-size car Mark reserved was a nice surprise. Laney set the cruise control to the speed limit and removed her foot from the accelerator. They passed a toll-booth and before long they headed north on I-25.

Maggie gazed out the window. Laney glanced to the left at the Rocky Mountains lining the western sky. They provided a majestic contrast to the flat land of the east.

Laney loved Colorado the first time she'd come. She loved the mountains. She loved how the wheat fields to the east looked like waving golden flags when the wind rustled through them.

Maggie turned away from the window and toward Laney. "Are you excited about what your aunt may have to say?"

The interstate stretched ahead. A well-worn path she'd taken many times when she'd flown home for breaks. Was this path the only way to learn the truth about *her* child? Dividing lines zoomed by.

"In one way, I'm excited. In another, to be totally honest, I'm scared to death." She met Maggie's gaze in a quick glance then returned her focus to the highway. "I know this whole journey has been for a reason and I've loved seeing the hand of God in everything we've encountered. From you hiring Eric to coming on this trip with me."

Her fingers wrapped tighter around the wheel. "As much as I trust God in so many areas of my life, there are still areas I hold onto so tightly He can't work in them. I just can't seem to let go where my past is concerned."

She clicked her blinker and veered around a slow moving minivan. "Holding on has become a security blanket. If I let go, I'm afraid of what I'll find underneath. It all makes me wonder—if I can trust so well in some areas and not in others, do I really have faith?"

Maggie adjusted her seatbelt. "You know, I'm certainly no expert in trusting God, but I think it's kind of like trusting ourselves. There are some areas in my life, like my work, I'm confident about. Others, not so much. Like having friends and moving forward. Ask my husband, he'll give you a dissertation on my doubts. I don't know about faith, but I believe it's human nature to doubt. In your case, maybe where you've seen God work you can let go. In the areas you haven't, you still want to hold on. Isn't there a saint or someone in the Bible who doubted?"

"Yes, Doubting Thomas."

"Maybe we all have a little bit of Thomas in us. Some of us more than others. I must admit, Laney, I've never thought about trusting God before. I had too many reasons not to."

"What about now? After what we've been through?"

"I don't know." Maggie turned back toward the window.

This was the first time Maggie willingly discussed the

possibility of God playing a role in their meeting. Laney remembered what Maggie had shared about her past and about living with the grief of a missing child. Laney reasoned her faith and trust in God had been easy until now. She'd never been really tested before. Could she have trusted Him if she'd been through what Maggie had? Could she trust him now?

Lord, be with us. Give me Your peace and give Aunt Elaine peace with what's in her heart. And Father, draw Maggie to You. Let her see Your hand in her life.

The car's air-conditioning and the *whoosh-whoosh* of the tires on the highway provided the only sound in the car for the next several miles. Laney's mind revolved through the thousands of possible things her aunt could have to tell her. Maybe her child had died and her aunt couldn't bring herself to tell her.

After a long while, Maggie spoke, her gaze still fixed out the window. "Laney, I have a personal question, you don't have to answer if you don't want to."

"Okay."

"Why have you never pursued finding your child before?"

Laney stared at the Dodge pickup barreling down the road ahead. How many times had she asked herself the same question? Too many. Her answer never satisfied.

"I really don't know." She rolled her bottom lip between her teeth. "Maybe, I didn't think I deserved to be his mother, or even to be part of his life after I gave him up." She tapped on the wheel. "How pathetic is that? At the time, I thought the less I knew the less my mind could torment me. Which I guess is true, but I've regretted the decision every day of my life."

"Ironically, enough, I understand. What about later when you wanted a child?"

"By then it had been a few years and the feeling of unworthiness was steeped deep into my psyche. Besides, I told myself I loved my child too much to interfere in his life. It was how I reasoned pushing away any thoughts of the baby. Later after Bryan and I married, the longer I didn't tell Bryan the harder it became to tell him. So I just kept it from him. Even when I discovered the reason I couldn't have any more children was due to a complication during the delivery."

She slid her hand along the top of the steering wheel and rested her fingers on the cross brace in the middle. "In my demented thinking, I accepted my inability to have children as the consequence for the sins I'd committed. I also believed I didn't deserve to know my child."

Maggie flipped the air-conditioner vent near the window toward her face. "This sun beating in through this windshield is like a sauna."

"We can turn the AC up if you like." Laney reached for the dial.

"No. This is fine." Maggie paused allowing the silence to spread through the car. After a while she spoke. "Laney, God knows I'm not the poster child for confidence, but I can't believe that someone like you wouldn't deserve to know her child. What will you do if your aunt tells you where your child is? Will you go to him?"

Laney stared at the road. "I don't know. I really don't know."

CHAPTER 39

*L*aney veered off the interstate onto Exit 47. The familiar tug of the past drew her. How many times had she driven this route during her two years at CSU? Countless. A pang of regret ripped through her. She should have graduated. Not let the shame control her. Not let him scare her away.

Professor Joseph Mallory had encouraged her departure. Laney leaving Fort Collins helped him keep the façade of respected citizen, generous professor, and loving husband. If only those who held him in such high esteem knew the truth.

"You're remembering aren't you?" Maggie said.

"Yes, being here is bringing back all the memories, some good but mostly bad." Laney turned the visor to block the blinding rays streaming into the driver's side window. "I never exposed the professor. What if he seduced another unsuspecting freshman? If I'd said something I could have prevented that."

"Laney, you're talking to the wrong person if you want sound advice on not beating yourself up over the past. I've lived the past twenty years in a boxing ring with myself. I can tell you, it hasn't done me a bit of good. Knowing Paul was kidnapped with the intent to put him with an adoptive family has made me realize it wasn't because I was such a terrible mother. Those people knew what they were doing. Sometimes I wonder if the crying child was a setup."

Laney frowned. "Crying child?"

"There was a young girl and her four year-old brother in the park that day. Her brother fell off the slide and cut his knee." Maggie paused then exhaled. "The sister, in a panic, came running for help. I glanced at Paul before I rushed to the other child. He was busy patting sand into the back of his toy dump truck his sweet face so focused on the task. I didn't even think he'd noticed I'd stepped away.

I ran toward the crying boy, lifted him and carried him back to my table. There I wiped his knee and tried to calm his crying. During the process, I glanced a couple of times toward the sand box and saw Paul still playing. Once the boy settled and limped away with his sister, I turned back to Paul and he was gone."

"Just like that."

"Just like that. In an instant. I was no more than twenty feet away."

"How horrible."

Maggie tried to soften the edge of her fingernail. The torn nail snagged on her blouse. "Although Craig has never come right out and said it, I know he blames me."

Laney slid an emery board from her cell phone case and handed it to Maggie.

"Thanks." Maggie worked to smooth the unruly nail.

"I admire how you never gave up on Paul. When the opportunity to find the truth came along, you pursued it with passion regardless of what the truth might reveal." Laney sighed. "And, I'm sorry we didn't find proof for you. Yet, you're here helping me."

"It takes guts to do what you're doing. I couldn't let you do this alone."

"I trust the Lord has opened this door for a good purpose, but I have to admit I'm a little scared."

"Somehow I think it's okay to be afraid, as long as you don't let it cripple you and keep you from doing what you should."

"You're absolutely right. I believe your statement defines my faith."

"But I thought Christians were never afraid or had doubts. If they believed, there would be no doubt."

Laney smiled. "Nope. I don't know what type of Christians you've encountered. But, real Christians are real people. They are people who fear, doubt, make mistakes, stupid mistakes like not telling their husband about a baby they had years ago." She grinned. "... and they carry a semi-tractor trailer full of other ailments. I guess the difference is our faith can help us to overcome our mistakes, not be defined by them, and maybe cause us to think twice before repeating them."

Laney paused. She hoped her words were truth that spoke to Maggie's heart. "If you've avoided becoming a Christian because you thought you had to be perfect, then you've missed the blessing of having a wonderful relationship with a loving, forgiving God."

****

Maggie let the words sink in. What had she missed? She saw Laney's faith. Her being here proved the woman had a built-in sense of truth and desire to make things right.

Even if Maggie never felt comfortable praying to God or being part of Laney's religious world, she wanted her as a friend. She liked how she felt when around Laney. She respected her despite the situation they'd been thrown into. Or was it because of their situation?

Regardless, she accepted her. Ironically, this was the first time she'd allowed someone to become close to her. The reality unsettled.

Maggie raised her hand then hesitated. Should she? Finally, she rested her hand for a moment on Laney's shoulder. Would the tender touch convey her friendship? She wasn't a touchy-feely kind of person and didn't give hugs too freely—except to her tiny patients.

She gave a tiny squeeze. The act had taken less energy than she thought it would. Hopefully it made Laney feel better.

Silence commanded the car on the remainder of the drive north. Their silence was bred from quiet contemplation and the budding knowledge that their friendship didn't need a constant flow of words.

CHAPTER 40

Laney took slow deliberate steps, like walking through jelly, toward the chrome-sided hospital bed that stood in sharp contrast to the antique dresser and vanity in her aunt's room. Other than the bed, little had changed in her aunt's room, except for the overabundance of medications on the oak nightstand. As she approached, her aunt's labored breathing sent an icy chill through her. She rubbed her arms in an effort to rid her skin of the goose flesh.

She gasped as she stood next to the bed. The withered and barely recognizable form of Aunt Elaine took up barely half the twin mattress. This woman, her namesake, had been larger than life to Laney. Her admiration for Aunt Elaine had given them a special bond. Laney loved her—loved her like her mother until...until she'd convinced Laney to give her child away.

The thin parchment-like skin looked like it could tear as easily as a Bible page. Red polish partially worn off from her fingernails sent Laney back in time. Laney's heart swelled knowing Aunt Elaine would be upset to see her nails in such deplorable shape. Her aunt's nails were always impeccably manicured. The tap, tap, tap of her long red nails played through Laney's mind. The night they'd discussed what to do, Aunt Elaine drummed her fingernails on the table. Abort it. The words still sent a dagger through her heart. How could she have suggested such a thing? The small consolation came from choosing adoption over abortion. But soon after the growing ache spilled into every part of her being. It was the worst decision of her life. Giving away her child had not been the best thing for all involved. It had been the best thing for those who had wanted to hide the truth, because the truth would destroy their perfect world. Including hers. It was the thing she regretted most. Next to keeping the secret from Bryan.

Resentment stabbed. A sentiment she thought she'd shaken, but now she found vestiges of anger and bitterness lingered in her heart. They hadn't spoken in over two decades. What meaningful conversation could they engage in?

The handling of the adoption in a cold business-like manner by her aunt broke Laney just as much as giving away her baby. Then after...Aunt Elaine acted as though the whole event never occurred. Laney's relentless questions went unanswered—ignored.

After a few months, unable to bear the pain, Laney left school, left Fort Collins, and her aunt. Never to return. Until now. She battled the swirling storm of old emotions. The ones she'd left here. The ones she'd pushed deep down inside. The ones that surfaced whenever she thought of her baby.

Lord, give me grace and compassion for her. I don't want those old feelings to interfere with forgiving her.

A groan drew her attention back to the bed. Her aunt's paper-thin eyelids flickered. A labored breath escaped her lips.

"Aunt Elaine. It's Laney." Laney reached for her hand, but stopped midway and rested on the chrome side-rail.

"Laney, my sweet Laney." The croaky response filled the room and sent shivers through Laney. Sweet Laney?

Had her aunt forgotten all the pain she'd caused Laney?

Her aunt's lips twitched—an attempt to smile, maybe? Laney paused before leaning in closer. Tiny cracks dotted the rim of Aunt Elaine's lips. Laney drew in a deep breath. "Mark said you wanted to see me. I'm here."

Aunt Elaine lifted her skeleton hand and pointed with a long bony finger toward a chair in the corner. "Pull up that chair."

Typical. Commanding instead of asking. Even imminent death didn't change some things. Or some people. Laney retrieved the chair and placed it next to the bed.

"Look in there. The envelope." Her aunt pointed to the top drawer of the nightstand.

Laney slid it open. The familiar scent of menthol and eucalyptus drifted from its depths and captured her senses. If any smell defined Aunt Elaine, that was it. She'd had arthritis at a very young age and concocted homemade lotions to combat the meddlesome disease.

A bulky ochre envelope with Laney's name scrawled on the front, sat amid the tangled mass of lotions, books, eyeglasses, and an orange flashlight. She lifted the envelope, surprised by its weight.

Aunt Elaine pushed opened her eyes and stared for a moment, but the effort seemed to be more than she could handle. She lowered her lids, then spoke. Her voice, low and raspy, "I'm sorry. I'm so…sorry. Please forgive…me."

The words speared Laney's heart. How long had she intended to say them?

A barrage of responses and a ball of emotion jammed in Laney's throat. She'd never heard her aunt apologize for anything. Could she forgive her? Should she forgive her?

Her prayer came to mind. If ever she needed answered prayer, it was now. While part of her wanted to forgive Aunt Elaine, another part wanted to hold onto the anger and resentment. A stark reminder slammed—Laney had agreed to the adoption. It wasn't like her child was taken from her like in Maggie's case. She'd freely agreed to give up her baby.

Why was it so important for Aunt Elaine to apologize after all these years?

Laney brushed her fingertips on her aunt's skinny hand. The sunken skin between the bones created valleys along the top, ridges Laney's fingers dipped into. She'd seen those hands chop wood with the strength of any man. She'd seen those hands butcher a chicken. She'd also seen those hands crotchet an award-winning bedspread.

Each labored breath produced a gut-wrenching rasp sending Laney's heart into a tailspin. Her aunt struggled to survive. To breathe in life-sustaining air.

"Aunt Elaine. It's okay." Could she say the words and mean them? "I..." She inhaled. Lord, help me to let go. "I for...forgive you." She slipped her fingers around her aunt's hand and gave a gentle squeeze.

Aunt Elaine's gaze met Laney's. The sad, sunken eyes misted. When her aunt closed her lids, tears spilled along a path of wrinkles next to her temple. When she exhaled, a long and hoarse whistle accompanied the effort.

No.

Surely, her aunt had not held on just for this? "Aunt Elaine?"

A gentle squeeze from cold thin fingers answered. With what seemed supernatural effort, she opened her eyes again. "I never meant to hurt you."

Laney swallowed, her throat raw from the effort. The envelope weighed heavy on her lap. "I know you didn't. It's okay, Aunt Elaine. It was my choice."

Her aunt rolled her head from side to side on the flattened pillow. The action caused more tears to drip from her eyes. "No, it's not okay."

Laney cupped Aunt Elaine's hand in both of hers. Why was she so adamant about this? "I forgive you. I hold no ill feelings toward you."

"You will." Her voice barely a whisper, "You will when you find out." She closed her eyes and somehow Laney knew her aunt had fallen asleep. Please Lord, ease her pain.

She brushed the face of the envelope. Let her fingertips glide over her name. The letters were written with a shaky hand. Some letters darker than others where more pressure had been applied. Did this envelope contain the information about her child?

Laney drew the envelope to her chest and listened to the hoarse breathing of someone she'd loved struggle for life. You will when you find out. The words pierced through the long-built barrier around her heart.

Laney blew out a long breath. "Oh, Aunt Elaine. What have you done?"

#

Laney slid the chair closer to the hotel room's table. "I guess now is as good a time as any." She looked toward Maggie, who sat on the bed farthest from the table.

"Would you like to be alone?"

"No, not at all. I have a feeling this will take a lot of courage." Laney peeled the flap away from the side and poured the contents onto the table.

A photograph with faded colors captured her attention. It showed a boy sitting in front of a birthday cake. Ten candles glowed on top of the homemade cake. She lifted the photo and stared into eyes matching her own. She closed her eyes and let the image meld with the one she carried in her heart and mind. The image she'd burned into her memory on that March day so many years ago. Was this the same child? She flipped the picture. Alex Davenport, Tenth Birthday.

The image blurred as though looking through the old windows of her aunt's house. This must be her son.

She spread the contents until everything in the envelope lay flat on the table. Post cards, pictures, letters addressed to her, and an envelope from a state agency lay before her.

Waiting to be answered.

Waiting to tell the story of Alex, her son.

It had not been a closed adoption. The adoptive parent's

letters rested in Laney's shaking hands. They wanted him to know her. All these letters—their letters went unanswered.

She bowed her head. Lord, I need you right now.

Maggie's voice, soft and gentle floated from the other side of the room. "Laney, is everything all right?"

Laney nodded, but kept her head bowed. Suddenly, a mountain of questions assaulted. What kind of person had he grown up to be? Was he married? Was she a grandmother? The thought sent a flutter to her heart. A grandchild. She could be a grandmother. Would her child accept her into his life? She lifted a post card from the Grand Canyon and read the neatly written words.

Laney, we took Alex to see the Grand Canyon. It was such fun to see how excited he became. We're still thinking about you and waiting to hear how you're doing. Much love, The Davenports

Her chest tightened. She'd missed so much. How long had they waited to hear from her?

She lifted another photograph, the same ear-to-ear grin as in the first photo greeted her. He seemed happy. *I prayed for you every day.*

The state agency envelope sat on the table. Did the envelope contain her son's birth certificate?

She un-tucked the flap and removed the folded document. The aroma reminded her of the library. Old book smell, she'd called it as a child. She inhaled and let the scent work its magic, let it take her back to the day her son was born. As she unfolded the page, it fluttered in response to her shaking fingers. Finally, the truth.

The photocopied birth certificate touted worn edges and a single stain. A coffee stain. Did the certificate's condition prove her aunt's struggle with the truth all these years?

She scanned the page. Last Name: Davenport, First Name: Alex. Laney rubbed her thumb over the coffee stain. The commonness of the stain seemed disrespectful to the significance of the document she held. After all the years of wondering how she'd feel having the information she now held in her hand, she could've never imagined the rush of emotion. She scanned the document to take in the information she'd craved for so long.

He'd weighed seven pounds and three ounces. She'd missed the blessing of having that tiny weight in her arms. A nurse at her bedside had tilted the small bundle so she could see the round wrinkled face. She had burned the image of that precious face into her mind. And through the years the image had sometimes haunted, and sometimes comforted.

She pressed the fingertips of her hand against her clamped lips and squeezed her eyes shut. As though the action could dam the flood of emotions. Emotions long held back. Emotions rolling like a bulldozer threatening to break through. Now her aunt's words made sense. Aunt Elaine hadn't apologized just for her role in the adoption, she had apologized for this. For denying Laney the privilege of knowing her son.

She picked up a letter addressed to her. The postmark date—two months after Alex's birth. The return address was written in a firm but delicate handwriting from Prairieland, Texas. Why had she never gotten this letter? She slid her finger under the envelope's flap. The aged glue released with minimal ease.

Dear Laney,

We hope you are feeling well and have recovered from the delivery. Alex is such a good boy. He sleeps most of the night. When he does wake, he usually eats and then goes right back to sleep. He has a healthy appetite and his growth is right on target for his age. He is a fine boy.

We are grateful to you for giving us our dream. God used you to answer the prayers of a couple who had almost given up hope of ever being parents.

Please know we will be the best parents possible and will take good care of our precious son.

If you should ever want to visit, you are always welcome.

Sincerely,

Hank and Judy Davenport

Laney released a long sigh. A ball of emotion rose in her throat. How could her aunt have kept this from her? Why? She had a right to know. Laney lowered her head onto the table, onto the letter. The people who had adopted her son had invited her into their life. Into the life of her son. A new emotion boiled within. She slammed her fist on the table next to her head. How could she? She had no right.

Suddenly, the weight of Maggie's hand on her shoulder drew her attention. "Laney, is there anything I can do?"

Laney lifted her head. Maggie's compassion-filled eyes blurred before her. "My son's name is Alex." She spread her hands out over the pile of documents. "Look." She pointed to the last line of the letter. "They invited me. They wanted me to be a part of his life. She kept me from my son, my aunt kept me from my son. How could she?" Wet warmth touched her cheek. "How could she?"

Maggie slid her hand along Laney's shoulder. "I'm so sorry."

"You know she apologized and I was naïve enough to think it was because of her guilt over convincing me to give up the baby. But now, I know the real reason. She couldn't stand knowing she'd robbed me of him—not once, but twice. What kind of person would do that?"

As soon as the words escaped, Laney wanted to grab them from the air and shove them back into her mouth. Catch them before they reached Maggie. "I'm sorry. I-I-I didn't mean…"

Maggie lowered her eyelids then rubbed Laney's shoulder again. "It's okay. If anyone can understand how you feel, I think I can."

Laney reached for Maggie's hand. "I don't know how you lived with this kind of pain for so long. I feel like my heart has been ripped into a million pieces."

"Trust me. I didn't do a very good job."

"Seems to me, you've done the best you could."

Maggie grinned. "So, what are you going to do with this newfound information?"

"I'm not sure. It's all so new. Look at this." She pointed to the postmark on the letter. "They're from Prairieland, Texas. I wonder if they still live there?" She tapped her lips with the corner of the letter.

"There's one way to find out." Maggie slid across the room and reached for her laptop. "What's the name?"

"Hank and Judy Davenport." She thought about her dying aunt and examined her heart. Could she forgive her now? Lord, soften my heart. Let me forgive her.

"I got two Hank Davenports in Texas." She hopped from the bed with the laptop in her hand. "Laney, look, there's one in Prairieland, Texas. He's still there."'

"Oh."

"Aren't you excited about this? Here's a connection to your son—a chance to meet the boy you gave birth to." Maggie's fingers clicked through the keyboard. "Prairieland is a small farming community just south of Dallas off Interstate 45."

"I don't know. They have probably written me off. Look at all these letters. Not one was answered. Dear Lord, I bet he thinks I didn't want anything to do with him. He probably thinks I don't care."

Maggie returned to the chair next to Laney and gazed into her eyes. "He might think all those things. And there is nothing you can do about the past and what happened, but now you've been given a chance to make things right. You've been given this amazing gift. It's up to you what happens from this point forward."

Laney met Maggie's gaze. "You're right." She shook her head. "Did you hear what you just told me about the past? That's pretty good advice..." She smiled. "How did this happen? We came here to find the truth about Evan. Yet, we've found the truth about dozens of other missing children. Found the truth about my son. I feel so bad for you. How can you be such a source of encouragement to me, when I know you've got to be hurt by this?"

Maggie's fingers relaxed in Laney's grasp. "I don't know." She shrugged. "But I do know that there's a possibility for you to meet your son. It makes me happy to think you can know a son you never knew. I'm a little envious." Maggie grinned. "But, happy too. Besides…" She lifted one of the photos of Alex. "When we exchange photos, I'll have my answer."

Laney wrapped her arms around Maggie. At first, Maggie grew stiff, but slowly she relaxed returning Laney's hug.

The chirp of Laney's cell phone sounded. She smiled toward Maggie. "Thanks." Then answered her phone.

"Laney, it's Mark.".

CHAPTER 41

*M*ark's voice sent a chill through her. "Yes?" She waited.

"Mom's not doing well. The hospice nurse said she could go at any moment. She woke up for a moment and was rambling about you and a baby. She was pretty upset. She kept saying your name over and over and something about Alex needed his mother. I know the drugs are making her confused, but she asked for you again. Will you come?"

Would she?

Could she?

Lord, I can't do this alone. You'll have to carry me on this one. She exhaled and felt the edges of her heart soften. "I'm on my way."

"Thanks, Laney. She may not awaken again, but if she does I know you being here will give her comfort."

She closed the phone and stared at Maggie. "Aunt Elaine is asking for me again."

Maggie looked up from the laptop screen. "Living with regret is tough. Don't let her die with it. You'll both be free. Trust me on this one."

Laney reached for her phone and purse. "Would you like to come with me?"

"I think this is one you have to do on your own. I'll wait for you here."

Laney nodded then headed out the door.

A half-hour later, Laney sat in the rental car parked in her aunt's driveway. She'd finally found the courage to call Bryan and filled him in on how her aunt was doing. That was all she told him. Thankfully he hadn't asked a lot of questions, but encouraged her to take all the time she needed.

The rest she would have to tell him in person. No more deceptions. She'd also asked a special favor from him, one she hoped was the right thing to do. If not, she'd know for sure tomorrow.

She slipped her phone into her purse and walked toward the front door. Just as she reached for the doorknob, the door swung open. A young lady with dark hair stood on the threshold. "Oh, excuse me. I'm Angie Bourgeois, the hospice nurse. You must be Laney."

Angie accepted her offered hand. "Yes, I am. How's she doing?'

Angie's smile melted, but peace beamed from her eyes. "Not well. If she makes it through the night, I'll be surprised. But then again, I've been surprised many times. I'll stop back by in a few hours." Her southern accent drifted to Laney's ears.

Gentle warmth spread through Laney's heart. "You're not from here are you?"

"No. I'm from Louisiana. Here on a traveling assignment for a few months."

"Thank you for taking such good care of my aunt."

The nurse nodded then stepped aside. As she walked past Laney, she brushed her arm with a gentle touch. *Nice lady. I could never do what she does.* Her job required so much strength. How did she care for patients who would never be well again?

She entered the house. The aroma of death hung heavy in the air. Stale, musty, and old. Even the distant scent of moth balls and menthol didn't cover the pervading smell. She trudged down the dark hallway to her aunt's room. Mark sat in the chair she'd moved next to the bed earlier.

She whispered, "Any change?"

He shook his head then stood and rested his hands on top the side rails.

She stood next to him. Aunt Elaine's chest rose and fell in shallow erratic breaths. "Has she ever accepted Christ?"

Mark turned to her. Tears filled his dark eyes. "She did about an hour ago."

Laney exhaled. *Thank you, Lord.* Her aunt would know the grace of salvation. And if she awoke again, would know the mercy of forgiveness.

Laney wrapped her arm around Mark's shoulder. "And you?"

"A long time ago. I'm a pastor. Bet you didn't know that." He tried to smile, but his lips trembled. "I've been trying to reach Mother, but a barricade around her heart held her back." His green eyes misted with compassion. "I've prayed for her salvation every day for the past twenty years. This day is certainly bittersweet."

Laney thought about all she'd discovered in the past few hours. "It surely is. Why don't you step out and get some fresh air? If she stirs, I'll call for you."

"Thanks, I'll be on the patio." He hugged Laney and then left the room.

Laney lowered the bed rail and then scooted the chair closer to the bed. She cradled her aunt's hand in her own.

She took a deep breath and let the words flow. "Aunt Elaine, it's Laney again." She cleared her throat. "I hope you can hear. I have the envelope and I know about Alex. My boy. You shouldn't have kept him from me, but please know I forgive you. I know you did what you thought was best. You knew first-hand the struggles of a single mom. So I know you wanted to save me from that difficult life." She lifted the frail hand and kissed the valleys. "Thank you for making sure I got the envelope. Thank you for giving me back my baby."

Laney saw a flicker of movement beneath the thin eyelids, but no other response came. She lowered her head onto the bed and prayed. After a while, she left the room to find Mark. "She hasn't awakened."

"The nurse didn't think she would." He stood by the kitchen door. "Laney, I don't know what happened all those years ago to drive you away, but I hope we can keep in touch."

"I'd like that."

He reached into his wallet and retrieved a card. "If you ever need anything, I'm here. It means a lot to me that you cared enough to come."

He linked her arm through his and led her back toward his mother's room. Once inside, a new found peace settled through Laney's heart. Mark slid a rocker from the corner of the room to the edge of the bed. He motioned for Laney to sit. He placed his hands around his mother's wrist. "She's still with us. I bet she can hear us."

Laney smiled. "I bet she can."

He sat in the chair next to Laney and returned the smile. "Tell us about your life."

She leaned back into the cushion of the rocker and told Mark and Aunt Elaine about her wonderful husband Bryan and her amazing adopted son, Evan. She even told them about Maggie and how she came to be her friend.

And with the last words, Laney wasn't sure but she thought she saw her aunt's lips spread in a small smile.

****

Maggie's fingers tapped against the keyboard. Laney had left hours ago. Since then Maggie had discovered how far Prairieland was from Dallas then priced airline tickets into DFW. They'd come this far, surely Laney would want to see her son.

Maggie's search for information about Alex Davenport would be a surprise for Laney. Alex graduated the top of his class at Harvard Medical School. Knowing Alex had done so well should give her peace.

Maggie paused—her fingers hovering over the keyboard. Had she searched for Alex for Laney's sake or had she done this because it was what she'd become conditioned to do? For twenty years Maggie wanted to know her son had been safe and happy. Wouldn't Laney want to know the same about Alex?

The ugly monster of jealousy surfaced. But what about her? Would she ever have the evidence to prove Evan was Paul? To convince Evan he was Paul? To convince Craig? Or would she have to rely only on her instincts? She wanted what Laney had—proof. Tangible, irrefutable proof.

The last few days had created a volley of emotions and hope. One minute she rode high and confident she'd have the answers she craved, the next she dipped into the depths of darkness, unsure if she'd ever know the truth. She'd come so close only to have the joy of discovery snatched from her hands. How much more of this could she take? At least by focusing on Laney's quest, she could numb the sting of failure for a while. She hoped the pictures Laney had of Evan would be the only proof needed to let the world know her son lived and he lived as Evan Ellerby.

She glanced at her watch then around the room. Laney's nine-by-twelve envelope sat on the table. Nine inches by twelve inches was all the space it took to give Laney back her son.

She dimmed the light next to her bed and rested her head on the pillow. The last few nights had been nightmare-free, perhaps because her days had been nightmare-filled. Every dead-end brought back the empty ache she lived with for so long. Her brief moments of hope felt like a shot of pure oxygen. She wanted to keep that feeling. That hope.

Laney's Bible sat on the nightstand. Maggie reached for it, but stopped midway. What good would that do? *Why should I change my mind about God? What could He possibly do for me now?*

She turned away from the nightstand and the book and focused on her iPad. What she needed was proof. Then she'd have peace. Her phone chirped as she closed her eyes. A quick glance at the screen caused her heart to race. Craig's face and number filled her LED screen.

The *click* of the hotel room door, made her send the call to voice mail. *I'll call him later.*

CHAPTER 42

*L*aney slid the plastic card into the hotel room lock and turned the door handle. She used her body to push the heavy door. In the dim light, Maggie lay in the bed near the window reading on her iPad. Maggie sat up when Laney plopped onto the other bed.

She rubbed the back of her neck and shoulders. Fatigue seized her whole body. All she wanted was to fall into a deep dreamless sleep.

Maggie looked toward Laney and in the soft glow of the bathroom light. "Laney, are you okay? You've been crying."

"Aunt Elaine died tonight. She passed away while Mark and I sat next to her bed and talked. Quite peacefully." Laney rubbed both hands up and down her face. "There will be a memorial service tomorrow night. If you want we can head back the next day." She flipped off her shoes and plopped onto the pillow. "What a stressful day."

"I'm so sorry. Did you get to talk to her before she died?"

"She didn't wake, but I did talk to her. I forgave her. And I think she heard me."

"Wow, a very generous gesture."

"It wasn't a gesture. I really forgave her. I was able to let go and give it all to God."

Maggie said, "You're a better woman than I am. I'm not sure I could do that."

"You could. With God anything is possible." Laney punched her pillow into a more comfortable position. "Besides, her deception has clearly shown how important it is I tell Bryan the truth. I don't want to live keeping this secret. It's taken enough of our life already."

"How do you think Bryan will respond?"

She envisioned her betrayal on Bryan's face. Her stomach clenched at the thought. "I'm not sure. I know he'll be hurt. I hope he can forgive me. But if I've learned anything from this, it's that life is too short to live with deception."

Maggie nodded. "I'm glad you feel so confident about telling him."

"Maybe confident isn't the right word, but it's what I need to do." Laney stifled a yawn.

"How do you feel about seeing Alex?" Maggie asked.

Laney lifted her head and looked at Maggie. "That's another story."

"Don't you want to see him?"

"Of course, more than anything, but after all this time of thinking I don't care, he may not want to see me."

Maggie remained silent.

Laney rolled out of bed. "I better get changed before I fall asleep in these clothes."

She rifled through her suitcase for her nightclothes and then headed for the bathroom. A glance in the mirror confirmed her fears. She looked liked she felt—worn out. The green of her eyes lacked their usual luster. What if Alex didn't want anything to do with her? It was certainly his right after all this time.

Laney's heart went out to Maggie. Evan had done the same thing to her. Had his refusal to be tested been the catalyst pushing Maggie to find proof?

Maggie called from the bedroom. "Don't you think you owe him the choice?"

Laney turned the knobs of the tub releasing a jet flow of water. Maggie's question hung around her shoulders like a millstone she couldn't release. Maybe she did owe him that much—the chance to say whether he wanted to know her or not. But her showing up after all this time would surely disrupt his life. Did she want to do that? Having her life disrupted was something she could surely relate to.

****

Maggie smiled into the phone. "Thanks, Eric. It's nice to know that you're taking such good care of my patients."

"Ha, they're my patients now. You should have seen the look on Ms. Beauregard's face when I entered the room. I thought I'd have to call Tara in to save me."

"Why so?"

"Let's just say *Ms.* Beauregard is looking for a daddy for her little Tommy and it seems I met her criteria."

"Oh, no." She laughed. "Guess, she'll be asking for you from now on."

He chuckled. "Yes, she's already informed me. Give my sister-in-law a hug for me. Bryan told me about her aunt. So sorry to hear that. Laney didn't say much about her, but I'm glad you're there with her. Don't worry about the practice. Everything is going well here, but everyone does miss you and can't wait for you to be back."

She smiled. "See you in a couple of days."

Maggie ended the call with Eric. All her patients were being well-cared for. She enjoyed the feeling of relief and freedom. Something she hadn't had for a long time.

She punched in the numbers of Craig's cell phone. He was still in South Carolina. When he answered, his voice sent a long-lost stir within her. "Craig, hi it's me, returning your call."

"Maggie." His voice held a tone of excitement. "Great news. I got the contract for the Amsterdam Building."

"That's wonderful." Her heart sank a little with the news. He'd be traveling more often.

"How are things back home?"

Should she tell him? "Well...I'm not exactly at home right now." She paused. "I'm in Fort Collins, Colorado. Remember, Laney, the lady you met?"

"Yes, she came over to the house before I left."

"That's her. Anyway her aunt died and I offered to fly up here with her."

"You did? How nice of you. I can't believe you actually took time off work."

"Eric is working out well and able to handle things for a few days."

"I'm proud of you. It's about time. Maybe when I get back and before this project gets rolling, we can go somewhere together."

He sounded sincere. It was the first time he'd suggested going anywhere together in years.

"I'd like that," she said and meant it. It was a new sentiment for her. She thought of Laney's admission of telling Bryan the truth. That was what she needed to do as well—be honest with Craig. Tell him everything. Even if she didn't have proof about Paul, she knew Craig had a right to know. She'd take her chances on whether or not he thought she was crazy.

"We can discuss a place when I get home," she said.

He cleared his throat and paused. Maggie glanced at her phone. Had she lost the connection? "Maggie, I miss you."

She gripped the phone tighter. He missed her? Warmth spread through her, a feeling long absent from her life. The foreign threat of tears surprised her. "I miss you, too."

****

The next morning, Laney sat in the passenger seat while they drove to Aunt Elaine's house. She had promised Mark she'd help make the arrangements for the memorial service. Because her aunt had donated her body to science, there were no funeral arrangements to make.

"I know it's somewhere here in Luke." Laney thumbed through her Bible for a verse she wanted to share with Mark.

"I checked on flights from Denver to Dallas, we can fly out in the morning. Pretty reasonable too," Maggie said.

Laney's Bible verse search stopped and she looked at Maggie. "You checked on flights?"

"Yes, in case you wanted to go from here. We can fly into Dallas, drive to Prairieland then fly to New Orleans from Dallas."

"You think I should do this, don't you?"

Maggie stole a glance in Laney's direction. "My opinion doesn't matter, but yes, I think you should do this."

Laney looked down at her Bible. Would it be easier to do this without Bryan? Taking this step without him would be another form of deception. But…if she could meet her son and know whether he wanted her or not, when she shared with Bryan she'd have the answers to all his questions.

"I don't know. I think I'd like to call Bryan before making the decision."

"Will you tell him over the phone?"

"Probably not, but when I hear his voice, I'll know what to say."

Maggie nodded. "Sounds great. Let me know, if you want to go from here, I'll go with you."

Laney nodded and then resumed thumbing through her Bible. "Here it is. Mathew 7:7-8." It was the perfect passage for Mark. Although Laney was sure he already knew it. He was, after all, a pastor.

Maggie cleared her throat. "Well…"

Laney glanced toward her. "What?"

"Aren't you going to tell me what it's about?"

Laney's heart nearly sputtered out of rhythm. Had Maggie just asked her to talk about a Bible verse? "Well it talks about trusting God and believing that He wants the best for us regardless of our circumstances, but that He is faithful to His children." Laney lifted the Bible and began reading the verse to Maggie.

"Wow, is that the passage you were looking to share with Mark?" Maggie asked.

"Yes."

"That seems a little odd considering his mother just died. Don't you think?"

Laney marked the verse then closed her Bible. "I forgot to tell you, last night before she died she accepted Christ. Something Mark had prayed for his mother for years. It happened in God's perfect timing."

"Do you suppose I haven't gotten proof about Paul because I haven't asked?"

"I don't know. But I do know God knows our heart and the desires we hold dear. If it's in His will for those desires to be fulfilled, it'll happen."

Maggie remained silent.

Laney prayed. *Draw her to You, Lord. Give her Your Peace.*

Mark greeted them when they arrived. He kissed Laney's cheek. "Good morning."

She hugged his neck in greeting and then introduced him to Maggie. After the introductions were made, and Maggie offered her condolences, Laney turned to Mark. "I'm going to slip in Aunt Elaine's bedroom for a bit. I need to call Bryan."

"No, problem." He reached for Maggie's arm. "Maggie and I will have a cup of my favorite coffee. Shall we?" He pointed toward the kitchen.

Maggie smiled. "Thank you. The hotel coffee just didn't hit the spot."

Laney entered her aunt's room. The empty hospital bed stood as a stark reminder that Aunt Elaine was gone. She paused and placed her hand on the metal railing, just yesterday she'd held Aunt Elaine's hand from this same spot. "Lord, be with Mark. Give him your peace today." Two steps took her to the chair in the corner. She settled in and dialed Bryan's number. "Lord, give me Your words."

CHAPTER 43

*L*aney inhaled deeply. Two rings. Three. *C'mon Bryan, answer. Before I lose my nerve.* What would she say?

"Hello, this is Bryan." Laney looked at the number on her phone. She'd called his work number. Regret gripped. He asked about her aunt and how she was doing. She filled him in on the activities in Colorado.

"I miss you. I'm excited for you to come home. When do you think that might be?"

"Umm…that's what I was calling about. Bryan, there's been something I've discovered here that I need to look into. There's something we need to talk about when I get home, something from my past. But before then, I'd like to get as much information as possible."

"Laney, you're scaring me. Are you all right?"

"Honey, trust me, I'm fine. I don't want to go into this on the phone, but wanted to see if you'd mind if I took another day or two to gather some facts."

"Is…this about Evan?" His words were spoken with reserved caution.

She sighed. "No, it's not. It's about *my* past and something I should have done a long time ago. I'm sorry I sound so mysterious, but I promise I will tell you everything when I get home."

Silence filled the line for what seemed like an eternity. "Bryan?"

"I'm here." He cleared his throat. "Laney, I trust you. I know what I did was hard for you to accept. I hope this doesn't have something to do with my betrayal—

"No, not at all. It's not about you, it's me needing to clear some cobwebs so I can be the wife I need to be."

An audible sigh drifted over the phone. "I appreciate that you still want to be my wife." He paused. "Babe, I'm fine with whatever you need to do, you have my support. Keep me posted, okay?"

Her chest tightened from her spiked emotions. This man—her husband, was the best. "I will, it shouldn't take more than a day, two at the most. And, honey, would you pray for me? Pray that God will bring healing and provide the answers we need."

"You've always got my prayers, but I will pray for that specifically."

"Bryan." She lingered on the thought of her husband praying for and waiting for her without drilling her for answers. How lucky could she be? "I really do love you."

"I love you, too. I'd fly out there and be with you if I could, but there's no way I can leave during this shutdown."

"I know and I appreciate that more than you know. Maggie's still with me and she's promised to stay with me until I come home. She's become a good friend."

"Well, well. Who would have thought so much could change in a couple of weeks? God does have a strange way of opening doors. Oh, by the way, I sent the FedEx package you asked for to your aunt's address. You should be getting it today."

"Thank you, honey." The thought of what he'd sent made her smile. She couldn't wait to share it with Maggie.

"Laney, be safe and hurry home. I've got to run to my

meeting."

After she ended the call, she looked around the lonely room and the furnishings Aunt Elaine left behind. Was this it? The only legacy her aunt had. The awareness sealed her determination. Her legacy would be one of children and grandchildren who had stronger faith because they'd known her. That included her son, Alex. If he'd have her.

Laney joined Maggie and Mark in the kitchen. "Any coffee left in that pot from this morning?"

Mark slid a business card across the table to Maggie. "Yes, we made a fresh pot. Maggie and I have been having an insightful conversation."

Before Laney could pour her coffee, the doorbell rang. "I'll get it. I'm waiting for a package from Bryan, that must be it." She opened the door to a young man holding a large pizza box. "This is for the Elaine Burkett family. Paid for by her friend." He flipped the receipt over. "Professor, Joseph Mallory."

Laney's legs quivered. She leaned against the doorframe. The driver extended the box. *Professor Mallory and Aunt Elaine Friends?* The betrayal took her breath. The young man placed a note on top the box. "For the family." No envelop, just a note. The familiar handwriting sent her stomach rolling. *I'm sorry for your loss. - Joseph Mallory.* Even in death, Aunt Elaine still had the power to hurt Laney.

"Ma'am?" The young man still held the box. "This is yours."

"I'm sorry." She dug through her pockets and found several folded dollars and handed them to him. She took the pizza. It's warmth a confusing contrast to her cold hands. She stood at the open door long after the driver left.

Joseph Mallory. There'd been a day when the mention of his name would send bees swarming in her stomach. In a good way—a fun tingly feeling. A new one to her, unless she counted Richard Dryson from her junior year—the first boy she let kiss her. Poor Richard had been so nervous, he'd fallen off the log they sat on when he'd leaned toward her.

But Professor Mallory, he was the big leagues. He knew how to charm. Especially, a naïve country girl from southern Alabama.

It didn't take long for his name to turn her stomach into knots. In a bad way. His charm turned to selfish conceit when he found out Laney was pregnant. Of course, at that point he fessed up. He'd never had any intention of leaving his wife.

The warmth from the pizza radiated through her hands, bringing her back to the present. How could he and Aunt Elaine have been friends? She'd never given his name, only told her aunt it was one of her Professors. What a fool she'd been to protect the louse? But then again, she'd been so embarrassed she didn't want anyone to know she'd slept with him.

She walked through the house and placed the pizza on the table next to where Mark and Maggie sat engrossed in conversation. "Pizza, wow, just in time. I was going to offer to have one delivered. Laney did you do this?" Mark asked.

"No. A friend of your mom's."

"That's nice. Did they leave a name so I can send a thank you note?"

"Yes, it's on the top of the box."

Mark reached for the single piece of paper. "Professor Joseph Mallory." His lips pressed into a line and his eyes narrowed. "I can't believe he's still around."

"Me either."

"We called him the snake charmer when I went to CSU. He could charm anything."

Maggie glanced toward Laney with an arched brow. She jerked her head ever so slightly toward the pizza. Laney knew what she asked and nodded. Maggie held her gaze for a moment longer then smiled. "Well, there's no sense letting this pizza get cold, I'll get plates." Maggie stood and headed for the cabinets.

"They're in the top cupboard. Just left of the sink." Mark turned to Laney. "I meant what I said yesterday when I gave you my card. If there's ever anything you want to talk about, I'm only a phone call or email away."

Although, he'd moved away to another college by the time Laney had moved in with his mother, Mark had treated her like a younger sister the times he'd come home. And because he'd gone to Europe during the time of her pregnancy, he'd never been told about the baby. At least, she'd never told him and she didn't think Aunt Elaine had either. Did he know?

The doorbell chimed. Laney stood, maybe this time it was FedEx with her package.

She opened the door. And wished she hadn't.

CHAPTER 44

"*L*aney?" Joseph Mallory stood on the doorstep. The one person in the world she hoped to never see again.

She nodded and met his piercing gaze head on. It had sucked her in once when she was young and impressionable, but it held no power over her now. "Yes."

"I wanted to come by to express my regrets in person. I second-guessed the pizza thing." He shrugged.

Laney looked up and found, instead of the charmer smirk she expected, genuine compassion-filled eyes. His brown free-flowing hair was now salt and pepper and trimmed short. His beard sported patches of gray on his chin. She often thought about what she'd say if she ever encountered him again and all those words volleyed through her brain fighting to spew forth.

He shifted his weight. "Is Mark here?"

So he'd come to see Mark. Had he even considered she'd be here? "Yes, yes, come in." She backed away from the door.

He stepped into the house. "I just want to tell him how sorry I am, but Laney I'd like for us to talk if possible."

Talk? What could he possibly have to say to her? Could

she stand to listen to his lame excuses and meaningless reasons after all this time?

Give him the time.

The words settled her beating heart and gave her the peace that only came from the Giver of her faith.

She led him into the kitchen where Mark and Maggie sat with the pizza in the middle of the table. A plate with a large piece waited for Laney.

Laney introduced him to Maggie. She shook his hand, then cast a glance toward Laney. Her arched brows and compassionate gaze spoke volumes. She nodded encouragement and mouthed the words: *Be strong.* In their short time together, they'd developed a bond Laney had never thought possible.

Mark ushered Joseph Mallory into the living room after he declined sharing the meal. Laney lowered into the chair next to Maggie.

Maggie nudged her shoulder with her own. "How ya holding up?"

"I'm not really sure. Okay, I guess. I wasn't expecting to see him."

"What's he doing here?"

"Evidently he and my aunt were friends." She picked up the pizza and took a large bite from the tip.

Maggie wrapped her arm around Laney's shoulders. "I'm so sorry, Laney. You're being hit with a lot all at once."

Laney nodded. "Oh, that's not the best part. He wants us to have a little chat once he's talked to Mark."

Maggie's brows creased. "Really? Will you?"

"Yes." Slowly, Laney's lips spread. "Yes...I believe I will."

She swallowed the last bite of the pizza and reveled in the confidence bursting through her. There were things she needed to tell him and now would be the best time. Although, she'd just recently come to grips with her past, there were a few loose ends where Joseph Mallory was concerned.

"Thanks, Joseph, I'll be in touch." Mark walked back into the kitchen with Professor Mallory at his side.

Laney stood and stared at Professor Mallory. "Would you like to take a walk?"

His eyes met Laney's. "That would be nice." He bid goodbye to Mark and Maggie then walked with her toward the door. "Thanks for talking with me. I didn't think you would."

She opened the door and stepped out into the Colorado sunshine. The clear day still had a nip of coolness. "If you'd asked me yesterday, I probably would not have."

He matched her slow stride as they headed down the driveway and onto the sidewalk of the quiet street. The greens of Spring dotted the trees along the way. Laney remained silent. He had asked for this meeting so she'd let him begin. What could he possibly say to make her understand his actions all those years ago?

The cracks on the old sidewalk reminded her of the day she'd discovered she was pregnant. A visit to the campus doctor had confirmed the results. She'd walked up and down this sidewalk over an hour before she had the nerve to walk in and tell her aunt. Laney knew how disappointed Aunt Elaine would be. She also knew how hard it would be to tell her father. When Aunt Elaine had taken her in while she went to college, she promised her dad she'd take care of Laney.

"Did you know my wife died three years ago?" Professor Mallory laced his fingers behind his back and seemed to study the same cracks Laney did.

"No, I didn't."

"Leukemia."

Where was this conversation going? Did he want her to feel sorry for him?

He continued, "Her death shook me to the core. A shaking I needed for a long time. It kills me I didn't see things clearly while she was still alive. While she and I could enjoy our relationship. But I guess, God had other plans for me and for her."

Had she heard him correctly? Had this man, the professed womanizer, adulterer, and liar, found Christ?

A young woman pushing a double stroller approached. Laney stepped to the right off the sidewalk and Professor Mallory to the left. Two round chubby faces peered out from their matching Noah's ark blankets. Laney smiled at the mother, then glanced again at the babies. She'd never had the privilege of being a mother to a tiny baby.

When they rejoined on the sidewalk, Joseph cleared his throat. "Laney, I know an apology seems a weak consolation in light of all you've been through, but I think I owe you one. I'm sorry for the way I treated you all those years ago. I was a cad and a heathen for never taking responsibility for the baby."

Laney's feet planted to the cement. Where was this sentiment when she needed it? Of course, if he'd been this person all those years ago, their histories would be different. "I surely needed you back then. I was a love-struck young woman whose world rotated around your striking blue eyes." She glared at him. "You took advantage of me. You cheated on your wife. But the absolute worst thing—you abandoned your child."

Joseph Mallory focused on the ground and nodded as she spoke. When she paused, he met her glare. "I don't expect you to forgive me, but I am genuinely sorry." The corners of his eyes drooped and his usually sparkling blue eyes were dimmed by the moisture pooling there. "I'll never forgive myself for being responsible for you aborting our baby. It haunts my nights and will probably torture me for the rest of my life. It's a burden I have to bear."

Aborting the baby? Was his sadness only because he thought she'd murdered his child? Or did his remorse stem from his role in causing the situation to go as far as it did?

"You told me you would leave your wife. You assured me it was over between you two and you would get a divorce. How sad, my hopes rested on you leaving your wife. You took advantage of me being so in love with you. You used me and when I learned you never had any intention of leaving, I was devastated."

"I'm not proud of how I treated you and my wife. It haunts me. Makes me want to curl up and die. Neither of you deserved what I did. My only consolation is she's in heaven happy and I'm left here on earth to atone for my past. Alone. No children or family. Just me."

Should she tell him about Alex? About his son who lived despite Joseph's efforts? He had a right to know. Didn't he? A part of her heart wanted to clamp tight on the information. Let him suffer a little more—payback for the misery and pain he'd caused her. But the merciful part of her, the bigger part, couldn't do it. She'd accepted responsibility for the part she'd played in the affair. She knew he was married. She'd willingly participated in the affair.

He suffered. His repentance evident in the sadness spilling from his heart through his eyes. He couldn't fake the depth of sadness she saw. She didn't want the damage of an unforgiving heart. *Lord, help me to forgive him.*

Laney resumed walking. A small park on the corner invited with lush green grass and a bench along the edge. She strolled toward the bench and sat. As Joseph lowered next to her, a painful moan escaped. "Arthritis."

Sitting, she met his gaze straight on. "Tell me, what made you think I had an abortion?"

A spark flashed in the blue of his eyes. Like a lamp had flickered behind the irises. "When I didn't hear from you after…" He squeezed his lips together before he continued as though trying to repress emotions he didn't want to show. "…after I gave you the money for the abortion, I called. Your aunt answered. When I asked if everything was okay because you'd missed my class, she figured out I was the father and proceeded to give me a piece of her mind."

"Really." Aunt Elaine had known?

He nodded. "Called me a lousy piece of work for taking advantage of you. Said I didn't deserve to be a father and people like me shouldn't be allowed to procreate. She was pretty tough. Before we hung up, she assured me I would not have the privilege of the responsibility of a child. Her exact words were, 'your child doesn't exist.' So I thought she meant you'd had an abortion. You did, didn't you?"

Laney imagined Aunt Elaine giving Professor Mallory a shakedown. How did these two become friends? She shook her head. "I…I didn't."

His eyes widened allowing a sunbeam to reflect the blue. "You didn't. The baby. What happened to the baby?"

"I carried to term and had a boy. A boy, I gave up for adoption."

"A boy." He turned from Laney toward an elm tree across the street. "A boy." The side of his lip curled and the wrinkles in the corner of his left eye deepened. He turned back to Laney. "We had a boy. That is such good news."

We. Heat flushed through Laney's face and neck. How dare he make this sound like some joyous occasion? How dare he act like the proud father? Bile rose in Laney's throat and she fought the onslaught. The compassion she'd had for him earlier melted and all she envisioned right now was smacking him across his head. She slid her hands under her thighs. "Good news? Really, Joseph? Why couldn't you believe it was good news to have a boy when he was born?"

His jubilant grin dissolved. "Laney." He lowered his head then lifted it again. "I'm not that man anymore. I never *should* have been that man, but trust me, he's gone."

"I'm glad," she said. Her anger receded as fast as it had risen. She wasn't the same person either.

"Have you kept in touch with him?"

"No."

"Do you know anything about him?"

"I know he was adopted by a couple who live in a small

Texas town south of Dallas."

"He'd be what, about twenty-seven?"

"Yes. He turned twenty-seven three weeks ago." Twenty-seven years—a lifetime ago. *Thank you Lord, for all you've done to help me grow. To bring me to where I am.*

"Wow, it's so hard to comprehend. Here I am at fifty-seven finding out I have a son. The Lord is giving me this gift I surely don't deserve."

The Lord had grown Joseph Mallory, too. *Thank you, Lord.*

Joseph placed both his hands on his knees and slowly shook his head. "It's amazing. Have you ever tried to find him?"

She paused. "No, I just discovered information about him yesterday. Before, I didn't even know his name."

"Let me guess. Your aunt."

Laney grinned. "You got it. I never knew about the letters his adoptive parents sent me. They'd wanted me to be a part of his life. So I missed out. Missed all these years of his life. But..." She smiled and warmed when she remembered Evan. "...I have a wonderful son who is twenty-two, named Evan. My husband, Bryan, and I adopted him when he was two."

His lips spread into a grand smile. "I'm really happy for you Laney—happy things worked out for the best."

"It hasn't been an easy road, but the Lord has provided."

"It sounds like your faith has sustained you. I can't tell you the difference having Christ in my life has made. I'm a new man."

She laughed. "I see it."

A silent moment passed between them. Laney mulled over the harbored feelings she'd stifled since she'd last seen him—emotions lying under the surface ready to pounce if she let them. Today, even, she had to hold back her anger. Yet, right now peace blanketed her—a gentle reminder that God had her future firmly in his loving hands.

"Joseph, when I leave here, my friend Maggie and I are going to see if we can find Alex. If I do, would you like for me to give him your name and number?"

Lines deepened between his brows. "You'd do that for me?"

She nodded.

He reached into his back pocket for his wallet and retrieved a business card then paused with the card in mid-air. When he lifted his head and looked at her, moisture glistened against the blue. "It would mean a lot to me. I would love to meet him and get to know him. But…if…if he doesn't want anything to do with me. I understand. You tell him the truth about me. No lies. But he can call me if he wants to. I don't want to intrude on his life. It's his choice."

Laney lifted the card and slipped it into her pocket. "I know how you feel."

CHAPTER 45

*M*aggie placed left-over pizza into a plastic zipper bag while Mark folded the box to fit it into the trash. "Maybe Laney will want another slice when she returns," Mark said.

Pretty doubtful if the conversation had gone as Maggie suspected. Laney looked like a huntress leaving for her first hunt. A twinge of sympathy pinged for Joseph Mallory.

The *ding* of the doorbell drew Mark's attention. He answered it and returned with a red and white envelope. "Laney got an overnight letter from Louisiana."

Maybe a special gift for Mark? He laid it on the table.

Minutes later Laney walked in the door. Her face glowed with something Maggie couldn't quite determine. Peace? Satisfaction?

She waited for Laney to sit. "Is everything all right?"

Laney nodded. "I have so much to tell you."

"You got an overnight letter."

"Oh, yes, I had Bryan send something I needed." She smiled, picked up the envelope, and carried it into the living room.

Maggie remained standing in the kitchen. Although, she'd come here with the intention of helping Laney, something twisted in her gut—anxiousness to get back home. To have the information *she* needed. She'd waited twenty years, but now with the possibility of finally getting the truth poised just beyond her grasp, a tornado brewed within.

Maybe she'd been wrong to encourage Laney to visit Dallas. It would delay getting the truth she sought. Would she be able to handle watching Laney reunite with her son? Happiness for Laney still filled her heart, but something else vied for attention. Jealousy. She struggled to squash the unruly feelings, to keep the emotion from consuming her and causing damage to her budding friendship with Laney.

She was bigger than this. Better than this. Laney had promised a picture of Evan when they returned to Pecan Pointe. Maggie resolved to wait until then to know if Evan was Paul. Well, to have proof Evan was Paul. She already knew. In her mind and heart, she had found her son, now she just had to convince everyone around her of the truth.

****

Laney sat on the living room couch and glanced toward the door to make sure Maggie hadn't followed her. *Lord, I hope I'm doing the right thing. Please give me the perfect timing to do this.* She ripped the cord to open the envelope and reached inside for the precious contents—two pictures of Evan, one when they'd first brought him home and another a few months later. The photos were nestled inside a hand-written note. *Laney, I hope you know what you're doing. I'm still not sure about this, but I love you enough to trust you on this. Evan is doing well. He and Casey are spending a lot of time together. He sends his love. And I do too. Bryan.*

She held the letter to her chest. God had truly blessed her with a wonderful husband. He trusted her. The thought of returning home and sharing her secret still crushed her heart because she knew it would crush his, but she didn't feel the hopelessness she'd felt before.

She wrapped the photos with the note and slipped them into her purse. She'd know when the time was right.

A knock on the doorframe captured her attention. Mark

filled the entry. "Some of mom's friends are here. I thought you'd like to meet them. Also, we need to talk in private before we leave for the service."

Visitors filed in and out during the remainder of the afternoon. They brought food and condolences. At four o'clock, Laney and Maggie returned to the hotel to change clothes and freshen up for the memorial service at six. Laney had never gotten a chance to talk privately with Mark.

When Mark stood to give the eulogy, Laney didn't know what to expect, but she knew he would speak well of his mother.

"There's something I learned about my mother I didn't know before." He cleared his throat. "She had a heart for unwed mothers. Probably because she'd been one herself. You see, I never knew my father and my mother died with her secret. But in her desire to help other young women in the same situations, she has donated her house to be used as a home for unwed mothers who have no place to go. In addition, a generous donation from a local benefactor will help make her desire a reality. So I hope you all remember my mother for the woman she was, but more importantly for the legacy she leaves behind in this home. It will be called *Alex's Place: A home for unwed mothers*." Mark's moisture-filled eyes found Laney.

The sting of tears bit the back of Laney's eyes and a growing knot swelled her throat. Was this her aunt's way of trying to repair the damage she'd done by keeping the truth from Laney? And who was the generous benefactor?

After the service, Laney and Maggie walked toward the parking lot. Just as they approached the car, Mark fell into step next to them. "Laney, could we have a few minutes to talk? If you'd both like to, you can go back to the house or we can stop at a coffee shop."

Laney glanced toward Maggie while searching her purse for the car keys. "What would you like to do?"

"Could you drop me off at the hotel?"

"I can, but..." She turned to Mark. "...could you drive me to the hotel after our meeting?"

"Sure."

Laney offered Maggie the car keys. "Here, you take the car back. I'll ride with Mark."

Maggie hugged Laney then smiled toward Mark. "Have a good visit. Mark's a pretty sharp guy."

Laney looked into Maggie's eyes and saw a new sparkle there. What had caused the change?

Laney walked with Mark to his SUV. Silence hung heavy between them. What could Mark need to talk to her about? Had he found out about Alex? Surely, he would question why his mother had chosen to name the place like she did. He helped her into his vehicle then drove off.

"The memorial service was very nice. She had many friends." Laney folded her hands in her lap, then unfolded them. She tapped her foot on the floorboard. Why the nerves? The worst encounter was behind her.

"It was nice. I was surprised by all the people who attended. There were over two-hundred people there. Mother's reputation wasn't one of a friendly person. Professor Mallory enlightened me on her recent activities. Her passion for unwed mothers was well-known throughout the college community and she'd gotten a lot of respect for her fund-raising efforts. I'd call her and she'd tell me she was busy, but she never shared what she was working on. Now I know."

They arrived at the small coffee shop and found a table near the back away from the milling crowd near the counter. Once settled with steaming cups of coffee, Mark spoke, "Laney, I'll just come right out and say this. I know about the abortion, about Mallory, and my mother's role in the whole affair. Mallory told me the other day. I want you to know, if you need to talk I'm here for you."

Laney listened and absorbed the compassion spilling from Mark's eyes. He'd turned out, just as Laney suspected he would, to be a wonderful man. Any congregation was lucky to have him as their pastor.

She patted his hand. "Mark, I didn't have an abortion, it's what your mother led Mallory to believe. I had the child. Your mother gave me the documentation yesterday. His name is Alex."

Mark's face softened. "Oh."

She continued. "She gave me the adoptive parent's letters she'd kept from me. I was led to believe the adoption was closed. Now I know that's not the case."

"I'm so sorry she kept your baby from you. From both you and Joseph Mallory. It's no wonder she held on tenaciously until you got here. Such a heavy burden for her."

Laney nodded. A burden she wouldn't have had to carry had she only told the truth from the beginning. A guilt twinge pierced. Hadn't she done the same thing in her marriage? And hadn't she withheld forgiveness toward her aunt for all these years? What if she'd approached her aunt long ago with an olive branch? Perhaps, Aunt Elaine would have told her about Alex then and all these years would not have been lost.

Mark's eyes met hers. "Mallory is the generous benefactor. It's what we met about yesterday. He donated the money to get the home remodeled and started. Quite a substantial amount. The funds came from his wife's insurance money."

"Why wasn't it named after her?"

"He said Mother was adamant it be named Alex's Place."

Laney stared at the stream of heat rising from her cup. Just a month ago, she didn't know a thing about Alex and thought she knew everything about Evan. Funny how her world had been turned upside down in so short a time.

She told Mark about keeping the secret from Bryan and about how she and Maggie had become friends. He nodded when she needed affirmation, but mostly just listened with rapt attention.

When she'd told him everything, he simply smiled. "I love to see how God works in the lives of those who trust Him. Laney God has used you as a reflection of Him to Maggie, but also to all you've encountered here. I wasn't in the room with you and Mom, but I know you forgave her. I know you did."

"I did. But Mark, part of me didn't want to. Part of me wanted to hold onto the resentment."

"I know. It's the human part of us. Thinking retribution can be had by holding on to our grudge. Then we wake up and find a stone wall around our heart that keeps the bad stuff in and all the good stuff out. I'm glad you didn't let that happen to you."

"Sometimes I'm not so sure I haven't let it happen." She sipped from her mug.

"You haven't. If you had you wouldn't be here with Maggie."

"I suppose not. But now I have a decision to make. Do I fly to Dallas and find Alex? Or let him live his life thinking his mother didn't want to know him?"

Mark reached across the table and squeezed Laney's index finger. "Sweetie, I believe by the way you asked the question, you've answered it."

She smiled. "Perhaps you're right."

"I'll pray the situation with Bryan will open a new exciting door in your relationship. If he's the man you've described him to be, I know he'll forgive you. Laney, there's something else to think about." He shifted positions in his chair and leaned back, letting go of her hand. "God watched over those children, his children. Paul is not Maggie's. Evan is not yours, Alex is not yours. You were both given the privilege to give birth, but those children are God's and He is faithful to have watched over them all these years."

Laney nodded. Mark was right. Those boys were the Lord's and He had watched over them when Laney and Maggie couldn't. He'd sent others to care for them and to love them. In her case, Alex's adoptive parents and in Maggie's, she and Bryan. She had been blessed much more than she really knew. She'd been trusted despite the mistake she'd made. God had trusted her with Evan.

Mark continued. "By the way, I had this same conversation with Maggie yesterday. She told me about Paul and the kidnapping."

Maggie talked to Mark? *Thank you, Lord.* Was Maggie searching for more than just answers?

Had Laney been a good enough example to Maggie? Laney's intentions when this began had been to find the truth so Maggie could leave them alone. But now, the possibility Evan was Paul seemed more and more likely. She could lose Evan. And if Alex didn't want anything to do with her, she'd not have him either. She'd never get to know her son. A sliver of doubt snaked into her heart. The picture in her purse came to mind. Did she have what it would take to show it to Maggie? She thought so when she'd told Bryan to send it, but now she wasn't so sure.

Lord, I need you now. Help, me make the right decisions. Guide me in what to do, and say.

CHAPTER 46

*M*aggie stared out the window of the plane, only this time the ground served up patches of lush Texas farmland as they approached the Dallas/Fort Worth airport.

She leaned back and closed her eyes. The jealousy pang she'd felt earlier didn't stab as much today. Not since she'd spoken to Mark. His words had reached a place in her heart she thought had been sealed shut, hardened by the years. And the guilt.

His words wormed in and softened what she thought was hopeless. He'd said God had protected Paul. Regardless of what happened, God had taken care of His son until He brought them back together again.

She wasn't sure about the God part, but slowly she came to realize her life could have turned out much different. Had God been the one to protect her as well? It was a long stretch to attribute all the good to God and none of the bad, but Mark had been quick to point out God used bad things to show how good can come about. She still searched for the good from her mother's parade of men through their house. Maybe she wasn't looking hard enough. Maybe she needed to understand a little more about God.

"Maggie?"

She opened her eyes and turned toward Laney. "Yes?"

"What did it feel like when you first saw Evan?"

"First saw him the day he was born? Or in the restaurant

in Baton Rouge?"

"Baton Rouge."

"It's hard to describe. The first thing to strike me was his deep commanding voice. I've heard that sound for over twenty years from Craig. For a moment, I thought Craig had walked into the restaurant, returned from out of town." She leaned back again. "Then I saw the eyes, the eyebrows, the chin, every detail of his face stirred a memory. The prominent features of Craig were duplicated right there on Evan's face. I just knew. In my gut, I knew he was Paul."

She shifted her body to face Laney. "It's as though I've never been more certain of anything in my life. Like I'd been given this amazing gift after all these years of agony."

Laney nodded. "I understand." But her eyes remained guarded. Unbelieving. Sadness and uncertainty settled in the parts of her face usually perked with enthusiasm.

"What's on your mind? Something is bothering you isn't it? Don't you want to meet Alex?"

"I don't know if I can face him. What will I tell him? I gave him away. It was my choice to give him away." Laney pursed her lips and bit the inside of her lip.

"If you should decide to see him, tell him the truth. You were nineteen at the time. He'll understand your situation. And when you tell him what your aunt did, I'm sure he'll understand that also."

"I hope so. I'm worried about disrupting his life. He's probably done well without me. What will my showing up do to his life?"

Maggie nodded. She thought of Evan. Thought of Laney and Bryan's life and how her accusation had disrupted it. Should she have remained silent? Not brought her concerns to light? Was she being selfish for wanting the truth?

****

Laney dialed the Davenport's number she'd found on the internet while Maggie drove the mid-sized Chevrolet they rented. She waited through one, two, three rings before they stopped. "Hello." The gravelly voice sent chills through her.

"Mr. Davenport?"

"That's me. How can I help you?"

With heart pounding, Laney pulled in a deep breath. She told him her story and asked if she could visit.

"Little lady, we've been waiting a long time for this call. Come on over."

Her heartbeat rose. She wiped the palms of her hands on her jeans. "We're on our way." She couldn't believe he'd been so welcoming after all these years. Her heart calmed after she disconnected the call. The man who had raised her son seemed kind.

Skyscrapers, busy streets, and numerous billboards gave way to open meadows dotted with cows and free moving traffic as they headed south. The closer they got to Prairietown, the more her heartbeat pounded in response. Each passing mile brought her closer to finding her son. Would they meet face to face? Or would she only meet his adoptive parents?

Maggie pointed to the street sign approaching. "Look, the exit for Prairietown is twenty miles away. Then I think it's another ten miles from the exit."

Laney widened the screen on her phone and flipped through the detailed route directions. "That sounds right."

During the next few miles, Laney's mind wandered. What would she say? She rehearsed a string of words. Each sounding trite and empty. Would the Davenports like her? Want her to meet Alex? She would understand if they didn't.

The interstate changed to a two-lane road surrounded by open pastures. They remained silent through the drive. Laney's heart raced in anticipation of the encounter to come. Was she doing the right thing?

"We should be getting close to the house. It must be a farm," Maggie said. "That's all we've seen on this long road."

Had Alex liked growing up in such a rural and sheltered

place? Had he ridden a bike on this very road?

"Look, I bet that's it." Maggie pointed toward a small farmhouse. A tin roof reflected the bright afternoon sun from amid oak trees and a couple of large maples surrounding the house.

A rusted mailbox with the address hand-painted on the side came into view. A red reflector marked the entrance to the driveway. Maggie slowed to negotiate the turn. "This is it. Ten twenty-nine." She turned to Laney. "Are you still up for this?"

"My stomach is in knots. I'm not sure."

"Remember, you owe Alex. At least let him know you didn't abandon him." Maggie stopped the car at the entrance to the driveway and shifted into park.

"I could have told Mr. Davenport that on the phone." Laney ran her hands through her hair.

"Yes, you could have, but he didn't give you the chance did he?" Maggie looked at Laney.

"No, he just said to come over. He didn't even ask any questions."

"See, he wants to meet you." Maggie shifted again. "Ready?"

Laney fingered the door handle and exhaled long and hard. *Focus, Laney. Remember why you're doing this.* Alex had a right to know his mother didn't abandon him. He had to know he had been in her thoughts. She hated the idea he'd gone through life thinking she didn't want to know him.

"Okay, you can turn in."

Maggie steered the car onto the gravel driveway. Large potholes jostled the car—and Laney—side to side.

The front porch of the old farmhouse sagged on the end farthest from the front door. Maggie stopped the car next to a Chevy pick-up. A line of rust ran along the bottom of the passenger door. How many trips to town had the old truck made in its twenty or so years? Did Alex learn to drive in this truck?

Lord, give me your strength and the words. She gripped the door handle. All she had to do was open the door and walk to the house. A small step then a short walk, yet why did it feel like she was about to climb Mount Everest?

"You can do this." Maggie said. "Go on."

"Aren't you coming in?"

"Only if you want me to." Maggie rested one hand on the steering wheel and the other on the shifter.

"Are you kidding? I can't do this alone."

"Okay." Maggie turned the engine off, opened the door, then turned to Laney. "Let's go." She left the car and closed the door with a resounding thud.

Laney sat for a moment in the silence. Maggie's arched brow and questioning gaze from outside the car, prodded her onward. She exited the car holding the envelope of letters and photos. Each one sent to her so many years ago from the house standing before her. The house where her son had grown up, where she hoped he'd been loved and cared for.

A breeze blew in from the north lifting the dust from the driveway and rustling the leaves in the trees near the house. The gust pushed her forward. She climbed the rickety steps onto the porch of the house. With each step, the old wood groaned from her weight.

On the porch, she pulled on the rusted handle of the weathered screen door. The hinges croaked in resistance. She knocked on the worn wooden door. A quick inhale did little to calm her tattered nerves. She waited. And waited.

After a moment, shuffling along with a deep resonating bark sounded from inside the house. A scratchy voice filtered through the door. "Down, Ruffy, down boy."

The *click-clack* of the turning latch sounded and the heavy oak door parted slowly—as though seldom used. The old man holding the knob wore a face filled with wrinkles and the lines creased further when he smiled. "Can I help you, ladies?"

"Mr. Davenport? Hank Davenport?"

He nodded his blue eyes sparkled in the sun. "You must be Laney."

Laney held out her hand. "I'm Laney Ellerby, used to be Laney Pouncey. This is my friend, Maggie Langston."

He gripped her hand with both of his and met her gaze with warmth. "We'd pretty much given up on you." He grabbed the old beagle by the collar and opened the door wider. "Come in, come in."

Laney walked through the door, followed by Maggie. The small living room hosted two couches and a large overstuffed recliner. The TV tray next to the recliner overflowed with newspapers, television remote controls, a bag of corn chips, and several paperback westerns.

"Have a seat." He pointed toward one of the covered couches.

Laney lowered onto the edge of the couch closest to the recliner. Maggie sat next to her.

"Can I get you anything to drink?" he asked.

"No, thanks."

He descended into the recliner, and moaned from the effort. The beagle plopped on the floor at his feet. Its ears fanning on either side of his droopy eyes.

Hank Davenport turned toward Laney. "What can I do for you?"

Where to begin? She drew in a long breath. *Give me the words, Lord.* "I just recently found letters that you and your wife sent after you adopted Alex."

His brow creased. "Just recently?"

She nodded. "I never knew. My aunt told me the adoption was closed and withheld your letters and pictures."

He shook his head in a slow methodical way. "Why would she have done a thing like that?"

"She thought she was protecting me. And protecting Alex."

"He's wondered about you, these many years." His bushy, gray eyebrows moved closer together.

"Mr. Davenport, I'm not here to disrupt his life. I just want him to know I didn't turn my back on him. If I had known you wanted me to share in his life, I would have."

He stared at the floor. Did he believe her? After what seemed an eternity, he lifted his head and looked at her. "My Judy would have liked that. You know as much as she loved having Alex, her heart grieved for you. She couldn't imagine what you went through giving away your child." He paused.

Laney pushed back the lump of emotion rising in her throat.

He smiled a crooked little smile that made his eyes twinkle. "That's the only reason we sent those letters and pictures, it was her way of easing the pain she imagined you must have felt. When you didn't respond after the tenth letter, she figured you didn't want to be part of Alex's life. She went to her grave believing that. Prayed for you 'til the day she died."

Laney absorbed the words. Let them settle in her heart. Alex's adoptive mother had worried about her. Grief rushed in—for the lost time, for the lost relationship, and for the loss of her son. So much could have been different. Would she have adopted Evan had she been a part of Alex's life?

She couldn't imagine her life without Evan. Who would have adopted him? She and Maggie surely wouldn't be sitting here right now had her aunt told her about the letters. She marveled at God's way of creating meaningful circles.

"How long ago did she pass away?" she asked.

"Been two years this spring. But she was blessed to see Alex graduate from medical school. Got to see her son become a fine doctor." He pointed to an eight-by-ten photograph sitting on top a crowded table. A handsome young man wearing a cap and gown smiled while receiving a diploma.

She walked to the table and lifted the frame. Her son. The tips of her fingers brushed the glass over his smiling face. Those eyes. It was like looking into a mirror. Her son, a doctor. Mark's words flowed through her mind. God had taken care of her son.

He'd sent Judy and Hank Davenport. They'd nurtured him and raised him to be the person God had intended.

Thank you, Lord. He had brought good from the bad. "Mr. Davenport, how is he doing?"

He smiled and his eyes glimmered with sentiment. "Please, call me Hank." His lips spread wider. "He's doing well. Got a job at one of the big hospitals in Dallas. He comes to visit as often as he can, but calls everyday to see how I'm doing. Also, calls to check on ole' Ruffy here. Those two grew up together—Ruffy and Alex. When Alex turned ten, Ruffy here came to live with us." He patted the Beagle's head. "Our family has been blessed beyond measure. He's a fine young man. I'm sure he'd like to meet you."

His words bathed Laney like a soothing balm. A refreshing mixture of gratefulness and sadness mingled inside. She loved hearing about Alex, but regretted missing out. Was this how Maggie felt about Evan?

Her heart pained for Maggie. How had she handled the past few weeks? Having Evan so close and being sure he was her son Paul, and yet not being able to talk to him or hold him.

She returned to her place on the couch and squeezed Maggie's hand. "I can't imagine what you went through these past twenty-years." She hammered back the tears rising in her throat.

Maggie's eyes misted.

Laney remembered Hank and turned back toward him. "Do you really think he'd like to meet me?"

"Yep, I do. He's often said he wished he knew his real mom and dad, but he was always quick to say that didn't mean he loved us any less. He was always curious."

Curious? About her. The thought warmed her. "I don't know. Meeting him after all these years..."

Hank Davenport nodded. "He'd love to. I'm sure of it."

Laney lifted the envelope next to her. "You said he's in Dallas. We're flying out of there tomorrow."

"He is. You could probably meet up with him tonight. I could call him and tell him you're coming."

"No, don't call him." She reached into her purse and retrieved her card and Joseph's. "Here's my address and cell number, if you talk to him please tell him if he wants to talk to me, he can call. I don't want to intrude. Here's his father's card as well."

She handed both cards to Hank Davenport—a man proud of his son and confident in his love. One who had enough love as a father to share his son with this stranger—his son's mother. She admired his confidence.

"He'll probably call tonight. I'll let him know you came by." He placed the cards next to the phone on the TV tray. "I'll be sure to tell him you never knew where he was or how to get in touch with us. You see, we never told him about the letters and pictures. Judy didn't want him disappointed or hurt if you didn't respond. She was fiercely possessive of that boy." He laughed at the memory.

Laney knew they'd had a good relationship and Alex had been a major part of their lives. Her heart exploded with joy. God had chosen this wonderful couple to help her son be the man he was destined to become.

She and Maggie stood. "I guess, we've taken up enough of your time. Thank you, thank you so much for telling me a little about Alex."

Mr. Davenport rose from his chair in a slow deliberate move. "There's no hurry. I can tell you a lot more. We'd been married twenty-eight years when Alex came to us. There'd been many disappointments when Judy failed to bring her own child into the world and when several adoptions fell through because the birth mother changed her mind. That boy brought a lot of joy to this house." His gaze flowed with kindness. "But, we never did spoil him. He has a good appreciation of what the Lord provides."

Laney placed her hand on his shoulder. "Somehow,

Hank, after meeting you, I believe it. I'm sure Alex is a wonderful young man. I'm very grateful God chose you and Judy to be his parents."

His eyes watered and his unwavering gaze remained fixed on Laney. "I sure hate you had to give up your baby, but Alex was an answer to prayer. My Judy blossomed as a mama. She always told me she was doing what God had meant her to do when she became Alex's mama. Thank you, Miss Pouncey, for the gift you gave us."

Laney stared. Tears stung her eyes and words jammed in her throat. She inched closer to the door. If she didn't leave soon, she'd be nothing more than a puddle on the floor.

He lifted a small spiral-bound notebook and a pencil from his tray and scribbled on the top page. "Here's Alex's cell phone number and the hospital where he works. If you want to get a peek at him, he'll be working the emergency room tonight." He winked at Laney when he handed the page to her. "Be a shame to come all this way and not see him."

She pressed her lips together.

Maggie reached around and took the offered page. "You're right, Mr. Davenport, it would be. Thank you for the information. You're a very generous man."

Laney nodded. The action caused the tears welling in her eyes to spill onto her cheeks.

Maggie laced her arm through Laney's and led her toward the door, but before Laney walked through, she turned around and hugged Hank. She breathed in his woodsy scent mixed with menthol as she buried her face into his skinny shoulder.

He returned the hug then whispered in her ear. "God's plan is always sovereign. He takes care of his own."

"Bless you," she whispered.

She followed Maggie out onto the porch then down the driveway to the car. Although she didn't turn around, she knew Hank Davenport's gaze followed her. She didn't look back until she sat inside the car and Maggie started the engine. Hank and Ruffy stood on the porch. He waved as though to a friend who visited everyday. Laney learned a lot from Hank Davenport in such a short visit. He had just showed her the true meaning of grace.

CHAPTER 47

Maggie accelerated from the Davenport's driveway, and veered onto the country road headed back to the Interstate. They remained silent for several miles. What could they say?

Laney had been given the thing Maggie wanted. Laney's gratitude to the Davenports for taking such good care of Alex had touched Maggie. She'd thought the same thing about Laney and Paul. Had she shown Laney her gratitude?

Mark's words haunted Maggie. *God had taken care of your son.* At first, she thought the comment just a cliché to make her feel better. Now she wasn't so sure seeing how both Alex and Evan had been nurtured and well cared for. Maybe God *did* have some part in their lives.

Laney pointed to the driveway of an abandoned farm house. "Could you pull in here?"

"Are you feeling ill?"

"No, I'm feeling better than I have in a long time."

Maggie steered the car onto what remained of a driveway. A line of grass grew straight down the middle and threatened to take over the hardened dirt on either side. Maggie slowed and turned to Laney.

"Keep going." Laney pointed ahead. "Go to the end of

the driveway. There next to the old barn."

She pulled forward toward the barn. A small creek ran along the back of the building. Again she turned toward Laney. "Well?"

"I saw this place on the way in. C'mon let's get our feet wet." She leaned over and flipped off her shoes and socks.

Maggie watched then shook her head. "Are you serious?"

"As a heart attack."

"Okay. Race ya." Maggie stepped out onto the tall grass and started toward the creek.

"No fair. I can't run bare-footed."

When Maggie reached the water, she found a makeshift bench made with an old plank and two rocks. She flipped off her sandals then dipped her feet into the cool water.

Laney sat next to her and did the same. "This is nice." She handed Maggie something wrapped in a sheet of paper. "This is for you."

"For me?" Maggie grasped the folded paper. What could Laney have for her?

She unfolded the page. Her heart raced. Sweet memories rushed in. The picture of her son. He wore clothing she didn't recognize, but that face...that precious face. There was no mistake. It was the precious face of her two-year-old Paul. The baby taken from her.

Laney sat still.

Maggie gulped the blob of emotion choking her. Laney had given her the answer she so desperately needed.

The cool water around her feet felt cooler, more refreshing, as though twenty years of misery and despair seeped through her feet into the circling waters—cleansing waters. Brilliant blue filled the sky, and the sun—the glorious sun—warmed her shoulders and the top of her head.

Her son lived. What she had known from the deepest depths of her core, had now been confirmed. Her fingers held all the proof she needed. Real, physical proof.

She met Laney's gaze and although the image blurred, she knew Laney smiled.

Maggie clutched the photograph to her chest and allowed the flood to flow. Years of emotions spewed forth. Evan was Paul. "Thank you. You don't know what this means to me."

Laney brushed the top of her arm. "Honey, I think I do." Laney's fingers rested on Maggie's arm—comforting in silence. After a while she spoke, "That picture was taken the day after we brought him home. He squirmed around quite a bit, but the photographer finally got his attention with a toy dump truck."

Maggie squeezed her lids closed. The image of an overturned truck in the sand filled her vision. She swallowed a sob. "It was his favorite toy."

Laney continued. "He didn't sleep for the first two weeks. I sat in the rocker in his room and read books to him or rocked him until he fell asleep. Then sometimes in the middle of the night, he'd awaken crying. I thought it was because he remembered losing his family. Little did I know he still had a family missing him, loving him, and waiting for his return."

Laney's eyes drooped in the corners and drew Maggie in. "If it makes you feel any better, I love that boy with all my heart. I didn't sleep for nights on end sitting at his bedside. I wanted to be there in case he woke up frightened. Many nights I'd wake up to find Bryan sitting at the foot of Evan's bed. I didn't realize what a blessing that might be to you until I saw how Hank and Judy cared for Alex."

Maggie pulled the photo from her chest and stared at the round face and sparkling green eyes she'd dreamed about for two decades. His button nose and chubby cheeks still brought a smile. She turned to Laney. "Do you think God took care of our boys?"

Tears spilled from Laney's eyes. "You bet I do. And I thank Him for it. I pray you think so too." She squeezed Maggie's shoulder.

Maggie rested her head against Laney's and kicked up the clear water with her bare feet. "I believe I do. I actually believe He did."

She laughed and, for the first time in as long as she could remember, her laughter came from a place deep inside. A place where genuine joy spilled forth and bubbled to the surface. It felt good—felt great. Her laughter came from her heart.

No pressing questions festering and tormenting. No wondering if her son had been tortured or murdered. No nightmare thoughts strangling her mind. Her heart finally knew joy again. "Thank you, dear friend."

Laney grinned. "Guess what?"

"What?"

"When we moved into our house in Pecan Pointe, I prayed for God to send me a friend. A really good friend I could share my deepest and personal thoughts with. Someone who could be a Godly influence for me."

"Did you? Well, you got a friend, but I'm not sure about the Godly influence." She chuckled.

"Oh, I'm sure. Honey, you've taught me more about forgiveness and trusting God than any bible study I've ever done. Although you haven't had the faith in God, you believed in something. You believed Paul was still alive with unwavering faith and you had the courage to search for the truth. If not for you, I wouldn't have the courage to be here. To do what I'm thinking of doing next." Laney's eyebrows rose in a perfect arch.

Maggie smiled. "Hospital or Airport?"

Laney nodded. "Hospital. Two moms on a mission. That's exactly what we are. Maggie, you are a mom. Regardless, of what you think. To have the faith you've had and the love you've shown for Paul. Only a mom could have that kind of tenacity."

Maggie glanced back at the photo. Her precious son. Her baby. Returned to her. "I've dreamed of this day for a long time." She hugged Laney's neck. "Thank you."

Just as she did, Laney screamed and yanked her feet from the water. "Owww! I think a fish just nibbled on my toes!"

Maggie followed suit by jerking her feet out also. "Guess that's our cue. It's time to move on."

****

Laney stared at the sign, *Emergency Room,* with its red arrow pointing to the right.

Maggie followed the sign's instructions along a winding drive to a small parking lot. "I'll drop you off here." She pointed to a general parking lot about a hundred yards away. "And park there."

"You'll meet me in the waiting room?"

"Yes."

Laney nodded, exited the car, and then turned toward the doors. Behind them her son, the child she gave birth to, worked as a doctor. Worked as a life-saver.

Even in her craziest dreams, she never imagined him as a doctor. Was it because she thought he couldn't be successful without her for a mother? No, she had actually dreamed about him once. As an attorney who had scoured city hall to find the records of his birth mother. He'd stood on her doorstep with a three-piece suit and a bright red tie. She'd smiled when she'd awakened and taken the dream as a sign her son was well.

She scanned the parking lot. Maggie parked in a spot at the far end. It would take a while for her to walk to the waiting room. Laney started toward the double doors. As she neared them, they slid open. Parting the way. Saying, *Welcome, your son awaits.* But did he? Hank seemed confident Alex would welcome her, but what if he didn't? What if Hank didn't know Alex's true feelings?

She ripped her foot from the invisible nail fastening it to the cement and forced her feet to move forward, through the doors, and onto the glassy tile of the emergency room floor.

A middle-aged brunette looked up when Laney entered

the waiting area. "Can I help you?"

Could this person help her? Could she be the link reuniting Laney with the son she relinquished to the hands of strangers all those years ago?

Laney cleared her throat. "I'm looking for Alex Davenport, Doctor Alex Davenport."

The woman looked up. "Are you ill?"

"No. It's personal."

"Not a sales call is it?"

Laney shook her head. "No."

"Is he expecting you?" Her brows knitted together.

"No."

"You'll need to have a seat. He's seeing a patient right now. Who can I say is calling?"

Who could she say was calling? His mother? And old friend? He probably didn't even know her name. "Tell him I'm an old friend."

The receptionist eyed Laney from under lowered brows. "An old friend, you say?" She clucked her tongue. The sound vibrated throughout the open waiting area and went through Laney like a spear. "...Okay. Have a seat."

Laney turned toward the waiting area. Two rows of empty chairs filled the middle of the room and along the outer three walls. A television hanging from the top corner of the room played a rerun of an *I Love Lucy* episode. Laney lowered into the first chair of the row along the windows. What was she doing here? What could she possibly hope to accomplish?

Laney peered through the window to the parking lot. Maggie sat in the car, her cellphone near her ear. Sirens from a distance competed with the television as the parting song of the episode played. The TV music dimmed as the sirens intensified.

Maggie entered the waiting area and sat next to Laney. "Have you seen him?"

"Not yet. It would appear the receptionist is also the first line of defense to protect doctors from suspicious visitors."

Maggie laughed. "I'm sure they've seen some weird things here. People who do crazy things. Oh, Eric told me to tell you he sends his love. I almost slipped and told him we were in Dallas. Anyway, he's got everything under control at the practice. He said it's been busy but not crazy. Which is good. I thought I'd miss work more than I have."

"You've been a little busy." Laney's gaze followed the wailing ambulance as it pulled into the emergency room entrance. The siren died along with Laney's hope of seeing her son. Someone in there needed to see him more than she did.

The hope of seeing him lingered for a moment longer in her heart.

But she quickly abandoned it.

Because she knew—knew beyond any question—she didn't need to invade his world today.

She thought she needed to be here to reassure Alex he'd not been abandoned. But the clear reality boomed. She was here for herself. Not Alex. She wanted to know him. She wanted to see for herself that her son had grown into a fine man. This was about her and what she wanted.

She had no right to be here. No right to intrude on the life he had. One he'd carved out and made without her. Laney stood. "Let's go. I don't belong here."

Maggie stood next to her. "I thought you wanted to meet him."

Laney rushed toward the door. When she exited the hospital, she took a deep breath and let the cool spring air seep deep into her lungs. Let it cleanse the guilt and uncertainty from her.

When Maggie caught up to her, she placed her hand on Laney's shoulder. "What's wrong?"

Laney stared at the double doors she left. "I do want to meet him. But that's just it. It's what I want. Here I am at his work location. He's a doctor, for heaven's sake, and I'm here to totally throw this wrench in his life while he's at work." She took in another deep breath.

"What am I thinking? That I'd just waltz in and say, 'Hello, I'm your mother and I didn't know what happened to you, but just wanted to say hi and I didn't abandon you.'

She started walking toward the car with Maggie by her side. "How would he feel? Then what would I do? Leave? Leave him to get back to work maybe saving someone's life after I drop this bombshell on him?"

She reached the car and turned to Maggie shaking her head. "This is not right. I'm doing this for my satisfaction. To ease my mind. Not his. Can we drive back down to the farm house?"

Maggie's lopsided smile tugged at her heart. Did her new friend think she was crazy?

Maggie reached in her purse for the car keys. "Of course we can." She brushed the top of Laney's arm with her fingertips. "I hope you didn't come here because you felt I pressured you into doing this."

Laney stopped and turned to face Maggie. "No, not at all. I didn't know I felt this way until just now—until I imagined him caring for the person they delivered in that ambulance. He is just fine without me. He doesn't need me barging into his life. If he wants to know me, it'll be his choice. I'm not forcing myself on him."

"Then why are we going back to the farmhouse?"

"Because I want to tell him in a letter and I know Hank will give it to him. I don't particularly trust the sentinel receptionist in there."

Maggie remained silent and simply nodded.

Regret pierced Laney's heart. Had she hurt Maggie's feeling with what she'd said? What could she say to the woman who had become her friend?

They entered the car. Maggie started the engine and adjusted the air conditioning while Laney searched for words to say to Maggie. She inhaled, letting her chest expand. "Maggie, I'm sorry. I didn't mean to imply—"

"Stop. It's okay." Maggie's gaze rested on Laney. "I respect your feelings about this."

"I don't want you to think I'm judging you."

"I don't. Your situation is very different than mine. You have to do what *you* think is right."

Laney exhaled slow and loud. "Thank you. I'm so glad you're here with me."

Maggie smiled. "I am, too. Now find something to write on."

Laney searched her bag for the tiny notebook she used for her shopping list. Her note to Alex whirled through her brain. Could her fingers write fast enough to capture all she wanted to say?

Her laptop would be a blessing right now. Then again, no it wouldn't. She couldn't write this letter on a computer. The words from her heart had to flow through her fingers and be formed by the gentle stroke of her hand. With a pen. Her handwriting. Personal and with love. That was the only way she could give Alex this letter.

As Maggie backed the car out the parking lot, Laney steadied the notebook on her lap and let the words flow. She poured her heart onto the tiny lined pages, letting Alex meet her through her words

CHAPTER 48

Maggie followed the now familiar path south out of Dallas toward the farmhouse. Laney sat in the passenger seat deep in thought while her hand flew across the pages of her notebook.

Maggie pondered Laney's words about getting to know her son for selfish reasons. But surely there wasn't anything wrong with wanting to know your own child? Was there? Was she being selfish for wanting to know Evan?

Her heart had shattered into tiny twisted pieces when he'd rejected her. He'd not shown any interest in learning the truth. Did he care? Could he ever?

But…he was twenty-two. So young. Laney and Bryan were the only parents he'd ever known.

If she really loved Paul, should she let him come to her? Let him go? After all, she finally had the answer to her question. Paul was alive and safe. Could she—should she—do the same thing Laney had done? Walk away and let Paul come to her?

But wouldn't that be turning her back on him? The desire to get to know him, to show him how much she cared burned so deep in her soul that she didn't think she could do what Laney had done. She wanted to reassure Paul that she'd never leave him. Ever. And that she never stopped loving him.

"Are you sure this is what you want to do?" She asked Laney.

Laney paused, her fingers wrapped around the pen with its tip poised above the paper. "Yes, I'm sure. This is how things have to be in our relationship. But...that doesn't mean it's how it has to be with you and Evan." She reached over and patted the side of Maggie's arm. "You have to do what *you* believe is right."

Grateful for Laney's understanding, Maggie nodded. Laney turned back to her notebook and the pen danced across the page once more.

Do what she believed was right.

The words made the act sound like an easy task. The truth for Maggie was not easy. She'd been deceived a long time ago by her heart *and* her head. What she believed was right didn't always produce the best results for her.

She'd trusted her mother after her father left, she'd trusted her mother's new boyfriends like her mother suggested, and she'd trusted that her mother would take care of her.

That had *not* turned out well.

Then she'd followed her heart to help the little boy that day in the park. Again misery. That's when she'd lost Paul.

Could doing what she believed was right lead to anything but disaster?

When they passed the driveway to the old farmhouse and creek, part of Maggie's heart quickened from the memory of Laney giving her Paul's picture. Streams from the late afternoon sun ran across the weathered and rotting boards of the old farmhouse making the overgrown grass look planned. The place looked beautiful to her.

The vision would forever be planted in her mind. This is where she'd finally gotten the truth she needed. It didn't matter that it wasn't forensic proof. It was the answer her heart craved for far too long. Now a deeper craving replaced—to know Paul again. To share in his thoughts and dreams. Being part of his life would give her the joy she thought had been forever stolen from her. She couldn't just sit back and wait for him to come to her. Could she?

"There's the driveway," Maggie said. "Are you done with your letter?"

"Almost." Laney inched the paper higher to write on the last few lines of the page.

Maggie glanced in the rearview mirror. No cars. They were on a country road. "I'll stop here. With all those potholes in the driveway, he'll never be able to understand your writing."

"Thanks." Laney's lips curled toward her cheek while she remained focus on the page.

Maggie leaned back onto the headrest and let the cool air brush across her face and arms. The tangled mess of thoughts jamming her mind proved more confusing than anything. For now, she'd have to ignore them and concentrate on being here for Laney. Once she returned to Pecan Pointe, she'd figure out what to do.

Laney wrote on the edge of the paper. The adoptive mother of her son had become her best friend. How in the world did something like that happen? What were the odds? Could she have written this chapter of her life as such a far-fetched story? No. Not in her craziest dreams.

"I'm done." Laney clicked the pen.

"Have you said all you've wanted?"

Laney nodded. "Yes. Maybe." She let out a sharp exhale. "No...but it'll have to do until we talk...if we talk."

Maggie leaned forward then shifted into drive. "Okay, if you're sure."

"I'm sure."

"Then here we go...again." Maggie turned into the driveway and negotiated through the potholes.

Once they stopped in front of the house, Laney tore the pages from the notebook and folded them in half. "God, I hope this is the right thing to do." She opened the door and then headed for the farmhouse porch..

Maggie sat in the car and watched as Mr. Davenport welcomed Laney into his home for the second time. His generosity swelled her heart. Not only did he welcome her into his home, he was willing to share his son with her.

She thought of the photograph Laney had given her and realized Laney wasn't much different than Mr. Davenport. Could she have done the same thing if she'd been in their shoes?

She reached into her purse and retrieved the picture. Paul's smile tugged at her heart. She'd missed so many of those smiles. The tip of her index finger circled his tiny lips. How many goodnight kisses had she gone without? Especially at bedtime after she'd been the one to read *Goodnight Moon* to him.

Fate had been good giving her back her son. But had it simply been fate? Or God? Once again, Mark's words chimed through her mind. *God takes care of His children.* Her soul rested in thinking God had watched over her son until this time. A strange comfort now occupied the space in her heart usually twisted with grief. She had to admit, it felt good.

The high-pitched warble of her cell phone broke through the silence, startling her. Her lifeline back to Louisiana. She rifled through her purse and found her phone. Craig. "Hello."

"Good afternoon. I had a few minutes between meetings, so I thought I'd call and see how things were going. Are you still in Colorado with Laney?"

Wow, so much had changed since she'd last spoken to him. She wanted to tell him everything, but knew this was not something she could share over the phone. "Not quite. We're in Texas. Seems like Laney's aunt had some secrets to share with Laney about the son Laney gave up for adoption years ago."

"Really? Let me guess. You're helping her find her lost

son." His words carried an edge but not enough so Maggie could tell whether he was being sarcastic or not. But Craig and sarcasm didn't match. What did his tone mean? This was new ground for her. And for Craig.

"Yes, we've found him and I'm sitting in the car right now while she delivers a letter to the adoptive father."

Craig didn't respond. Had the call dropped? Maggie stole a quick glance at the LED. The call was still connected. "Craig?"

"Honey, how are you doing with all this? Are you okay?" He called her Honey. How long had it been? His tender words comforted. She paused and let them soak in. Let them nurture the mended parts. Let them pierce through the wall she'd cemented around her heart eons ago.

Would her voice work? She fought the swell of emotion threatening to take over. "Um...uh...when are you coming home?"

"My flight is scheduled for tomorrow afternoon."

"Can we have a quiet dinner tomorrow night? Something special. I have so much to tell you."

"Sure. Are you okay?"

She heard the questions in his voice and knew that finally she would be able to answer him truthfully. "I am." She smiled. "Perhaps, the best I've been in a long time."

Maybe. Just maybe. Laney's God would work things out for the best for all of them.

****

Laney explained the events of the past few hours to a surprised Hank Davenport. He nodded a few times, but remained silent.

When she held out the note to him it shook in her trembling fingers. "Here. It's all written in the note. Please, Mr. Da...er Hank, I'd be so grateful if you gave this to him. You said he comes here on weekends, right?"

He nodded.

"Would you add this to my card? He can call me if he wants." She gulped back the sob rising in her throat. "My door will always be open to him."

For the second time that day, Hank Davenport's eyes misted, and Laney fought to keep her own tears at bay. If she didn't, there'd be no stopping the avalanche. She'd lose all control and break down right in front of Hank and Ruffy. This is what God lead her to do. She had to trust Him.

"Thank you."

He met her gaze, the mist in his eyes thickened. "I won't be here forever, maybe not much longer, and our boy needs family. He needs you. I will make sure he calls you."

Laney tried to smile, but ended up pressing her lips together. She wrapped her arms around the feeble shoulders of Hank Davenport. But instead of his frailness, all she felt was the bold shoulders of the strongest man she'd ever met. Her hug lingered.

"Thank you." She knew she'd already said the words, but she hoped by repeating them she could convey the gratitude exploding from her heart. Besides no other words came to her and, if they had, she couldn't have voiced them.

She stepped onto the porch and turned back toward the house. Hank stood in the doorway, Ruffy near his feet. The beagle's eyes matched his owners. Sad. Droopy. He lifted his hand, her letter between his thumb and forefinger. "I'll see he gets this."

She smiled and prayed he saw her appreciation in the simple act. When she entered the car, a grinning Maggie greeted her. "Well, what did he think?"

"He thinks I should have spoken to Alex. But he'll see him this weekend and give him the letter."

Maggie squeezed her hand. "I'm sure he'll do just that. The rest is up to Alex."

Laney met Maggie's gaze. "And God." She placed her hand on top of Maggie's. "Thank you for coming here with me. You've been a good friend and I know we haven't known each other for long, but it feels like longer. Are you ready to head back home and deal with the repercussion of all the truths we've discovered?"

Maggie smiled. "The truth will change things for us, won't it? I'm ready. Are you?"

Laney returned her smile. "I think so. I don't think I could have done this without you."

The muted strains of Vivaldi sounded from Laney's phone. "The world just doesn't go away does it?"

Maggie laughed. "Nope. Not even in the middle of Nowhere Texas."

Laney lifted the phone from her purse. "It's my hubby." She connected the call. "Hello, sweetie."

"Laney, where are you?" His stressed voice knifed a red alert right through her.

"I'm sitting in the car with Maggie." She braced herself. "Why?" She swallowed not sure she wanted to hear his next words.

"It's Evan. He's been in a terrible accident."

CHAPTER 49

Maggie forced herself to focus on the road. A silent Laney, thumbed the edge of her cellphone. Maggie white-knuckled the steering wheel. It had been five miles and Maggie's nerves were winning in her battle to remain calm.

She couldn't stand the silence any longer. She couldn't stand not knowing. "Laney, can you talk now?"

Laney inhaled sharply and then nodded. "I think so." Her hoarse voice puffed the words in short raspy pants.

She drew in another lungful of air. "Evan and Casey were driving home from Grand Isle." The words flew out with her breath. "A vehicle ran them off the road and they slammed into an embankment south of Gonzales."

She paused and stared at the road as though she'd forgotten what she was doing. Maggie waited.

"Oh, dear Lord, please. Please, let him be all right." Laney sighed. "They're at Baton Rouge General. Casey is in stable condition. Evan's in ICU." She rested her head on the passenger window.

The words came. Maggie took them in. They butchered her heart into millions of chunks of raw flesh. How could this be? Had she found her son only to have him snatched away again? What kind of cruel God would do such a thing? If this was the God Laney trusted, the one she prayed to, then she wanted no part of Him.

Laney's whispered prayer broke the forced vigil. "Please Lord, protect him. Save him, Lord, for me and for Maggie."

More words. This time they mended some of the broken pieces of her heart. Laney prayed for Maggie's needs too. She held onto her faith and trust for both of them. Her love and pain spilled into the spoken words. Her sentiment spoke of a future—one for all of them.

Had Maggie placed more into the words than Laney had intended?

No.

Laney trusted God.

Maggie didn't.

That was the difference between them. Laney prayed to God for an expected outcome, but trusted enough to accept God's will, while Maggie questioned why He would allow such a horrid thing to happen.

Maybe. Maybe if she could just say a simple prayer she would feel hopeful. Like she wasn't sitting under a stack of lead blankets banning together to crush the life from her.

Maybe she could find a stitch of optimism in the fabric of this crazy life and understand why the woman sitting next to her calmly prayed to a God she believed with her whole heart would answer her prayers.

Why was this woman now her best friend? The one who had been the mother she was supposed to be to a boy that was supposed to be her son.

Would Maggie ever understand how Laney could pray for their son to be saved so they could continue to love and spend time with him? It didn't make sense.

The more she tried to arrange the pieces into a coherent whole, the more the image blurred. Was this how Laney's God showed himself? During times like this?

If only she could be more like Laney, she'd find faith and calm during these times and know they had a purpose in her life and reflect that faith to those around her. If only she could be that person right now. If only life had not sucked so much out of her.

She ventured into the dark place—returned to the torment familiar to her. Her comfort zone, but one that provided no comfort. What if Paul died and she lost him? Again. Could work sustain her like it had before? Or would she find herself in the dark abyss—snatching away any promise of light?

The warmth of Laney's hand on her forearm brought Maggie back. She wrapped her fingers tighter around the steering wheel as though the act could keep her mind fixed on the road only, and not fly to the sanity-stealing places— ones offering nothing but pain.

Maggie wanted to close her eyes. Release the million tears banging to be set free. Instead she took a deep breath and concentrated on the approaching exit.

"I'm scared, really scared." Laney's voice, quivering and weak, touched the place Maggie fought to avoid. It was where fear controlled with a ruling fist.

How could she comfort Laney when her own heart lay open in her chest? And where had Laney's trust and faith gone? Surely, she wouldn't be afraid if she trusted.

Maggie tucked a strand of stray hair behind her ear, careful to keep the car between the lines. "What are you afraid of?"

Laney slid her hand away from Maggie's arm, and from a sideways glance, Maggie saw her twist her fingers together in her lap.

"Oh Maggie, I'm afraid..." The words spewed from her wavering lips. "I'll lose Evan and never see Alex. I'm afraid while I was chasing after one son, I may lose the other. And although I trust God's will to be done, I'm a little afraid of what His will is. Scared I'll...I'll be forced to fully understand what you lived through. To have my son taken away." Her last words were barely a whisper, cloaked with the strain of choking tears.

Fear. Maggie knew the monster too well. He'd lived with her and controlled her thoughts and actions for longer than she cared to admit. Could this be the breaking point where she let him conquer? Or where she cast him into the fire? Where she chose not to let him dictate how she felt or acted?

Her words could change the direction of her mind. All she had to do was find the strength to say and believe them. She took a deep breath and decided.

"We'll face this together." She stole a glance toward Laney. "I'm afraid too, but let's not let the fear take over. We don't know all the details yet. We'll know more when we get to the hospital. For now, and even if it's just right this minute, we have to believe Paul...um...Evan will be fine. That he'll pull through. I refuse to believe my son would be given back to me only to be taken away again."

Laney let out a long sigh. "You're right. I know you are, but for a moment, a brief moment, the fear took over. It wrapped itself around my heart and squeezed my breath away."

Maggie's own heart jolted to Laney's words. She knew all too well that feeling. "I know." She reached over and squeezed Laney's hand. "I know."

The remaining miles to the airport trudged along despite Maggie's pushing the limits of the law, as well as the accelerator. Just hours earlier, the landscape had fascinated. Now it tormented. Its expansive fields and pastures only emphasized the distance left to travel before they could be where their hearts craved to be.

If only she could blink her eyes and be at Paul's bedside. But then what? Would she tell him she was his mother? How could she? That would be the last thing he needed or wanted to hear. A shiver snaked its way the length of her spine, making her whole body tremble. How could she play the role of mere bystander while her son fought for his life?

****

Laney stared out the plane window on their nonstop

flight to New Orleans. *Thank you, Lord.* They'd gotten to the airport on time for the next available flight.

The patchwork of earth below served as a cruel reminder life went on. Rivers flowed. Crops grew. The earth changed. Had God been preparing her for this day? Dare she think of the possibility of losing Evan? No parent should lose a child. Life wasn't supposed to be that way. Of course, Laney knew things didn't always turn out as expected. Sometimes quite the opposite.

She glanced at her watch. They would be in New Orleans in less than an hour. Still too long. She wanted to be there now.

The powder blue of the sky caressed the pillow-like clouds reflecting the late afternoon sun. She felt as though heaven was just beyond the clouds and her prayers were closer to God.

The view blurred as she let her mind drift. Her precious Evan lay in a hospital bed perhaps fighting for every breath while she was off searching for another son—a son she'd kept from her family. *Please Lord, protect Evan.* How could she tell Bryan about Alex now? She couldn't deliver such a gut-punch while he wondered if his son would survive. *Lord, guide me. Show me the path you want me to follow.*

She leaned back into the seat, allowing the flow of overhead air to embrace her. "Maggie, you asleep?"

"No. Just thinking."

"Really?"

"Yeah."

"Want to share your thoughts?"

"I'm thinking it might not be a good idea for me to be at the hospital. Maybe I could just call you to get updates?"

Laney's eyes flew open when she turned to Maggie. "What? Why would you think that?"

"Because I don't want to upset Evan or Bryan. If my being there upsets Evan...keeps him from...I just don't think it's a good idea for me to be there."

Laney sat up straight and glared at Maggie. "Listen to me. I believe you when you say Evan is Paul." She touched Maggie's arm causing her to open her eyes. "I believe you. You have every right to be with me at the hospital. If you don't want to go into his room, I understand, but there's no reason you and Craig can't be sitting next to me and Bryan in the waiting room."

The skin beneath Maggie's eyes sagged. "I want to be there for you. And also for me. But I won't go into Evan's room. Okay?"

Laney nodded and fought the rush of tears gathering in her throat. "Don't believe for one second you're not a good mother."

Maggie's lips parted. She brushed her fingertips along her cheekbone. "The same goes for you, Laney Ellerby."

CHAPTER 50

*M*aggie waited in the waiting room while Bryan and Laney disappeared through the double doors toward the Intensive Care Unit. Maggie slouched in the chair and rested her head on the back. The position only comforted for a few minutes. She shifted again. And then again. Unable to get comfortable, she stood and paced along the row of empty chairs. A gray-haired man who sat in the far corner left with two teary-eyed women.

Her body ached from all the traveling, but also from all the emotion. She'd barely been able to follow the speed limit from New Orleans to Baton Rouge. So much had happened since she and Laney left just days ago. So many revelations had changed the course of their lives. Laney would never be the same, whether she ever heard from Alex. But he had been loved, cared for, and had grown into a fine young man.

Maggie would never be the same. She'd found Paul. Who also had been loved and cared for. Her heart longed to get to know him, but not at the expense of his happiness. She would leave when Bryan and Laney returned. But could she go home to an empty house while the son she'd dreamed about lay in a hospital bed just a few miles away?

She closed her eyes and inhaled the heady aroma of the hospital. The rush of carts and the steady hum of conversation flowed in to lull her into the familiar. Memories of medical school and residencies rushed back. She'd done her first residency at Oschner Medical Center in New Orleans. But she'd never been on this side. Never had a loved one needing hospital care.

Her mother had died at home in bed with her first love— a bottle of gin. The neighbor had called her a week later when an old boyfriend had returned and discovered her mother's body. At that point, Maggie had not grieved. She'd lost her mother long before. Her mother died a year after Paul's abduction. She still grieved for her son. There was no way she could grieve for her mother—for the woman who'd never cared for anyone but herself. Yet, her heart ached that her mother had died alone.

She paced along the opposite row of chairs. Why would she think about her mother today of all days? Old memories imposed. Their haunting presence came at the worst times. How could she be any support here when mired in the chains of her past?

A slight tug on her shoulder brought her back to the waiting room. Laney's tear-stained face filled her view. "Would you like to see him?"

See Paul. How could she? She vowed she wouldn't. Yet…here was Laney asking—offering the very thing she wanted so desperately. What would keep her from falling down into a melted puddle of flesh right at the foot of his bed? "How…how is he?"

"He's unconscious. They've preformed a craniotomy to relieve some of the swelling. The next twenty-fours hours are crucial." Her bottom lip stuttered making her chin quiver. She extended her hand to Maggie.

Bryan wrapped his arm around Laney's waist. He nodded when Maggie met his gaze. Their encouragement propelled her forward. She reached for Laney's hand before any inner demons could change her mind.

Each step toward the double doors seemed to take every bit of remaining energy. How could she see her son in this state?

Laney slipped her arm through Maggie's and guided her forward. "Brace yourself. He doesn't look like himself. He's-he's..." She lowered her head and kept pushing Maggie toward the doors.

Beeps and hisses snarled as she entered. A form lay in bed surrounded by an army of life-supporting devices—sentinels to protect her son or at least preserve the life he struggled to hold on to. Laney gently guided her toward the bedside. "Go on."

Maggie gazed upon his face and gasped. The swollen eyes and crimson cuts along his cheeks and forehead changed him into someone she didn't recognize. The acute resemblance to Craig was gone. Instead, the gruesome aftermath of a tragic accident remained. But beneath the horrific swelling, bruising, and lacerations was her son. Her baby boy. Suddenly, she didn't see a twenty-two-year-old man, but the two-year-old baby who'd been snatched from her. Her heart ached from the memory but also from the emotion. Could she bear losing him again?

She wrapped her arms around her sides. The tender pieces of her softened heart cried out. She longed to whisper in his ear. *You have to be well. You have to come back to me.* He couldn't leave her. Not again.

"Please, please. Lord, please. Save him." Dare she? The whispered words mingled with tears from deep within her throat. And when they escaped, competing with the sounds from the electronic watchmen, they came back to her just as foreign as when they'd left her lips.

Laney approached and linked her fingers through hers. "Please, Lord. Hear our prayers. Two mothers who love this child. We know you've taken care of him. Please continue to watch over him. To bring him back to us."

The words seeped into Maggie's heart and she cradled

them there. Hoping they would be enough to heal her son.

****

Laney succumbed to the assault of tears. She thought the storm she'd cried with Bryan had depleted her, but the new stream proved otherwise. She brushed the blurring flow with the back of her free hand.

When she released Maggie's hand, Maggie reached down and adjusted the sheet near Evan's chest then grabbed his hand. With tender brushes, she stroked his fingers, then his palm and forearm. "Come back. Please, come back." Her whispered words drifted into the room, and were consumed by the cavalry of machines. She bent over and placed a gentle kiss on the bandages covering his forehead. Only a few more minutes of visiting hours remained.

At first, Laney doubted whether bringing Maggie back to Evan's room was the right thing to do. But she had let her heart lead her. Let God lead her. And, she was glad she did.

Maggie turned away from the bed her eyes glistening in the florescent brightness. Laney met her gaze and her throat tightened at the sadness in Maggie's eyes.

When Maggie wrapped her arms around Laney and gave her a gentle hug, she swallowed to keep the rush from flowing again. Maggie's whispered words gently brushed her ear. "Thank you. Thank you so much. I'll be waiting for you just outside the door."

Alone with Evan, Laney yearned to tell him everything she'd learned in the past few days. She wanted to talk to him as though he sat next to her wolfing down a meal she'd prepared for dinner, but she couldn't escape reality. Evan lay before her on the brink of death. She stood closer to his bed and slid her hand beneath his. The warmth of his palm surprised her. Had she expected him to be cold? The thought clinched her chest and sent another wave of hot tears to her cheeks.

This would be the last time she would allow her tears to

flow. Evan needed her. Bryan needed her.

"Evan, it's Mom. Honey, I know you can pull through this. Hang on, sweetie. Hang on." She bowed her head and said another silent prayer asking for healing. Asking for the strength to be a reflection of Christ in the midst of her current storm. Thanking God for carrying Evan this far. She also thanked Him for drawing Maggie closer.

CHAPTER 51

The streetlights of the winding road to Pecan Pointe cast eerie shadows on the hood of Maggie's car as she steered home. With one hand, she rubbed the top of her shoulder and the back of her neck. She couldn't wait to get into her shower. Sleep in her bed. Yet, would she be able to sleep? The past few nights she'd enjoyed the most delicious nights of rest. The best she'd had in years despite hard hotel mattresses. Maybe the rest came because she finally had the answers she sought and her mind finally let go.

But what about tonight.

Once she reached her driveway, she waited for the gate to open, and then the garage door. When she finally entered her house, familiar smells welcomed. The scent of green apples and cinnamon drifted from the pottery bowl filled with the potpourri mixture. She hadn't even noticed the scent before she left. Being away had offered a new perspective for both her olfactory senses as well as her heart.

Her cell phone's ring grabbed her attention. Craig. She couldn't wait to share all she'd learned with him. "Hello."

"Hello. So where are you tonight?" She heard the smile

in his teasing words.

Her heart sank when she realized the first time he saw Paul would be in a hospital bed where his son struggled for life.

"I'm home. Just walked in." She dropped her purse on the counter.

"Oh, good. I've reserved an earlier flight. I should be in around nine in the morning."

Maggie sighed. Good. She wouldn't have to wait all day to speak to him. Planning what she'd say and how to say it. "Why don't I meet you at the airport, I'll take a cab we can ride home together?"

"Sure…is everything all right?"

"It's a long story. Not one I can do justice to over the phone. I'll fill you in when I see you."

"Okay…but," he paused, "now you've got me wondering what's going on."

"I'm sorry. I'll take you to breakfast and tell you everything. Please, trust me on this one."

"Fine, I'll trust you."

"Thank you. And Craig…I'm really looking forward to seeing you tomorrow. I've missed you." A moment of silence made her wonder if he'd heard her.

"I've missed you, too."

She jotted down his flight information. After she hung up, the surprise in his voice lingered in her ear. It had been a long time since she'd told him she'd missed him when he left. Then again, it had been an even longer time since she actually missed him. Missing him felt good.

Maggie showered and prepared for bed. Before she turned down the covers, she placed the picture of Paul Laney had given her on her nightstand. Next to the framed one she'd kept there for two decades. She slipped between her cool sheets under the comforting down blanket, and stretched. She tensed each muscle in her legs and torso then relaxed them. She repeated the same with her arms and shoulders.

Her bed should be a welcome relief to the uncomfortable chairs of waiting rooms and airplane seats. It was hard to believe this morning she'd been driving around Texas.

Maggie nestled her head into the soft pillow and released her body to sink into the memory foam mattress. Her eyes remained focused on the smiling face of her son. She closed her eyes and willed her body to slumber, but thoughts rattled through her brain. Would Paul survive? And what if he didn't make it through the night?

Craig. How would he accept the news? Bryan and Laney. Would their marriage survive if Paul didn't? And how would Laney's secret affect their lives? The questions flittered in and out. Taking turns dominating her mind.

She turned to her right side and punched her pillow to create a cradle for her head. Once again, she tried to sleep.

When she closed her eyes, images of Paul's two-year-old face danced through her mind. The sweet curve of his chubby cheek soon morphed into the swollen, bruised, and lacerated face of a twenty-two-year-old. Her eyes flew open to escape the haunting vision.

She flipped the covers off, jumped to the floor, and then raced to her closet. She slid hangers looking for something comfortable. Something to wear to the hospital.

What had she been thinking sleeping here alone? No way would her mind allow her body to rest while Paul's life hung by a thread as fine as a spider's web.

The need to be there proved much stronger than her need for sleep in a comfortable bed. She scanned her closet again for something that might work for Laney. Her new friend was nearly the same size. Maggie's closet held a few ensembles in different sizes. Thanks to her days of trying to relieve the guilt and pain by eating and then fasting.

Navy sports pants with a matching jacket stood out. She ripped it from the hanger and folded it into a small satchel. A soft cotton shirt went in as well as a pair of fresh socks and underwear. She rifled through the multitude of beauty and hygiene products she'd collected over the years.

Several went into an extra cosmetics bag then into the satchel. Confident she'd gotten everything Laney might need, she headed toward the door, but not before stuffing both photos of Paul into her purse.

#

The now familiar smell of the waiting room wrapped around her and, as unpleasant as it was, it welcomed. Somehow, she belonged here. Sitting on the hard uncomfortable chairs, breathing the stale air, smelling the antiseptic mixed with, God knew what, and squinting to the harsh florescent lighting. She belonged as close as possible to Paul. And to Laney.

Laney and Bryan huddled in corner chairs. Laney's head rested on Bryan's shoulder, her eyes closed. She wore the same jeans and the short-sleeved, pull-over she'd worn in the Dallas hospital earlier today. Only a few hours ago, but yet, it seemed a lifetime. When she approached, Laney stirred but didn't open her eyes.

Maggie locked gazes with Bryan. He smiled then nodded toward the chair next to him. She handed him a bag filled with sandwiches. Then whispered. "Thought you might be hungry."

He accepted her offering. "Thanks. Unbelievably, I am a little hungry." He opened the bag in a slow deliberate move careful not to wake Laney.

"I also brought some things for Laney. Change of clothes and items to help her freshen up some. Any more news on Paul..." She shook her head. "I'm sorry...Evan?"

"He's lost a lot of blood and used the supply the hospital had. He doesn't need any right now, but if surgery is needed, he might. They're calling for donors. His blood type is not very common. AB I think. But I think he's a universal recipient so Laney and I have donated.

Yes. Confirmation. Paul had the same blood type as Craig. Could the blood type and the photographs be enough to convince Craig that Evan was Paul?

"Oh, good. I'll head down to the lab and donate. My

husband actually has that blood type. His flight comes in at nine. I'm sure he'll be happy to donate also." She glanced at her watch. Seven hours before she had to tell Craig his son, missing for twenty years, lay in a hospital room in Baton Rouge near death's grip.

They would miss the morning visiting hours and would have to wait until after lunch to see him again. If he regained consciousness, she'd forfeit her time. He didn't need any confusion in his life right now. It would be a blessing to forgo seeing him if it meant he had awakened.

She leaned her head back on the seat and listened to Bryan's soft chews on the turkey and ham sandwiches she'd brought.

In her mind, a sweet prayer for Paul circled her thoughts.

Not that she knew how to pray.

She only knew what she wanted for Paul and if she couldn't give it to him, then maybe God could. And if it took asking God—the God she'd turned her back on when He'd abandoned her—then she would ask for Paul.

****

Laney awoke with a start and focused on the waiting room. She'd dreamed of the day Evan had come home to her. His sweet eyes and gentle smile filled her vision and left her feeling comforted, secure. Then reality crashed like a hammer to her head. A dull throb in her back from the uncomfortable chair made her shift. The pain in her head out-ranked the one in her back. Last evening had drained her of all emotion. She felt empty and disheveled like a wrung-out dishrag. The lead ball in her chest once serving as her heart, cast a consuming pain overshadowing both her head and her back.

Maggie slept in the chair next to the empty seat where Bryan had been. When had she returned? The last Laney remembered she'd bid Maggie goodnight at eleven. She checked her watch. Four a.m. She extended her legs and pumped her feet back and forth and then stood and extended her back. Where was Bryan? His empty chair sent a jolt of alarm through her. Had something happened to Evan? Her pulse raced at the thought. *No, he would have awakened me.* Just as she lifted her arms out in front of her and stretched, footsteps to her left drew her attention. Bryan slid his hand along her back and spoke into her ear. "Good morning, sweetie."

She stood and kissed his cheek. "Hey, babe." She peered into his eyes and saw the wonderful father and husband she'd been blessed to have. How could she have kept her secret from him for so long? Why had she not trusted he would understand? He'd always been there for her. He'd always looked out for her.

She wrapped her arms around him and squeezed. The comforting weight of his arms pressing around her offered a safe-haven in the current raging storm. Two as one who stood against the forces threatening to change their world forever. Threatening to rip their family apart. For a moment, she opened to the emotions. She let them run through her, letting Bryan's strong arms and body absorb them.

He whispered into her hair. "I love you. Honey, hang on. He'll be okay. God's got this."

"I know. I really do, but sometimes I forget. Thank you for reminding me." She rested her head on his chest and allowed his arms to support her. "I love you, too."

Soon, she'd have to tell him about Alex, but not now. She couldn't be responsible for adding another burden to his already burdened heart.

She pressed her cheek into his chest as he increased the pressure around her shoulders. The thumping of his heart sounded loud and strong in her ear. With each pulse, her own heart responded. Their rhythm matched. In the shelter of Bryan's arms, she knew she could take on anything the world threw at them.

He handed her a small white bag. "There's a table out here, if you're hungry." He guided her toward the door then stopped. "Oh, I almost forgot. Maggie brought you some clothes and stuff." He pointed to a satchel on the floor near Maggie's chair.

Although she had not eaten since the small snack on the plane yesterday, the thought of food made her stomach roll, but freshening up did sound good. But then again..."What if the doctor comes looking for us?"

"It's early. He said he usually makes rounds between five and six."

For some reason, the urge to share her heart with Bryan swept over her. It was as though she had to tell him now or she'd lose the desire and the courage. "Um...I didn't tell you everything about our trip to New Orleans and Colorado. There's a whole lot more."

He led her to a small table in a small room near the waiting area. They sat. His gaze found hers. There she found pools of compassion. So deep she wished she could just jump in and let the emotion envelope her. Would revealing her secret to him change that?

"Honey, I know you have something to share with me. I sensed it the minute I saw you. Also, the fact you invited Maggie to see Evan spoke volumes about what you'd uncovered. Don't feel you have to say anything right now. Let's just stand together, all of us, to pray for Evan and support each other until he's better." He drummed his fingers on the laminate tabletop. "I had a lot of time to think while you were gone."

"Really? And what have you thought about?"

He leaned back into the plastic-backed chair. "If Evan is Paul, which, from your actions and Craig having Evan's rare blood type, makes me think he is. It's not something we conspired to do. It just happened and now we've got to deal with things the best way we can. We've got to trust God. We've got to trust that our love for Evan and our faith is strong enough to help us share Evan with his biological parents. I can't imagine what it's been like for them. They deserve to know their son."

His words hung in the air between them and Laney absorbed them with her heart. She knew Bryan spoke the truth and she hoped he'd feel the same about Alex, her biological son. She hoped he loved her enough to share her with the son of another man.

Should she tell him? Something inside caused her to hesitate. His concern for Evan occupied everything he did right now. It didn't seem fair to increase his troubles just to ease her conscience.

CHAPTER 52

Maggie paced the floor near the baggage claim area. She glanced at her watch, nine fifteen. She scanned the area for Craig's lanky figure. The monitor showed his flight as being on time. How would she tell him all that's happened? He would be shocked by the turn of events.

"Hey, lady." Craig's sparkling eyes beamed down on her. "Breakfast?"

"Craig!" She wrapped her arms around him and squeezed his neck. When they parted, his huge grin and wide eyes made her smile. The emotional hug had surprised them both.

He put his arm around her shoulders. She missed the closeness. Had Craig been the one to distance himself or had it been her? She'd been so consumed by her guilt and pain she'd pushed him away. She understood that now. Finding Paul brought a new perspective to her life.

Maggie draped her arm around his waist and allowed him to guide her toward the luggage carousel. He looked down at her. "It's so good to be back home." He squeezed her shoulders. "With you."

His words spread warmth through her. "I've got a lot to

tell you. So much has happened this week."

"Sounds like you and Laney connected. Do you think you two will become good friends?"

She smiled. "Oh yeah. We already have."

"Have you? That's great." He graced her with an enchanting smile then reached for his bag and heaved it off the belt. "I'm ready to hear about your mysterious adventures."

Once again, she put her arm around Craig's waist and gave him a gentle squeeze. "It will take a while."

Thirty minutes later, they settled into a popular breakfast restaurant and surveyed the menu. "I'll have the pancakes and fruit." Maggie handed the menu back to the waitress.

"I'll have the hungry man." He also handed back the menu then smiled at Maggie. "I'm starved." He reached across the table and grabbed her index finger. A broad smile stretched across his face. "Tell me about your week."

She took a gulp of water. "Craig." She locked her eyes on his. "Paul is alive. I saw him. Two weeks ago."

His brows arched, shoulders stiffened, and his brilliant smile faded. His widened eyes met her gaze. "You think you saw Paul? Two weeks ago? Why didn't you tell me?"

Maggie curled her index finger around his. "I'm sorry, but honestly Craig. Would you have believed me?"

His shoulders relaxed and the angle of his jaw softened. "Probably not."

She told him all the details, about the striking resemblance, and all the connections. About Laney seeing Craig at the cleaners and about Laney's help in New Orleans. While she relayed the events of their time at Hazel's, the waitress interrupted with their order. Maggie slid the photographs from her purse onto the table next to Craig. Then poured warm maple syrup over her pancakes while Craig surveyed the pictures.

"Laney gave me that one." She pointed to the photograph not in a frame. "She took it a couple of days after he came to live with them."

He held the photos side by side. "It's Paul. There's no mistaking those eyes and smile."

She continued with the details of their search for Paul's records.

"Mr. Mouchaux's brother had a warehouse—"

Craig's hand, holding a fork filled with scrambled eggs, stopped midway to his mouth. "What did you say?"

"Mr. Mouchaux, Henri. The Ellerby's attorney. His law firm set up all the adoptions. And we think was responsible for the abductions, including Paul's."

"Henri Mouchaux, Henri Mouchaux. Where did I hear that name?" He creased his brows, deepening the lines on his forehead. Then a glint of recognition relaxed the muscles. His eyes clouded then his cheeks drained leaving a pale facsimile of his face. He whispered. "Henri Mouchaux, the Garrison Group's attorney. Oh, no. It can't be."

"Craig, what is it?"

"Do you remember the shopping center I designed then lost the bid on?"

"That was a long time ago."

"Twenty years."

A shiver akin to a thousand ants crawling on her skin ran the length of her body. "Craig?"

"One of their investors tried to get me to overbid the job. By one hundred thousand dollars. He said he could guarantee I got the job, but it would cost me. He wanted fifty thousand dollars and said I could keep the other fifty."

He sipped from his coffee cup then ran a trembling hand through his blonde hair. "I reported him to the group. They gave him his money back and kicked him off the project. He lost a lot of money on that deal. His name was Henri Mouchaux."

Maggie gasped and when the full reality hit her, her hand flew to her mouth. "Oh, no. Craig, Paul's kidnapping wasn't random? Do you think Mouchaux did it as revenge? Targeted us?" Her hands began shaking and her stomach twisted. She lowered her fork.

"It's very possible. When Mouchaux found out I'd told the group about his proposition, he threatened to ruin me." Craig exhaled and shook his head in slow back and forth movements. "I never connected the kidnapping to Mouchaux. It happened a couple months after I lost the bid. I figured he'd talked the group into not trusting me. That was his payback—me losing the bid."

Maggie remembered how disappointed Craig had been he'd lost the job. He'd moped for weeks, but he'd never said anything about Mouchaux's threat.

All those years she thought Paul's abduction had been due to her carelessness. The small consolation she'd been targeted took some of the guilt away. She'd given them a small window of opportunity and they'd been like vultures waiting to snatch her son.

"I can't believe he could do this. What kind of person is so cruel?" She went on, telling him about the payment Bryan Ellerby had made.

A line formed when Craig pressed his lips together. "So Bryan paid Mouchaux to take our son." The blue of his eyes changed from soft, sky blue to a steely, cold gray. "Laney, your friend's husband paid to have my little boy, my baby, taken from me." He stood, threw several bills on the table and rushed out the door.

She sat. Stunned into silence. Never had she seen Craig act this way. Never seen him so angry. Not even after Paul had been taken. She hadn't had a chance to tell him the truth about Bryan's part in the payment. She stood on shaking legs and followed the path Craig had taken toward the door. She found him sitting in their car, his head resting on the steering wheel.

Maggie slid into the passenger seat. Quiet sobs filled the car. Craig crying? Not Craig, the man who stood strong and emotionless during the entire investigation into Paul's abduction. The man who never showed his emotions. Who always looked at things from a rational point of view.

She reached for his shoulder, stopped midway, then reached again and let her hand rest there. "Craig?" she whispered. "Honey, don't blame Bryan He didn't know about Mouchaux."

"Then why did he pay him?"

"He thought the payment was to move their names higher to get the next available child."

"Besides..." He lifted his head and stared at her. Large drops glistened in his eyes. "...it's my fault. I was responsible for our son...for losing...for..."

"You can't blame yourself. You had no idea. You did the right thing," she said.

He remained silent. His Adam's apple bobbled along his throat. He reached for her and brushed her cheek with the back of his fingers. Then after he let out a forceful gust of air, he spoke. "Maggie, oh, my sweet Maggie...I...blamed you. I didn't want to, but I did. I thought you'd neglected our son. I'm so sorry. I'm so sorry."

His words cut through to a place in her heart that had lived in dark denial for so long, the truth's illuminating light scorched. She wanted anger to rise from the ashes and lash out at Craig, but something else filled her. His pleading eyes, tempered with soothing compassion, healed. Because now she knew. Now she could deal with what they'd both avoided for twenty years.

"I knew you blamed me," she said. "But somehow, I also knew how hard you tried not to."

"Can you ever forgive me?"

Forgive him? Did she have the capacity to forgive the ache, the neglect, all the time lost in blame and denial? Their future depended on forgiveness. Healing depended on forgiveness. Their happiness depended on it, too. Did she have any other choice but to forgive?

She nodded. "Yes."

He embraced her. "I love you."

"I love you, too."

He pulled away. "I can't believe our son is alive. When

do I get to meet this young man who you think is Paul? Who looks like me?"

She met his gaze. "Ah, honey, that's the sad part. He was in a horrible car accident yesterday. His prognosis is questionable, but he's stable right now. The hospital is asking for blood donors. Craig, he has the same blood type you have."

"I'll be happy to donate. But Maggie that's not solid proof this boy is Paul. I know there's a lot of circumstantial evidence here."

"I know. But these things are more than coincidence. The puzzle pieces fit. And he looks exactly like you."

"What about DNA testing is that an option?"

"It's always an option, but Paul..er..Evan refused."

"We could get a court order."

"Yes, we could. But Craig, is that what we want? I don't want to force him."

Craig nodded. "I guess you're right."

"Ready to go to the hospital?"

He paused. "I guess the Ellerbys will be there."

"Yes."

"I'm not sure I can face Bryan. He paid Mouchaux? What kind of man pays someone for a child?"

Maggie closed her eyes. The situation was too complicated for words. She faced her husband. "You'll have to meet him. I think once you do, you'll understand."

He stood and extended his hand to her. "We'll see. I'll donate first."

Maggie placed her hand in his, but the doubt she saw in his eyes caused a sliver of fear to prick. What if Craig and Bryan squared off?

****

Laney leaned against Bryan while trying to absorb the words from the doctor who stood at the foot of Evan's bed. He met Laney's gaze. "The CT scan looks good. The swelling has dropped. But we've had to put him on dialysis. His remaining kidney is failing. Right now his best bet is a transplant."

"A kidney transplant. How can we test to see if we're compatible?"

"Our lab can tell you more. You can go down there to get the details."

A moan stirred from the bed. Laney rushed to Evan's side. "Honey, it's Mom. Evan, talk to me."

He moaned again. "Mmm."

Bryan stood beside Laney then placed his hand on the handrail. "Son, you're going to be all right. Hang on."

"Daaaad. My head hurts."

"I know, son. The doctor will get you something. You're going to be okay." Bryan turned toward Dr. Thomas. "Right doc?"

"Yes, I'll get something for the pain. Evan, are you hurting anywhere else."

"Sore all over."

Laney rested her head on Bryan's shoulder to let his strength support her, absorb her pain. Then she reached over and patted Evan's hand. "You rest now. You need your strength to heal." The words tumbled out with a mixture of tears. She fought to be strong. Evan needed her as a pillar of strength, not a quivering tower of gelatin.

After they said goodbye and encouraged him, the doctor ushered Bryan and Laney out the room. He paused at the nurse's station to give instructions.

Laney laced her fingers through Bryan's. As they turned the corner toward the waiting room, she saw Maggie and Craig seated at the far end. Her heart fluttered when she saw her best friend. The sensation increased when she saw Craig's face. She tried to avert her gaze but the pull proved too strong. She wanted to lose herself in Craig's perfect features. She imagined her son's face looking like that again—even if Craig's features were those of someone over thirty years older.

She rushed to them. When Maggie stood she gave her a hug. "He woke up."

"Really? Oh, that's great news." Maggie's brow relaxed then tightened again. She turned to Bryan. Laney followed her gaze. "Bryan, my husband, Craig."

Bryan's eyes widened and his mouth parted, but he didn't speak. He stared at Craig and after a long pause, he finally spoke. "My goodness, the resemblance is uncanny." He extended his hand in an unhurried motion. As though someone else controlled the act. "Mr. Langston, you are the spitting image of my son..." He paused. "...our son."

Craig's posture stiffened and his shoulders squared. "Mr. Ellerby." He accepted Bryan's hand and shook it. "We just returned from the lab."

Bryan's brows creased.

"Donated blood," Craig said.

"Oh, yes. Thank you."

Laney looked toward Craig. "Hello."

"Laney, hello."

"Tell me everything about Pau...sorry, Evan?" Maggie shook her head.

Laney smiled. "It's okay. He woke for a moment." She relayed what Evan had said and the latest update on his condition.

Maggie lifted fisted hands. "That's great about the swelling. Thank goodness."

Bryan held up a hand. "He's not out of the woods though. He lost a kidney and his remaining kidney is malfunctioning. He needs a donor. They've added him to the donor list but it could be a long time before he could get a compatible match."

Maggie reached for Laney's hand. "No."

"We'll get tested to see if we're a match. We know the odds are against us but it's worth a try."

Maggie and Craig locked gazes. Laney felt she could read their thoughts. Would they also be tested?

Craig turned to Bryan. "Can we see him?"

Maggie spoke up, "Honey, if he's awake. Seeing us may be a shock. Our presence may be too much for him right now."

"I'm sorry. I didn't even think about what seeing us would do."

CHAPTER 53

*A*fter Laney and Bryan left for the lab, Craig turned to Maggie. His jaw set. "I'll get tested."

Maggie smiled at her husband. Emotion thick in her throat. The sentiment started at the base of her heart and worked its way through all the pain and torment of the past to explode onto her lips. She hoped Craig saw her smile for exactly what it was. He'd made her a very happy woman. He believed Evan was Paul. Why else would he be willing to donate one of his kidneys?

"Are you serious?" Maggie asked.

"Yes. If I'm a match, then that will further prove he's my son." As though afraid he'd hurt Maggie's feelings, he reached for her hand. "Our son."

"Yes, our son. Which means we *both* get tested. I want him to have every fighting chance."

Craig nodded. "Hopefully, I'll be a match and we'll never have to consider putting you through that surgery."

She locked her fingers through his and allowed his strength and warmth to support her while they waited for the Ellerbys to return.

After what seemed an eternity, Laney and Bryan walked

into the waiting room. Laney's eyes drooped at the corners and the bags beneath Bryan's eyes seemed to have doubled in size since he'd left.

Maggie stood. "Laney what is it?"

"Well, the good news is because Evan's blood type is AB, he's considered a universal recipient, so we were able to donate blood. The not so good news, they test for something they called HLA. They told us the odds were not in our favor because we were not his biological parents." She averted her gaze and then lowered her eyelids as though she lacked the energy to keep them opened.

Maggie wrapped her arms around Laney's shoulders. "Craig and I will go. We'll both get tested. " She looked back toward Craig. He nodded.

Laney returned Maggie's hug and held onto Maggie as though she was a life preserver and Laney was drowning.

Maggie's phone rang breaking the bond between the two women. She glanced at the phone and frowned when she didn't recognize the number. "Hello."

"Maggie, it's Hazel. I remembered something after y'all left. Mr. Mouchaux said something about an attorney friend of his holding some files from the warehouse. I contacted the police and told them about it. They contacted the man and he still had them in his archives. They found all of them. Oh, and they found Salter and brought him in for questioning."

Was Paul's file there, too? Maggie's hand trembled as she transferred the call to the speaker so Laney could hear. "So the police have all the files?"

Maggie looked at Laney who mouthed, *Evan's?* Maggie nodded.

"Yes. But I have a copy of the Ellerby's file and wanted to get Laney's number from you so I can get her address."

Laney stepped closer to the phone. "I'm right here, Hazel." She gave Hazel her new mailing address.

"I'll get this out by overnight mail today. You should get it tomorrow. Oh, and would you keep this between the three of us?"

Maggie glanced toward Bryan and Craig. They both nodded. "Sure," Maggie said.

"Okay." Laney's brow tightened. "But Hazel, I don't understand."

"Let's just say it helps to know a certain Detective's mother."

Maggie and Laney thanked Hazel. "Oh, Hazel, please pray." Laney told her about Evan's condition."

"Oh, Laney, I'm so sorry. I'll call all my prayer warriors and have them praying for Evan. I'll call Rosie, too. She'll get the word out."

Once they'd said their goodbyes, Maggie disconnected the call and turned to Laney.

"Pretty powerful woman there. I bet her phone is burning up calling all her friends asking for prayers. I suppose Detective Thibodeaux's mother is one."

Laney nodded. A weak smile curled the corner of her lips. "Yep, I'm sure she is. I shudder to think of what pressure Hazel used through his mother to get the Detective to give her a copy of Evan's file."

The day dragged on as they sat together waiting for the next visiting hours. To Maggie's relief, Bryan and Craig chatted and found they had much in common.

Not much changed over the evening.

The next morning, Maggie checked in at work and discovered her schedule was full. Eric had done a great job and carried the full load while she traveled. Today they switched places, she carried the load while Eric spent the day with Bryan and Laney at the hospital.

She needed to focus on her patients. They needed her today and as much as she wanted to be at the hospital, she knew right now her place was here.

The morning flew by. The usual number of ear infections, chest congestions, and other maladies typical for children filled her time. She had a two hour break between patients during lunch so instead of catching up on paperwork, she decided to drive to the hospital.

When she entered the waiting area, Eric, Bryan, and Laney stood. "Maggie, you're just in time." Laney lifted a FedEx envelope.

"Is that what I think it is?" she asked.

"It is." Laney linked her arm through Maggie's "C'mon." She led her to the last row of chairs where Eric and Bryan had formed a circle. Bryan and Maggie sat on either side of Laney.

Laney took a deep breath. Maggie followed with a sharp inhale of her own. Laney ripped the envelope open and slid out the documents. A familiar manila folder rested in her palm. She peeled back the cover. The front sheet was the typical entry sheet Henri Mouchaux completed for each of his clients. Attached by a paperclip was a photograph of Laney and Bryan. Their younger smiling faces stared from the Polaroid.

Maggie's phone rang. Craig. She walked to the hallway and answered the call. "Hi, honey."

"I'm downstairs at the hospital and wanted to know if you had a moment to meet me here."

Wow, Craig at the hospital. He really cared. *Why didn't I ask him to come with me?* "Craig, I'm in the waiting room. Come up. We have the adoption file."

Maggie returned to her seat and let them know Craig was on his way.

Laney rested her hands on the folder. "We'll wait for him." She glanced at Bryan. "We *all* deserve to know."

Moments later Craig entered the room. His breath short. "What did I miss?"

Bryan answered, "Nothing yet."

Craig stood behind Maggie and looked over Laney's shoulder as she opened the file.

Maggie glanced toward Laney. They both knew the next page contained a list of possible candidates. She lifted the edge and flipped it over. There before them, like all the other files, was the page of candidates. Midway down the list was the proof they needed. Staring back at them—Paul Langston, Pecan Pointe, LA.

Laney lifted her hand to her mouth. Craig ran his hand through his hair and Bryan pressed his lips together while shaking his head.

After a moment, Laney broke the silence. "Maggie, now we all know what you knew all along. Evan is Paul."

Craig's facial features tensed. He kissed Maggie on the cheek. "My sweet Maggie. You knew. You knew all these years." He stepped away. "I think I'll head down to the lab." He looked toward Laney and Bryan. "Our son needs a kidney and I think I might have one I can spare."

"Are you okay?" Bryan looked toward Laney.

Laney smiled. "Yes, I am. If I have to share my son..." She linked her arm through Maggie's. "...I can't think of a better woman to share him with. "

Bryan walked toward Craig. "I think I'll walk to the lab with Craig."

"Hey, wait for me. I'm coming, too." Eric followed.

Maggie wrapped her arm around Laney's shoulder and watched her husband, Bryan, and Eric leave the waiting room. Each believing like her that Paul had been found.

Gratitude spilled from Maggie's rejoicing heart. "Thank you, Lord. Thank you."

As Eric and Bryan entered one elevator another one opened and several women exited. Rosamie Chabert, Hazel's sister led the group. Behind her, Maggie's friend and Elizabeth's mother, Grace appeared. Maggie rushed to her.

"Grace, you're here." She spread her arms and Grace embraced her. "Oh, Maggie, it's so good to see you again. I'm so sorry. Rosamie filled us in on the way over."

Maggie glanced at several faces standing behind Rosamie, Elizabeth's included. Maggie recognized several of the women. She'd seen them around Pecan Pointe, knew who they were but had always been too busy and too closed off to meet them.

Grace stood back. "These are a few ladies from Rosamie's Bible study group. Elizabeth talked me into visiting with her last night and when we heard the request...well." Grace paused, tears forming. "We had to come." She pointed toward an elegant lady about Maggie's age with golden brown hair wrapped in a French twist. "This is Jacqueline Dugas used to be Ledet. Her husband, Frank went to law school with me and Jacob. This is Sylvia Duplantis, her husband, Douglas is also an attorney we knew from Tulane. They're partners in Ledet, Arceneaux, Dugas, and Duplantis. The big firm in Baton Rouge."

Maggie extended her hand to each of the ladies. "Nice to meet you."

Maggie glanced toward Laney. "Grace, Elizabeth, Rosamie, Jacqueline, Sylvia, this is my very best friend, who has just moved to Pecan Pointe, Laney Ellerby."

Rosamie stepped forward and cupped Laney's elbows. "It is a great pleasure ta meet you. My sistah has told me so much about you. We won't stay long. Jus' stopped by to let you know we are here for both of you and are praying for your boy." She glanced toward Maggie. "Yours too, from what I understand. We know that all things happen in God's perfect timing."

Maggie pushed back the rush of tears and simply nodded.

Grace handed Maggie a basket filled with homemade snacks. "We brought these. We each added a little something. Rosamie, of course, added her famous pralines. Mama made the blueberry muffins. We're all thinking of y'all." Grace wrapped her arms around Maggie. Her closeness brought back the nights they'd helped one another study. Grace pressing to get into law school while Maggie worked to fulfill her lifelong dream of being a Pediatrician. They'd been good friends. When Paul had disappeared Maggie had pushed Grace away. A pang of guilt twitched her heart. Maybe now they could rekindle their neglected friendship even though Grace lived in

Biloxi.

After the women left, the waiting room took on a quiet calm. The words from the prayers they'd prayed for Maggie and Laney lingered. Hanging on like a perfumed mist sweetening the air and their hearts. For the first time in her life, Maggie embraced the peace she'd denied herself for far too long.

CHAPTER 54

Several days later, Maggie and Craig walked into Paul's private room. They shared the news they'd received—Craig was a viable donor. Laney and Bryan stood at his bedside along with the portable dialysis machine. His bruises had turned a kaleidoscope of yellows, purples, and greens.

"Mrs. Langston, hello, again." Paul sat upright in the electronic hospital bed. His gaze lingered on Craig. "Wow, I can see why you thought I was your son." He turned to Maggie. "He looks like an older version of me." He smiled and shrugged. "Sorry about the older part."

Craig walked to the bedside. His first visit to the son he had not seen in over twenty years. He extended his hand. "Craig Langston."

Paul lifted his right hand. "Evan Ellerby."

The vein in Craig's neck pumped. Maggie knew how much hearing her son identify himself by a different name stung. "It's nice to meet you. Have your…parents told you why we're here?"

"Yes, evidently you're a donor match. Mom told me. You're my biological parents. And you're willing to give me one of your kidneys."

"That's true." Craig nodded. "I am."

"I don't know how to thank you. Your gift means a lot to me. I don't know what to say. I can't imagine what you went through all those years. Can you tell me how, you know, it happened?"

Maggie cleared her throat and met Craig's gaze. He nodded. She stepped closer to his bed and let her fingers brush the sheet next to his arm. "We were at the park..." She told him the whole sordid story and several times she paused to fight the onslaught of tears.

His eyes glistened in the florescent lights. "Mrs. Langston—"

"Please call me Maggie." Mother. Mom. Mama.

"I'm really sorry for the way I acted at Uncle Eric's house. I didn't mean to come across so coldly. It was such a shock..."

"You don't have to apologize. I think we were both in shock. I know when I looked into your face, I certainly went into shock." She laughed in an effort to ease the tension in the room.

The corner of his lip curved. "I'm thankful to God that he brought us back together."

Maggie's heart twitched. Gratitude overflowed. Maybe God's hand *had* moved to bring her son back to her.

****

Four weeks later, Laney folded Evan's T-shirt, and added it to the pile of his clothes. It had been a little over two weeks since his surgery and he recovered more each day. Gaining strength and returning to his old self.

She'd returned to her youth group last Sunday and found that she'd missed them. A month and a half passed since her visit to Hank Davenport's Texas farmhouse and still no word from Alex. At first, the vigil at Evan's bedside had occupied her mind. Next the surgery and recovery dominated her waking days. But now, with Evan home and doing better, Alex entered her mind.

Wouldn't she have heard from him by now? Mr.

Davenport seemed so certain Alex would want to meet her. Could the old man have been wrong?

Laney returned to her preparations. In celebration of Evan's recovery, they were having a Fourth of July party at their new home in a couple of weeks. Maggie promised to help. Craig would attend depending on how he felt. His recovery was taking a little longer than Evan's.

"Honey, do you need some help?" Bryan appeared in the archway separating the kitchen and family room.

Her heart pounded. She'd prayed for guidance on when to tell Bryan about Alex. Prayed for the Lord to open the door so she could clear everything between them. Now seemed like as good a time as any. "Actually, I'd like to talk with you. Is Evan okay?"

"Yes, Casey is with him if he needs anything, she'll get it for him."

"Good, let's sit out on the deck. I'll get the coffee."

"Sure. I'll help. This sounds serious. Everything okay?" He reached for the coffee cups.

Laney carried the filled carafe. If he only knew. The anxiety Laney thought would press on her wasn't there. She'd prayed about this moment and knew the Lord would protect their marriage.

Once on the back porch, they settled at the outdoor table. Although the balmy night withheld any natural breeze, two ceiling fans whirled, churning a slight, though warm, draft.

Bryan sipped from his cup then leaned forward and grabbed Laney's hand. "So what is so important you didn't insist I take out the trash." His laughter echoed under the small porch.

She laughed along with him. "Very funny. But you still have to take out the trash later. In all seriousness, I do have something important to share with you."

Rapt attention replaced the jovial glitter in his eyes. "I'm listening. Is Evan okay?"

"Evan's fine. This isn't about him." She sat upright in

the wrought iron chair.

"Remember I told you I lived with my aunt while in college?"

He nodded.

"Well, as a Freshman at CSU, I had an affair with my English Lit professor."

Bryan's brows crunched and his hands twitched in hers.

"I got pregnant."

His eyes widened. "You what?"

"Got pregnant."

He shook his head. "Laney, what...what are you saying?"

She lifted her palm and gently stroked his cheek. "Let me finish." She told him everything. No more secrets between them.

His focus so intense she had to avert her gaze. His silence made her pulse race. Was he angry? She couldn't tell.

"So Maggie and I visited Mr. Davenport."

"So." He paused and stared at her. "That's where you and Maggie went."

She let out a long sigh. "Are you upset? Do you hate me?"

He held her hand and slowly shook his head. "Ah, sweetie. I don't hate you. I am upset because you didn't trust that you could tell me. Guess I know how you felt about me not telling you about the payment." He gave her hands a gentle squeeze. "Is it possible Mr. Davenport forgot to give Alex the letter?"

"I don't know. But Bryan I want to know how you feel about this."

He pushed his breath through pursed lips. "Laney, it's been a crazy couple of months. So many things to take in. I found out the boy I claimed as my son really is the son of another couple. He was kidnapped from them and not the person we were told he was. Now my wife of twenty-five years is telling me she gave birth to a son before we met that she gave away and didn't trust me enough to tell me about. This is tough. The two people I thought I knew most in this world have made me question. Question myself."

"But..." He brought her fingers to his lips and kissed the tips. "Laney there is one thing I don't question, no matter what happens." He embraced both her hands in his. "I love you. That will never change. I'm hurt you didn't trust me or our love enough to share this with me sooner. But I guess I'm not in a position to say much after the secret I kept from you."

"I'd say that's a little different."

"Maybe, but Alex is not a bad thing. I would love for you to get to know him. For him to be a part of our family. But honey, please don't be too hard on yourself if you don't hear from him. There could be any number of reasons he hasn't called."

She leaned forward and gave him a tender kiss. "I know. You're right. I tell myself the same thing. Bryan, thank you. Thanks for being such a wonderful husband and for understanding. I should never have kept this from you. Honestly, I never thought I'd see my firstborn again."

"If it's God's will for Alex to be a part of your life, then it will happen. You've done your part, now the rest is up to God." He lifted her chin with his index finger and pressed his lips to hers. He pulled away and whispered in her ear, "okay?"

"Okay." Bryan was right. God had opened the window for her to pour her heart out to Bryan and he'd taken the news well. She just needed to trust God would do the same for paving the way for Alex to be in her life. "Bryan?"

"Yes."

"I love you."

"I love you, too."

Thank you, Lord. Laney's heart lifted and the constant lead ball she'd carried in her stomach disappeared. She didn't realize how much of a burden she'd carried with her secret.

#

The next Sunday, when Laney entered the building, Tamara greeted her at the door. "He's here, Mrs. Ellerby. Caleb is here."

Caleb? Yes, Laney had forgotten calling Tamara's boyfriend and inviting him to join their group. Had it really been less than two months? It seemed so long ago. So much had happened to change the way she viewed herself and the world. Today she had a special class planned and she prayed her lesson would reach into the hearts of her students. "That's exciting Tamara. Any reason why he came today?"

"No. He called and said he would pick me up for church."

More students filed in, including a tall boy with long dark hair Laney suspected was Caleb. Her suspicions were confirmed when Tamara introduced them.

Once all her students were seated, she sat on a large pillow within their circle. "Today we'll be continuing our discussion about purity."

Several groans emanated from the opposite side of the room. Mostly boys who usually served as the class clowns. "Anybody want to open our group in prayer?"

Tamara raised her hand. Laney nodded toward the young girl.

She bowed her head and began. "Father God, thank You for our time together today. Lord, guide each one of us to follow Your will, seek your guidance, and open our hearts to accept what You have for us. Father, thank You also for healing Evan and making the situation with the Ellerbys one showcasing how good you are to Your children. Amen."

Laney kept her head bowed, but smiled at the sincerity of Tamara's prayer. She settled into the pillow then met the gaze of each of the students.

"I'd like to share a story with all of you." *Lord, give me the words and the strength.* "This is not an easy story to share, but I believe something a friend said a long time ago is true. God uses the broken places in us to reach others. I hope my story will reach some of you."

She shifted her position and glanced at Tamara. The young girl smiled and winked. Funny how the teenager was now Laney's encouragement. They'd swapped roles.

Laney began, "When I was in college..."

She told her students her story and shared with them the pain she'd lived with because of her poor choices. She hoped her mistake would be a glaring example of what not to do. She drove the point home—how the consequences of her choice still tormented and affected her family today, almost thirty years later.

She searched their hearts through the engrossed eyes focused on her. Usually, at least one of her students would fiddle with a cellphone or some other distraction while she taught, but not today. Each student gave her their full attention. They seemed to absorb her words.

"Any questions?" she asked when she finished.

Devin, a shy boy who rarely spoke raised his hand. "Do you think he'll call?"

"I'm not sure, but I've turned the situation over to God and trust what's best is what will happen."

Catherine, sitting next to Tamera, asked, "what did it feel like to give away your baby?"

Laney paused. How could she put into words what she'd felt?

She inhaled and shifted into a better position to meet their attentive gazes. "It felt like someone opened my chest and ripped a part of my heart out. Although it heals over time, the pain never really goes away. I wouldn't want any of you to know what that feels like."

One of the class clowns shifted in his chair. He flipped a lock of hair from his eyes then asked, "what about the dad?"

"Well, at the time he wanted me to get an abortion, even gave me the money to do it. But I couldn't. I couldn't take my baby's life. He never knew I had the baby."

She told them about her aunt's role in keeping the truth from Mallory. "I know he regrets the past. Probably more so than I did. He's a Christian now and has come to realize the sins of his past have been forgiven, but he's paid a hefty price through the consequences."

The young man stared at her for a moment, then his eyes glazed over as though he'd traveled to another place. "Do you think he regrets doing what he did?"

"Yes, he does. After all this time he told me so."

"Then everything is good now, right?"

"Yes, but just because we know God forgives with His infinite grace, doesn't mean we can blindly walk in sin. Yes, we'll be forgiven if we truly repent, but know this: sin has consequences and sometimes those consequences are costly to us and the ones we love."

She sensed she may have gone a tad bit too far in the preaching department. A couple of kids focused on their cell phone. Tough words sometimes had a way of pushing them away. She wanted to let the importance of what she'd said sink in and didn't want to dilute the message by going further. "Okay, any more questions? Thoughts?"

The sounds of birds chirping outside the classroom window was all that could be heard. "Very well. If any of you ever need someone to talk with or have any questions, I'm available. Everyone have my numbers? She pointed to the corner of the board where she'd written them the first day she'd arrived.

She closed in prayer and stood to gather her belongings while her students filed out the room. In the quiet, she bowed her head. *Thank you Lord, for the strength and the words.*

"Mrs. Ellerby?"

Laney looked up. Jessica a quiet girl who'd been in her class the last three Sundays stood next to the door frame. "Yes?"

Jessica walked closer into the room. "I got half-way

down the hall then felt this overwhelming pressure to tell you this..." She pressed her lips together. "Thank you for sharing your story. I know it was hard. You see my boyfriend and I have...well, we've come close a few times and I've always been the one to stop. I've been thinking lately I might want to...or maybe..."

She lowered her gaze and drew imaginary circles on the corner of Laney's desk. "I don't know, it seems my resolve has weakened and I was thinking I would go further, maybe all the way. But what you said to us today really made me think about the consequences. Made me want to wait." She lifted her head and Laney met her sweet blue-eyed gaze. "Thank you, Mrs. Ellerby for sharing."

Laney resisted a rush of tears. She couldn't give way to the emotion because once she did, she wasn't sure how far the wave would take her. She slid her hand along the bone of Jessica's tender cheek. "Thank you, honey, for being brave enough to come back here to tell me. It means a lot."

After Jessica left the room, Laney stared out the window. The leaves on the large oak tree blurred into a melted green canvas. The chirping birds dimmed into the background. Their sounds lost by her friend's words vibrating through her brain. *He uses the broken places. He uses the broken vessels.*

CHAPTER 55

"*Y*our pain pills." Maggie handed Craig a glass of water along with his 4:00 p.m. medication. Although it had been a little over two weeks since the surgery, Craig was ready to resume his normal activities even though his body wasn't.

He leaned forward in the recliner and winced. "I'm ready for this soreness to go away. Have you spoken to Laney? How's Evan?"

"She called this morning. He's doing well. He actually went for a walk around the block yesterday and is whining about wanting to drive."

Craig gulped down the pills then relaxed in the chair. "Do you think he'll ever accept us as his parents?"

Maggie pondered the question. "I don't know, but it really doesn't matter. He's alive and doing well. Craig, for the first time in my life, I believe God protected Paul."

Craig arched an eyebrow. "You really believe that?"

She nodded and a smile spread her lips. "Yeah, I think I do. Look at the chain of recent events bringing us to this point at this time. It has to be more than coincidence. When Evan needed a kidney, we were in his life. Craig you were given the awesome privilege to give our son a second chance at life. That is no accident. I still have trouble trusting completely, but I see things in a different light now. And it's okay if Evan isn't an active part of our life. I know he's safe. Now I can rest."

"That's a far cry from where you were just a few months ago."

She shrugged her shoulders. Could she voice her thoughts and feelings out loud? She swallowed through the emotions threatening to choke her. Her heart lifted as though a guiding hand kept her from falling prey to the familiar demonic tortures she'd endured for many years.

Somehow God's hand stirred in the midst of her life. Why? She didn't deserve it. She didn't know exactly how or why, but she knew this newfound peace was no accident. A quick glance at her devoted husband shifting to find a comfortable pain-free position reassured that her feelings were not just emotion, but came from a certainty she'd never known before.

She sat on the arm of Craig's recliner. "Now that I know it wasn't anything I did wrong, it makes things easier for me."

"What do you mean?"

"The pain of losing Paul consumed me. I lived thinking it was my fault." She laced her fingers through his. "I thought I didn't deserve to be loved or to love. If I loved you, I was afraid I'd lose you too. Everyone I ever loved left. First my Dad, then Paul. I couldn't stand to lose you, too."

Craig looked up at her. "You know you're the love of my life. I've always loved you. Ever since that day in the grocery store. Your sweet smile and funny grin when those oranges rolled off the table will always be a memory I treasure." He lifted her hand and pressed the back to his lips. "It's one of the memories that kept me going when I thought I'd lost you."

Maggie ran her fingers through Craig's hair. The

memory warmed her. Reminded her of what she felt for him. "I knew the day you helped me chase those run-away oranges you'd be my husband. I'd never been so sure of anything in my life."

"Then how could Paul's disappearance drive such a wedge between us?"

"I don't know. At first, I just didn't want to feel anything because it hurt so much. Then after time, it became a way of life. I felt you blamed me which only fueled my self-blame. Then later, even when I wanted to open my heart, I couldn't. It was as though I followed this irreversible path. And fear. Afraid if I opened to you, the pain would take over and I'd drown in it."

He rubbed his index finger along the top of her hand. "I'm as much to blame. I was afraid I'd push you away. It was easier to bury myself in work than to face the reality of our shattered life. But I never once thought about living without you."

She met Craig's compassionate gaze. "Thank you for standing beside me all these years. I know I wasn't the best wife I could have been, but I think I'd like to start fresh."

Craig's lip curled slightly toward the right, highlighting a small dimple Maggie adored. "Don't be so hard on yourself. I wasn't the best husband. We both let the situation turn us away from the other." His lips spread to reveal an endearing smile. "I'm all for a fresh start."

Maggie straightened on the recliner's arm. "Craig?"

"Yeah."

"I'm thinking of joining a Bible study that Rosamie leads. She's a self-appointed mentor of women here in Pecan Pointe."

"That sounds wonderful."

"I also think I want to try this church thing. Laney invited me to go with her this Sunday. Would you come with me?"

He ran his hand through her hair then cupped her cheek in his palm. "Sure I'll go. I can't tell you what it means to me to see you like this. Not only do I have my son back, in whatever way he'll have us, but I'm so grateful I have my wife back."

The doorbell sounded. "I'll get it." Maggie brushed a gentle kiss on Craig's lips before she stood and headed for the front door. His words warmed her heart.

As she approached the foyer, a tall lanky figure stood in silhouette through the beveled glass. It couldn't be. Or could it? She quickened her steps and opened the door. Yes, there on her welcome mat shifting from one foot to the other stood Paul. Alone.

The slight breeze from flinging the door brushed across her face. "P—Evan, hello. It's good to see you out and about."

He nodded.

She stared and remained still.

So did Evan. Only his face changed. His uncertainty flashed on and off like a neon sign. For a moment, she thought he might turn and flee. Finally, her senses awakened and she slid aside. "Come in."

He pinched his bottom lip with his thumb and index finger and resumed the familiar weight-shifting dance Maggie knew so well. She'd lived with its inventor for the past twenty-five years.

His uncertainty carved a hole through her. The image flashed of Paul at Eric's house the first night she'd seen him. She wanted her presence to give him comfort. Peace. Not this soul-twisting angst. She reached out to him. "It's okay, we're glad you came, please come in."

He lifted one foot over the threshold then hesitated. "I hope I'm not intruding. Maybe I should have called."

"It's fine. Craig was just asking about you. He'll be glad to see you."

He entered. Each step measured and slow. Similar to a hungry animal being offered food by a stranger. He stopped just inside the door allowing just enough room for her to close it. "Is he doing okay?"

"A little sore, but he'll be fine. C'mon, he's in the living room."

He stared for a moment and in a second, his eyes exposed the two-year-old boy who had lifted his hands in a gesture for her to pick him up. A rare treat. At two, his independent streak usually prevailed. She placed her hand on his arm and guided him toward the living room. He let her.

"Craig, there's someone here to see you." She guided Paul to the couch next to the recliner.

"Hey man, it's good to see you." Craig extended his hand. "Look at you walking around. Did you drive over?"

"Casey dropped me off." Before he sat, he turned to Maggie and blinked several times before he spoke. "I came to see both of you."

Fear as real as the day she'd lost him in the park, rushed in. Was he here to tell them he wanted nothing to do with them? Here to say a quick thank you for the kidney, but that's where the connection stopped?

Relax. Breathe. Remember, it's his choice. Remember, he's alright. Remember, he's alive. She inhaled and lowered herself to the couch. Paul did the same. Her son sat less than a foot from her. The woodsy scent of his cologne drifted toward her. Quite different from the smell of animal crackers.

The room seemed to grow—become a large cavern filled with years of questions, pain, doubt, fear, guilt. The widening space dictated the tone. Maggie watched Paul. Drank in his presence and wondered what he'd be like had he lived with her. She dared to venture into the unknown and grab at possibilities she knew were futile. He hadn't lived with her and Craig. He'd lived with Laney and Bryan.

Paul glanced at Craig then at Maggie. "I have something to say." The words broke through the room's increasing pressure, and released its hypnotizing grip.

Maggie exhaled and waited.

Paul shifted, took a deep breath and with it he

transformed. His shoulders lifted higher, his jaw tightened, and his chin lifted. "First, I'm Evan Ellerby. I've been Evan Ellerby for as long as I can remember." He exhaled and met Craig's gaze, and then turned to Maggie. "But I've come to accept I'm also Paul. I owe both of you for my existence, but I owe Laney and Bryan for my life. I've thought a lot about this." He chuckled. "Hospital rooms have a way of making you think. But what I am today is a combination of all of you. You gave me life and nurtured me for two years. Mom and Dad picked up from there and guided me into what I've become. So I'd like to know, would it be possible for me to be part of your lives as Evan, the person I am today? Not the toddler you lost twenty years ago. I don't know how to be Paul. Can you accept recognizing Laney and Bryan as my parents? Is that something that could work?"

Craig looked at Maggie with a deep questioning gaze. In the shift of his eyes, she knew what he was thinking. She knew he approved of the arrangement, but he wanted to know if she did. And in that moment, the moment his eyes enveloped her with his caring compassion, she knew it would be fine. She also knew, she would have to recognize Paul as Evan.

She nodded.

Craig spoke. "Evan, I believe that would be just fine. We'd love to have you in our lives in whatever way you want. We'd like to get to know you."

Evan's shoulders lowered. A subtle shift. He smiled toward Maggie. "I'd like to get to know both of you."

Maggie remained silent. Proud. Words jumbled in her throat and formed a dam holding back the flood. Prayer had proved to be a powerful part of where she was today. Faith, even the fledgling one she harbored was proving to give her strength she'd never had. Maybe it was time she delved deeper into where that faith could lead.

After all, the person sitting next to her was more than just her son, he was a special young man. *Thank you, Lord.*

Epilogue

"*D*aisies. My favorite." Laney accepted the bouquet from Maggie. "Thank you. I'm so glad you're here."

"The turkey smells delicious." Maggie kissed Laney's cheek and wrapped her arms around her friend. "Thanks for the invitation."

Laney pulled back and met Maggie's gaze. "Are you kidding? We couldn't have Thanksgiving without you and Craig. You're part of the family."

"Stop right there. Hold that pose." The electronic click of the digital camera let them know Evan had captured their friendship in a photo. He walked toward them and placed his arms around her and Maggie. "Hey Mom one and Mom two, how's it going?" A Cheshire cat grin plastered his face.

Maggie glanced at Laney. "He's your son."

Laney arched her right eyebrow. "Nope, I'm not claiming him. He's yours."

"Hey no fair, you both have to claim me."

Both Maggie and Laney shook their heads and laughed.

Evan's grin spread further. "I see how it is." He walked over to Laney and kissed her cheek then did the same for Maggie. "Thanks for cooking. This smells wonderful."

Maggie squeezed his shoulder.

As he walked out the room, Maggie called after him. "Send that picture to my home email address."

"You bet."

Laney basted the turkey, its skin transformed from pale to golden brown. After Maggie carried a steaming 9 x 13 casserole of cornbread and crumbled pork dressing into the dining room, she popped back into the kitchen. "What else can I do?"

Laney pointed to a mahogany box. "The silverware."

After Maggie left the kitchen, silverware box in hand, Laney squeezed more turkey drippings over the taunt brown skin.

The Langstons had become good friends. They spent weekends together with Evan and Casey. Laney was proud of Evan for accepting Craig and Maggie. And to Laney's surprise, she welcomed Maggie's role in Evan's life and in hers. She loved sharing her son with her best friend.

The roar of a football game drifted in from the living room where Eric, Evan, Bryan, and Craig watched the game. Casey would come later after she had dinner with her grandmother at the local nursing home.

There was only one thing missing.

Alex.

Laney's chest tightened. No word from him. The day would be perfect if . . . She shook off the thought. It was his choice. He had a life of his own.

Rosamie's words floated through her brain and her heart. *Everything is in God's perfect timing.* She'd shared about Alex at their second weekly meeting. The group of wonderful women were praying.

She'd done all she could—made the first move. No point pushing the issue further. If Alex chose to stay out of her life, she would respect his choice. But on days like today, she couldn't help but dream. Couldn't help but imagine what having Alex and his family as part of their lives would be like.

Maggie slid her arm around Laney's waist. "You okay?"

"Yeah, I guess. I can't help but think about Alex."

"Why not call? By some strange fluke, he may not have gotten your note."

"Mr. Davenport promised he'd give it to him. I'm pretty sure he got it."

"I'm really sorry." Maggie hugged Laney a little tighter.

Laney sighed long and heavy. "Thanks, I guess I need to shake out of this. All in all, I'd have to say I'm pretty well blessed."

"Maybe he just needs more time. Doctors are really busy and maybe right now you'd be another responsibility he might not be able to handle. Maybe after the holidays…"

"Maybe." She slid the oversized oven mitts over her hands and pulled the turkey from the oven.

Laney's table setting formed a festive layout with an open place of honor for the golden bird.

"Turkey's ready."

Bryan appeared in the dining room, carving knife in hand. Craig walked in, followed by Evan and Eric. "Everything looks and smells wonderful."

Each found their seat and waited. Bryan looked toward his son. "Evan would you like the honor of blessing the food?"

"Sure." Evan cleared his throat and began. "Lord, thank You. Thank You for how You've worked in our lives and brought us together. Thank You for two sets of loving parents. Wonderful parents. My children will be blessed as well. Lord, You've taken hard circumstances and changed them for good. We are grateful for Your faithfulness. And we know Your timing was perfect. Bless this food and our time together. Let the fellowship be such that it makes up for the lost time—" The door bell rang and he lifted his head then continued. "In this we ask through Jesus, Your son. Amen." He stood. "Sorry, that must be Casey, she's early."

Laney glanced around the table. Maggie's gaze met

hers. Moisture pooled in her eyes. She loved Evan. They both did. And Laney loved that her son was the recipient of so much.

"Mom, it's for you." Evan entered the room followed by a man carrying a toddler.

The tall figure, blonde hair, and huge smile matched the picture she'd seen in Mr. Davenport's living room. Alex. Could it be?

Laney stood, but her feet cemented in place. Her son here. *Oh, Lord.*

She rested her hand on the back of the chair and looked into his eyes. The familiar blue she saw every morning in her mirror stared back.

"I'm sorry. I know I should have called, but we were on our way to Disneyworld and before I knew it, I was in your driveway."

Laney moved one foot forward. Would the gelatin towers replacing her legs hold her? Alex. Here? In her dining room? Holding her…grandchild? Could this be true? Could God have answered her prayer? Their prayers?

She swallowed the ball of raw emotion and scrambled to find words. Before a coherent sentence formed, Bryan stood and walked toward Alex. "Please come in. I'm Bryan Langston, Laney's husband."

"Alex Davenport." He pointed to the sweet girl in his arms. "This is my daughter, Jamie." Then he turned and encompassed a petite blonde-haired woman who stood at his side. "And this is my wife, Katie."

Maggie appeared next to Laney and firmly nudged her forward. "Go to him. I'll get two more place settings."

Laney nodded. She lifted her foot and walked toward Alex. He watched each calculated move. She moved closer and when she reached Jamie, the little girl smiled at her. Laney's heart exploded. *Oh, Lord. This is so much more than I imagined. So much more.* She reached out to Jamie who grabbed her finger. "Well, aren't you a sweetheart?"

She turned to Alex. "Thank you." She gulped back the

lump threatening to explode into a sob. "Thank you for coming. I'm Laney Ellerby."

"I'm Alex Davenport, your son."

My son. Thank you, Jesus. She grabbed his hand and held it and then pressed her lips tightly together. *No, no crying.*

"I would have been here sooner, but I didn't find your letter until last week when I went through Dad's things. It was in his Bible. He passed away two nights after your visit." Alex's eyes glistened when he looked at her hand in his. "We shouldn't have barged in like this especially on Thanksgiving. I don't know what I was thinking."

"I told your father you were welcome here anytime. No phone call needed. I meant that." She turned to Katie. "It's nice to meet you."

Maggie arranged two place settings while Evan slid the chairs out.

Laney clutched Alex's hand tighter and looked into his eyes. "Please stay. We have plenty. I would love to spend time with you and your beautiful family." She turned back to Katie. "Please."

Evan linked his hand through Alex's arm. "Hey, I'm Evan, Laney and Bryan's adopted son." He pointed toward Maggie then Craig. "That's Maggie and Craig Langston they're my biological parents." He chuckled. "So you see, you'll fit right in. You've got to stay."

"Are you sure?" Alex glanced toward Laney.

"Sure? I've never been more sure of anything in my life." She pulled him toward his seat.

****

Maggie glanced around the table. Bryan and Eric chatted with Alex. Craig and Evan compared drumsticks. And Laney...Laney rubbed noses with the granddaughter she held for the first time. Maggie's heart danced for her best friend.

And for herself. Maggie marveled at how blessed she felt at this very moment. Her son had grown into a wonderful young man. That hadn't been by accident. Maggie's heart stirred with gratitude. Laney believed that God watched over their children when they couldn't. Looking around the room and deep inside her healed heart, Maggie found she believed it, too.

ABOUT THE AUTHOR

Marian Pellegrin Merritt is an award-winning author who writes stories that blend her love of the mountains with her deep Southern roots. Her work has appeared in newspapers, magazines and online websites.

She holds a Bachelor of Science degree in physical therapy and an accounting certificate from the University of South Alabama.

This Louisiana native writes inspirational Christmas Romances and Women's Fiction from the home she shares with her husband and a very spoiled Labradoodle.

To learn more about other books in The Pecan Pointe series and Marian's other books, visit: www.marianmerritt.com

Thank you for sharing your time with Maggie and Laney. I hope you loved reading about them as much as I loved writing about them. Readers are very important to me and I love hearing from you, please drop me a line at: marian@marianmerritt.com

The Moon Has No Light – Recipes

Rosamie Chabert's Famous Pecan Pralines

1 (14 oz) can of Condensed Milk
3 Cups of sugar
¼ Cup butter
3 tsp White Corn Syrup
½ Cup Water
½ tsp Vanilla Extract
½ tsp Almond Extract
5 cups shelled Pecan Halves

Combine the first 5 ingredients in a heavy sauce pan and cook until the "Soft Ball" stage on a candy thermometer (234 to 240 degrees).
Add Vanilla and Almond extract and pecans.
Heat until the mixture starts to thicken.
Drop by spoonful onto greased parchment paper. Let cool.
Remove and place in an airtight container.

Dominique Gaudeau's (Grace's Mother) Blueberry Muffins

2 cups flour
1/3 cup sugar
2 tsp baking powder
½ tsp salt
1 egg, lightly beaten
¾ cup milk
½ cup butter, melted
1 cup fresh blueberries

Combine dry ingredients. In a separate bowl, combine egg, milk, and butter and mix into dry ingredients until moistened. Fold in blueberries. Spoon into greased muffin pan or one filled with muffin cups. Fill each approx. 2/3 full. Bake at 425 degrees for 20-25 minutes or until tops are golden brown.

Laney's Cajun Cornbread and Crumbled Pork Dressing

4 8.5 oz Packages Corn Muffin Mix (no sugar)
2 sticks of Butter
1 cup onion, chopped
½ cup green bell pepper, chopped
¼ cup celery, chopped
2 TBLS garlic, minced
2 TBLS parsley, dried
1 LB ground pork
1 LB ground beef
2 cups chicken stock
1 ¼ cup Cream of Mushroom Soup
1 TBLS Salt
2 TBLS Cajun Seasoning
6 eggs, well beaten
3 cups Milk
1 cup green onion, chopped

Prepare Corn Muffin Mix per package directions using 1 stick of butter to grease pan. Bake as instructed then cool.
In a 4-qt pot, heat other stick of butter on high until melted then add onion, bell pepper, celery, garlic, and parsley. Sauté for approx. 5 minutes.
Add ground pork and cook until pork begins to turn brown, breaking up pork in crumbles. Add ground beef and stir well, breaking up ground beef also. Continue to cook meat until completely cooked. Remove from heat and drain any excess grease.
Add chicken stock and return to high heat. Bring to a boil for 10 minutes then add Cream of Mushroom soup and stir until well blended. Add salt and Cajun Seasoning. Blend well. Reduce heat to low and simmer for approx.. 15-20 minutes. Remove from heat.
In a large bowl, crumble cornbread well.
Preheat oven to 350 degrees. Slowly mix crumbled cornbread and mix meat mixture until blended.
Add milk to mixture and mix well. Add beaten eggs and green onions and mix until completely blended. Grease 9 x 13 pan. Spread cornbread mixture evenly in pan and bake at 350 degrees Fahrenheit for 25-30 minutes.

The Moon Has No Light –

Discussion Questions

1. Dr. Maggie Langston's son was abducted 20 years ago. She steadfastly believes he is still alive. As a pediatrician she is reminded daily of the child she lost. Do you think her career choice is a healthy way for her to live? Why, or why not?

2. We see Maggie struggling with the attention of a young colleague. What pitfalls did Maggie fall into that many women in unhappy marriages also fall?

3. Do you believe Maggie's career path and her inability to accept that her son is gone is the reason for her unhappy marriage? Or do you believe there are other inherent problems that exist and they're using their missing child as an excuse? What are some things you see that contribute to their unhappiness?

4. We see Maggie's beautiful home, her expensive car, and lacking for nothing material. She and her husband have prosperous careers that most people envy. What does the Bible say about this world and its earthly treasures? If you could share Christ with Maggie, how would you encourage her?

5. Laney and Bryan seem to have the perfect life. A good marriage with Godly influences. Yet, there is a crack in their relationship's foundation. Bryan's secret about paying to "move up" in the line for the adoption could be considered harmless by many. After all, some would say, "What Laney doesn't know doesn't hurt her." How is this

thinking harmful to a successful marriage? And why are secrets, even done for the good of the other, harmful? How would you say this IS harmful to Laney?

6. Laney also has a secret she's kept from Bryan. How is Laney's secret harmful?

7. Emma, Laney's friend warns her, "Be careful what you pray for, it may come to pass." What does she mean by this? And why is she warning Laney? Have you ever prayed for something you knew was right, yet when your prayer was answered it wasn't a true blessing? Discuss if you feel led.

8. Both Maggie and Laney allow a negative emotion/feeling to control their thoughts. What is it and why is it keeping each woman from receiving the true measure of God's grace and what he has promised each of us?

9. We see how a single sinful act by Laney (sleeping with her married professor) set into motion a life-long string of consequences, worry, and regret that involved many people. Is this what you've seen happen with sin? What do we see God do when both women pray for his guidance?

10. Laney's cousin Mark, the preacher, reminds Maggie that our children are God's and that he watches over them when we can't. For those of you who are parents, how hard is it to believe this? And how hard is it to back up our belief with complete trust and faith? What is the best example we can give our children to prove we trust God? What does this do for us? And for our children?

www.ingramcontent.com/pod-product-compliance
Lightning Source LLC
Chambersburg PA
CBHW051408170626
46809CB00006B/2070